VIOLENT DESIRE

ARIANA NASH

Violent Desire

Ariana Nash - ***Dark Fantasy Author***

Subscribe to Ariana's mailing list & get the exclusive story 'Sealed with a Kiss' free.

Join the Ariana Nash Facebook group for all the news, as it happens.

Edited by LesCourts / Proofreader Jennifer Griffin

Edited in US English.

Version 1 - June 2022

www.ariananashbooks.com

BLURB

Twelve immortals, twelve outcasts, one mission.

To kill their own kind, before it's too late.

Detective, killer, vigilante. Eric Sharpe is tired of watching criminals walk free. When a low-life drug dealer kills his partner and escapes justice, Eric plots his own revenge. His plan is faultless but for one thing: the handsome, mysterious man who arrives moments before Eric's plan comes to fruition. Not only does the mysterious man know Eric's an undercover cop, he knows exactly what Eric did fifteen years ago—an event so traumatic Eric has been trying to bury it ever since. And the mysterious man? Fifteen years ago, Eric killed him.

Now he's back to reclaim what's his: Detective Eric Sharpe.

Immortal, predator, vampire. After betraying himself and the Blackrose Brotherhood fifty years ago, Zaine can't afford another mistake. There's one rule above all others the Brotherhood stand by. One rule that can never be broken. Never, ever *care*. All Zaine has to do is hunt and kill the savage nyktelios vampires and keep his head down. And he was doing just fine until he saved Detective Eric Sharpe from a vicious vampire attack. He can't stop thinking about the intelligent, handsome, haunted man. Walking away is the right thing to do, but the detective and Zaine are hunting the same killer—a vampire who knows more about both of them and the Brotherhood than anyone realizes.

A vampire seeking to bring down the Brotherhood for good.

Zaine can't walk away. Eric *won't* walk away. The vampire must be stopped, Brotherhood rules be damned, and they'll go down fighting together to end him.

Violent Desire is the first book in an all-new MM paranormal romance series. Each book features a new MM couple ending in a HEA/HFN.

Content warning: These are adult books with dark content. There will be graphic, on-page depictions of sex, torture, drug use, and swearing. These vampires do not sparkle. They're relentless in their mission. They do bad stuff for good reasons, and some do good stuff for bad reasons. They DO NOT CARE. They have been described as psychopaths with fangs. Read at your own risk.

CHAPTER 1

Before love and life, before day and night and time itself, *Chaos* birthed the primordial First Order of Beings, Nyx and Erebus. *Night* and *Darkness*. From their volatile union, came the Second Order of Beings. *Time* itself gave chaos *Order*, the land rose up toward new stars, and oceans plunged toward the underworld. Our world was formed. Only then came the gods.

But all things began in Chaos.

And all things shall end with Her.

- *Partially destroyed ancient carvings, City of Knossos, 7000 BC*

Eric

. . .

VERGIL SWEPT the pile of poker chips toward his chest and rubbed his hands together. "Clearin' you out tonight, bitches."

Eric chuckled and tossed his bad hand of cards on the table. "You could warm us up before you screw us over."

The other five men around the table jeered and laughed, giving up their cards one by one. More insults bounced back and forth. Whiskey sloshed into glasses. Poker chips clacked. Familiar sounds, familiar people, and the same fake smile on Eric's lips accompanying the churn of hatred in his gut.

Vergil grinned and launched into a description of how he'd fucked one of the club's dancers the night before, then left a roll of cash for her so she *knew her place.* Skinny from a drug habit he couldn't afford and with prison ink etched across his knuckles, nothing stuck to Vergil, the low-life piece of shit. Not even the law. He'd so far escaped serious prosecution, as though he had his own guardian angel looking out for him.

That angel would be looking the other way tonight. Eric was going to make sure of it.

The dealer, another low-life dick named JB, dealt another round. Smooth playing cards skipped across green velvet cloth. Eric took a peek at his hand and sipped his whiskey, taking just enough to wet his lips. Nobody noticed his glass hadn't been refilled in hours. The others were well on their way to being drunk, with no idea they had a cop among them.

It had taken months to get to this chair, to this table. Weeks of fake smiles and cheap drug deals. Just enough to get him on Vergil's radar but keep out of jail.

Eric's ma had always said there was a thin line between criminals and cops. He hadn't understood what she'd meant at the time, and then she was gone. He understood now. When you looked in the eyes of your partner's four-year-old daughter and told her that her daddy wasn't coming home and you couldn't catch the bad guy who killed him, that line between good and bad got real blurry.

Eric had been that kid once too, realizing the world was fucked up and nobody was going to bring his family back.

He was so fucking tired of the bad guys winning.

Which led to this table, this night, and Vergil sitting opposite, his shit-eating grin cutting across his too-thin smug face.

The game went on, Vergil getting louder by the hour. Music thumped from the club above. The occasional clomp of boots passed the door but nobody dared enter. Game nights were sacred.

Eric won a few rounds, just enough to keep them on their toes. By the time midnight rolled around, Vergil's gang was loose-lipped, drunk, and high from the lines of coke JB had cut an hour ago. Primed and ready to go down.

"Hey, man, you not drinking?" Vergil asked, on his feet and opening a fresh bottle.

Eric waved the comment away. "Hell yeah." To prove it, he picked up his glass and gulped the whiskey down in one. These days, it no longer burned.

Vergil leaned in close and refilled Eric's glass. "What about a Charlie chaser?"

Eric glanced at the lines of white powder on the sideboard. "I'm good."

"You sure?" Vergil's blue eyes narrowed. "It's grade A. Might even be your product?"

"Could be." Eric chuckled, shifting a little in his chair to keep Vergil in his line of sight. The prick was jittery. When he got like this, his moods swung from being your best friend to an enemy in a blink. He'd cut a man a few weeks ago for being late to a game just like this one. Poker was his passion and his vice. One of many.

In this room, Vergil controlled what went down, and that included his generous supply of cocaine.

The door rattled. When he'd arrived earlier in the evening, Eric had made sure to position himself facing the door—having his back to the only exit was a bad move—so now when it swung open and a six-foot pillar of suave male sophistication strode in, he had the best view. Mid thirties, raven black hair cropped close but longer on top, and startling blue eyes. The newcomer didn't spare a glance for anyone and approached Vergil without missing a step. He had to be the club owner, someone in charge, but Eric's intel hadn't revealed anyone like him.

The man's hand landed on Vergil's shoulder, turning him on his feet. Vergil's face betrayed his alarm, although his quick smile vanished that mistake a second later. The suave man bent his head and whispered something into Vergil's ear.

Vergil's wired, jittery movements instantly stilled, as though someone had pulled his plug from a socket.

"Uh huh, yeah." Vergil nodded. "You sure?"

The rest of the group found their cards fascinating. A

few tossed a couple of jokes around, but Eric didn't hear a damn thing. The man squeezed Vergil's shoulder, and those cold blue eyes briefly skimmed the table, the cards, the men, before finally coming to rest on Eric.

Recognition jolted through his veins, bright and sharp, almost painful, and with it came a sizzle of sudden lust derailing his thoughts from the real reason he was here and steering them deep into the gutter. Fuck, the guy was a feast for the eyes. And... familiar. Eric's mouth suddenly dried and his heart thumped. He turned his face away and sipped his drink, and by the time he'd recovered, the new arrival had turned on his heel and left.

Vergil snorted, adjusted his jacket, and cleared his throat. He braced his hand on the back of Eric's chair. "Nothing like the boss showing up to ruin the mood."

"Who was he?" Eric asked.

Vergil's hard crow-like eyes fixed on Eric. "None of Your Fuckin' Business is his name."

Eric laughed some and raised his hands, hoping to soften Vergil's wrath. "Whatever, just askin'."

"Why?" Vergil smirked. "Huh? Why you wanna know?" He slid an arm around Eric's shoulder and brushed his cheek close to Eric's, smelling of whiskey and pungent aftershave. "I saw you lookin' at him. You hard for him?"

The others snickered.

Panic flittered in Eric's heart. They couldn't know he was gay. It was just the usual macho crap guys threw at each other. "No, man. Like I said, just curious."

Vergil snorted, patted Eric's shoulder, and backed off. "Don't worry, everyone wants to fuck the boss man. But mostly, he fucks everyone else. Bit of advice, stay away from him, eh? Unless you wanna get your balls cut off and your hands nailed to a wall."

"Yeah." Eric chuckled again. "Right." He glanced at the clock. Almost twelve thirty. A few more hours. "Are we gonna game or what? I'm warming up. Gotta win my cash back, right?"

"Sure..." Vergil's smile bloomed. "Just one thing." He wiped his thumb across his nose, swept to the sideboard, and scooped up the mirror with neat lines of icing laid out for snorting. "Get some of that in ya, eh? You're making the rest of us look bad." He laughed and the others jeered.

Eric's racing heart fluttered more. He smiled, knowing his smiles were always charming. "I deal it. I don't do it."

"I deal it. I don't do it," Vergil mocked. "Yeah, 'cept now you do."

"That's not our deal. Remember? I said I'd get you the stuff, but I never take my own product. There'd be nothing left to sell."

All the humor vanished from Vergil's face. His smile stayed, but it was a crocodile smile, full of teeth and menace.

Vergil reached behind him and plucked a gun from his lower back. He laid it on the table with a heavy *thunk*, making the poker chips dance. "Tonight you fucking do. Or I might start thinking you're not who you say you are."

"What?" Eric tittered to cover his racing heart. "What are you fuckin' talking about?"

"I dunno, man. Just a little birdie in my ear telling me you're a fuckin' *cop*?" Vergil grabbed Eric's jaw and pressed his mouth against his cheek. "So take the gear or I put a fuckin' bullet in your brain."

The suave man had told Vergil who Eric was, whispered it in his ear moments ago. How had he known? Who the fuck was he? *Shit...* With a snarl, Eric jerked his head free of Vergil's grip, grabbed a hundred-dollar bill from the pile of cash on the table, rolled it tightly, and snorted a row. Sparkling tingles numbed the back of his nose and throat. He snorted the second row and sat back, tossing the bill back into the pile. "Now get on with the fucking game, Vergil. Or are you too afraid to lose?"

Vergil's sudden laugh cracked like a whip. "I knew you were tight, bro."

"Whatever. Sit your ass down. Calling me a cop, you prick. What the fuck?"

"Not me, man. Not me." He snickered. "We're tight. I seen you do shit no cop would do. Bad intel is all. Someone has it out for you, my bro."

The game started up again. Five minutes, that was how long Eric had before the coke fully kicked in. He'd planned to have events take a turn near the end of the night when the club was closed and Vergil's men were too high to count their own fingers. That wasn't going to wash now. In five minutes, he'd be too jacked to do anything.

He didn't plan on dying here tonight.

Vergil's gun gleamed on the table between the stacks of poker chips and half-empty whiskey glasses, left there from his earlier threat. Eric had brought his own. It would have been weird not to. But his had been surrendered as part of the game's rules. It sat in the cupboard by the door with the rest of the group's weapons and phones.

A plan formed in his thoughts, a way for this to play out differently. *Use Vergil's gun. Wipe it down afterward.* He could imagine the sloppy police report: *Gang game night gone wrong.* Although the coke was also kicking in, making anything possible.

He tapped his foot under the table. Heat flushed through his veins.

He flicked open the first few buttons of his shirt.

12:40 a.m.

His heart raced, rattling his ribs.

His old partner, Grahams, hadn't deserved a bullet to the back of his head. He'd been the best kind of cop, a few years off retirement. He'd fucking made Eric who he was today. These pricks had to pay—dealers, killers, rapists. Vergil was the tip of the iceberg. The men around this table wouldn't stop. And the law couldn't touch them.

Somebody had to.

Vergil sat slanted in his chair, cards raised, blinking slowly. Eric held his gaze. He had a decent hand. He could win with it. "All in." He shoved his chips into the center of the table.

"Oh fuck!" one of the others blurted. "Hell no." He folded, laughing. "You fuckers are insane."

The subdued lighting brightened, sparkling in Eric's vision. Around the table, the rest folded, all but Vergil. He wouldn't fold. His pride wouldn't allow it.

"You're bluffing." The prick skimmed his tongue across his bottom lip.

Eric shrugged. "Try me."

Vergil's smile opened, lips lifting into a smirk. He shoved his chips forward. "All in, motherfucker." He fanned his cards open on the table.

The moment hung suspended, trapped between clarity

and chaos. Eric's heart tripped. He sucked in a breath, adrenaline and coke racing, and lowered his cards with his left hand while with his right he snatched Vergil's gun, flicked the safety off, aimed, and fired. The round smacked a neat hole through Vergil's forehead, jerking him back into his chair. Blood and brain matter splattered the wall behind him. Someone yelped. Eric swung the gun and pulled the trigger. The gun kicked, and another bastard fell. He got a third shot off, killing another one.

JB kicked the table over, scattering chips and whiskey. He bolted for the cupboard and the weapons inside. Eric swung, aimed, fired. The round slammed into the plasterboard above JB's head. He dropped and flung open the cupboard. A gun flashed in his hand as Eric ducked behind the table. One of the other pricks, Kendric, lurched in, flinging himself at Eric's gun arm. Eric jerked back, Kendric stumbled against him, and the round went through Kendric's skull at point-blank range.

So fast, shit!

JB fired into the table, wood splintering.

Another guy fled for the door. Eric fired, and the guy fell.

"You fucker!" JB shrieked. High on alcohol and drugs, JB didn't stand a chance.

Eric ducked his head out from behind the overturned table and took the headshot. JB's body slumped, his eyes open and empty.

A sudden, startling quiet declared the chaos over. Done. Eric's body thrummed, his skin prickling and heart beating like a drum in his head and chest. He'd done it. He'd killed them.

The door opened.

Eric raised the gun. He'd drop another one—he had to, to make sure he wasn't seen. But it was the suave man who entered the room. Cool eyes surveyed the bodies. He stepped over one fallen body—and Eric's mind must have glitched because cold hands suddenly clamped around his throat, his back struck the wall, and he was pinned, dangling from the suave man's hands, staring into those icy blue eyes without having seen him move. The gun was gone, torn from his hand so fast his fingers burned. But he couldn't see where it went. Couldn't see anything, just the man. He was everything.

"You," the suave man growled.

Eric blinked. His heart pounded so fast it might burst from his ribs. The others were dead. He'd killed them. But this one... this one was different. He hadn't been part of the plan. And he'd seen Eric's face. He had to die as well. But the gun was gone, and the iron grip of the man's hands tightened like a noose around Eric's neck. He bucked, tried to shove him back, but it was like trying to shove a brick wall.

"I know you," the man purred, his cheek suddenly hot against Eric's. "Fifteen years ago—"

The memories struck like vicious, barbed hooks sank into his past and yanked them to the surface. Fifteen years. That night.... A night that had lasted forever. He'd witnessed something he'd been trying to forget ever since.

"No." The single word squeezed through his gritted teeth.

The suave man's warm, wet tongue swept up Eric's

cheek. "You taste the same now as you did then, Sweet One."

Memories flashed. Coming faster now the lock holding them back had broken. Blood and tears. He had tasted both on his lips that night. Terror flashed through him now, setting him ablaze. But fear wasn't all he was feeling. Maybe it was the coke or maybe he was out of his mind, but the sensation of the man's warm cheek against his snatched his breath, tingled his skin, and filled his cock, as though his body *remembered* this more than anything else. His skin craved touch. His cock ached.

"Such a rare gift," the man whispered. His words tickled Eric's ear, slid inside and coiled around his soul. "Do not worry. To kill you now would be such as waste."

He pulled back, blue flame alight in his eyes, teeth glistening behind his smile.

"Put him down," a new voice said, a voice so different and unexpected that it slapped Eric's desire away.

Eric's thoughts and mind glitched again. He didn't see the man let him go, just fell to his knees, gasping through his constricted throat. The past and the now blurred in front of his eyes. His lungs burned, his heart beat so hard and fast it threatened to burst. Heat surged through his veins, burning him up from the inside out. His head spun, the room moving and the figures within it swirling too fast to track. Bad coke or just a simple old heart attack, either way Eric was in trouble. If he could just *breathe*... He lifted his head, trying to see through his swimming vision.

The suave man and the blond-haired new arrival wrestled up close, trading bone-cracking blows. The suave man had the intruder against the wall, repeatedly slamming punches into his middle. The intruder wore twin gun holsters. He held a single gun in his right hand, startling blue eyes fierce, and fired three muffled rounds into the other man's chest—but the man didn't slow. He roared, pulled the intruder from the wall, and flung him from one side of the room to the other, through the toppled poker table. He landed inches from Eric, shook his head, looked up, and... *smiled.*

Were those... fangs?

What the fuck? What was in that coke?

Eric's vision blurred, and darkness mixed with floating stars flooded his vision. His head thudded in time with his heart, and all at once, the heat and the hurt dragged him under.

CHAPTER 2

ric

ERIC GROANED awake from a dreamless sleep, guts roiling. Saliva pooled in his mouth, giving him just a few seconds' warning. He stumbled from the bed, down the short hall, into the bathroom, and heaved the contents of his stomach into the toilet. Shivering, he clung to the bowl until the nausea passed, then dragged his sorry ass back to the bedroom.

His head thumped, but even through the fog, alarm bells rang at the sight of the neatly folded pile of clothes at the foot of his bed. The blinds were closed. He blinked, frowned, and glimpsed the glass of water on the bedside table next to a bottle of Tylenol.

There was no way he'd set all that up before falling into bed last night. He didn't fold his clothes even when he wasn't hungover and coming off a high.

Holy shit, someone had been here. *Could still be here...*

He grabbed his backup Beretta from his bedside drawer and checked every room in the apartment. It was clear, no intruders. But the security chain on his apartment door was still fixed in place. That couldn't be latched from outside. Whoever had been inside had left another way...

More heat thumped through his head and down his neck. He couldn't think. His bones and body ached like he'd gone ten rounds with a pro boxer. Padding barefoot back to his bedroom, he dropped to the edge of the bed and glared at the glass of water and the pills next to it.

Last night... Shit, he didn't remember getting home. Didn't remember much...

His phone beeped from the pile of clothes. He rummaged around, found the phone, and frowned at the message on-screen.

Z: If I were you, I'd burn the clothes

Who the fuck was Z and why was his number in Eric's phone? He crouched and grabbed the pants from the pile. A whiff of whiskey and the metallic smell of blood burned his nose, flip-flopping his guts all over again. Blood speckled his hands too. A blood-encrusted poker chip fell out of his pants pocket and clattered to the floor.

"Shit..."

It *had* happened. All of it. The poker game, using Vergil's gun to smoke every last bastard at that table. Vergil—the fucker—was dead. Justice had finally been done. He'd expected to feel something, some kind of relief, but he felt... nothing.

His phone pinged in his hand again.

Z: *Take the pills*

The Tylenol?

Who is this? Eric tapped out, then deleted it, unsent. He had to be smart. Whoever Z was, they'd been in his apartment, knew about the clothes, about last night. Had Z brought him back? He couldn't remember. He'd killed Vergil, he recalled that vividly, but afterward... whatever happened was all mixed up in a bad hit of cocaine.

His phone pinged again. "Jesus—"

Nate: *Where are you?*

The time on his phone read 9:30 a.m. Eric rubbed at his face. "Shit." He was supposed to have met his partner, Nathaniel Saville, at the precinct by 8:00 a.m. Nate would be pissed. Pissed enough to come by. The last thing he needed was the keen-eyed detective poking through his apartment with the evidence of last night's massacre *right there.*

I'll be 30 mins, he sent back, then ditched his phone and grabbed a trash bag. The clothes went inside and he tossed the bag in the closet, then threw himself into a hot shower, dressed, collected his badge, skipped breakfast, and hurried out the door.

"Morning, Eric," his neighbor Caroline trilled as she locked her door. Her pug, Jimmy, leaped at his leg.

"Mornin', Caroline." He forced a smile, ignoring how it almost split his skull apart, and patted the little dog's head. "Can't stop—running late."

"Give my thanks to the nice man from last night, would you?" Caroline asked with a warm smile. "Jimmy got out and I thought he'd be gone down the stairs and I'd never see him again, but he caught him, quick as a whip."

"Er, right, sure. I'll do that." *Nice man?* He hurried down the hall.

"Elevator's still out," she called.

He threw her a wave. "Thanks." And took the stairs down to the parking lot. His black 1970s Dodge Charger waited in its bay. He hopped in, winced at his gray-faced reflection in the rearview mirror, started the car on the first turn of the key, and swung her out of the parking lot. The drive downtown gave him time to turn over what he knew. And none of it was good. He had no idea if he'd cleaned his prints from the murder scene at Vergil's club. He couldn't remember *leaving*. He'd killed the prick with his own gun—there was satisfaction in that—but where was that gun now? It would have his prints all over it.

He thumped the wheel. "Shit!" He was better than this. All his plans, months of setting it up, and he'd left goddamn evidence all over the crime scene.

Last night had been a fuckup of epic proportions. He could only hope nobody called it in. Vergil's crew wouldn't want cops crawling all over their business. And Vergil wasn't important enough to make waves. Maybe it would all slip through the cracks, exactly as Eric had planned when he'd set this up. He'd planned for everything except the suave man.

An image flashed in his mind—blue eyes, as sharp and clear as crystal. *You taste the same now as you did then, Sweet One.* Pain flashed through Eric's head, short-circuiting his thoughts, making them flare. Horns honked. The car in front loomed large in his windshield. He slammed his foot on the brake and the Charger screeched to a halt in traffic. Drivers honked around him.

His gut lurched, but already emptied, it had nothing to hurl up.

He clung to the wheel and breathed. More horns honked. *Just breathe...*

Memories tried to swim in front of his eyes. He furiously blinked them from his head. No, he wasn't remembering *him*—the demon from his childhood dreams. The demon he'd once tried to tell a shrink about and had quickly learned to keep his mouth shut if he wanted to keep his career as a cop, wanted to make detective, wanted a normal life where the only monsters were the sick fucks he put away.

He couldn't do this. Not today. Later. He just had to get through the morning and ride out whatever his head was trying to tell him.

He eased the car back into traffic.

His phone rang. *Nate.*

"Hey," Eric answered. "Sorry, man. Bad rice or something. I'm fine now. I'll be—"

"We got a case. Times Square," Nate said in his flat, professional voice. "Meet you there."

"On it." *A body at Times Square?*

His mind switched from trawling the past to focusing on the present. Work, he could do. He was fucking good at it. A new case to sink his teeth into was exactly what he needed to cover up his trash fire personal life.

TRAFFIC SAT GRIDLOCKED down Seventh Avenue. Eric blipped the hidden sirens and lights fixed behind the

Charger's front grille and inched the car through, then parked up alongside the marked NYPD cruisers. He clipped on his badge, grabbed his sunglasses, and climbed out into the painfully bright sunlight.

The circus waited up ahead. Fluttering crime scene tape, uniformed cops, and people trying to jostle to get the best picture with their phones, most of them tourists. A white tent had been thrown up around the victim to keep prying eyes out and preserve the evidence, although considering the body was on a bench in the middle of New York's busiest intersection, the forensics team was going to have its work cut out sifting through what was and wasn't relevant.

Detective Nate Saville waited outside the tent. He jerked his chin, eyes narrowing. With his tanned skin and dark hair, he had the boyish good looks that blew up social media, which was why the chief had made him the poster guy for the precinct's homicide team. The press loved Nate's wholesome good looks and straight-as-an-arrow attitude. He was a damned good detective too, full of ambition and a savage desire to right all the wrongs. Just like Eric had been before a mountain of shit had rolled over him.

"You all right, Sharpe?" Nate asked, his tone lifting some.

"Yeah... good."

Nate handed Eric disposable shoe covers. "Victim is John Capaldi, thirty-nine-year-old white male, Citegroup banker. Phone was in his pocket. Forensics have it bagged for data recovery. No wallet, likely stolen. He's been here since at least 6:00 a.m."

Since 6:00 a.m.? Right at sunrise. Eric nodded and slid all the personal shit aside, absorbing the information, and when Nate lifted the tent flap, Eric ducked inside.

The victim, a substantial male, sat slumped on the bench as though he was just taking some weight off his feet for a few moments. The photographer took the last few photos while Patricia Luscombe, the forensic investigator, a dour woman who disliked anyone with a beating heart, stood nearby. "Sharpe," she said. "You look like shit."

Eric removed his shades and tucked them in his shirt pocket. "Thank you, Pat. It's wonderful to see you this fine New York morning."

Pat reminded Eric of one of his middle school teachers none of his classmates had liked but all of them had damn well respected because they all knew, when she got angry, shit hit the fan. Slim and tall, even in flats, Pat ran on coffee and a sarcasm so dry it verged on verbal assault. She hated Eric for some reason he hadn't figured out. That didn't stop him from liking her.

"Who found him?"

"Street cleaner. He's outside, and like the rest of us, he's been waiting for you to grace us with your presence, Detective," Pat said.

"Sorry, ma'am. Bad night."

"Not as bad as Mr. Capaldi's."

Pat handed Eric a pair of gloves. He tugged them on and crouched in front of Capaldi's slumped form.

"No blood," Pat explained, coming around to stand behind Eric. "He wasn't killed here."

"Who drags a body to Times Square and sits him on a

bench before dawn?" Eric thought aloud. "Someone must have seen something. Cameras?"

"Gomez is looking into it," Nate said. "No luck so far. Apparently some kind of power outage happened right around the time this guy gets propped up here."

Bad timing, and not unusual. The whole downtown grid had been glitching lately.

Capaldi had no obvious wounds. For a fresh death, it was surprising how slate gray his skin already was, with lips so blue they were almost transparent. But there was nothing that immediately screamed murder—no stab wounds, no bruising. No blood. "What killed him?"

"Exsanguination."

Eric twisted and looked up at Pat. "You're joking?" He knew she wasn't. Pat rarely joked.

She leaned in and touched the bluish marks on the man's neck. Once puckered, the bruise opened, revealing two small puncture holes.

"Syringe?" Eric asked.

"Undetermined. But the diameter is too wide for a surgical syringe."

"Someone has a vampire fetish?" Nate suggested.

Weirder things happened every day in New York.

Eric let his gaze roam the man's slumped figure. At his wrists, a fresh tinge caught Eric's eye. He carefully pulled back the man's sleeve with gloved fingers. Bruises mottled the victim's wrists. He'd likely been restrained but he hadn't fought, not the way a man his size could have. Eric perused the scene, taking all the tiny details in and filing them away so his mind could turn them over later. "Anything else I'm missing?"

"We've got fibers under his nails and snagged in his clothes but the scene is remarkably clean." She sounded impressed. "Someone knew what they were doing."

Why hide the evidence but then leave the body out in the open? His headache threatened to make itself known again. He popped his shades back on. "All right, let's talk to the guy who found him."

The chat with the cleaner revealed Capaldi had been sitting dead on the bench for hours. The street cleaner had been picking up litter around the bench, knocked into him, and realized the guy wasn't getting up anytime soon. A hundred people had probably walked by Capaldi before his murder had been called in.

Eric reiterated the need for camera footage—the scene was overlooked by hundreds of office building windows. Someone had to have seen something.

"You think it's a message?" Nate asked, climbing into the Charger's passenger seat. "Leaving him out in the open like that. Why else would the perp go to all the trouble of moving him?"

"Good call." The theory had merit. "Whoever left him there has balls. You don't walk a body through Times Square and sit him on a bench unless you're confident you're not getting caught. Capaldi isn't small, either. It takes muscle to move a dead body. It takes a lot of muscle to move a big dead guy."

"So we're looking for a male with brass balls. Or a buff female."

"Right. Or two people..." But that didn't feel right. Two people carrying a third? Too conspicuous. Nothing about the scene felt right, as though they'd missed some vital and obvious piece of evidence, but Eric's thoughts had stalled. He'd think on it. It would come to him later. "Let's head to Capaldi's workplace, chat with the colleagues. See what they have to say." A deep throb of pain radiated up the back of Eric's neck. He rubbed his forehead.

"You sure you're all right?"

"Uh-huh. Just need to make a stop—grab some painkillers." He should have taken the meds left out for him, just like Z's text had suggested. But Eric wasn't thinking about that, or who Z was, or what had happened the night before. He had a job to do, and until it was done, nothing else mattered.

CHAPTER 3

aine

ZAINE HUNG BACK from the organized chaos of the crowd gathered around the crime scene. He caught glimpses of the detectives but kept his head down, blending in.

Eric Sharpe appeared to be coping well, considering last night's events and the state Zaine had left him in. If it hadn't been for his steady pulse, Zaine would have been forced to drop him off at a hospital or worse, take him back to the Atlas compound. Mikalis would have skinned Zaine alive if he'd brought a cop home. *Better to let them die than expose the Brotherhood.* Zaine knew the rules. It just so happened that sometimes he broke them. Not last night, though. He'd figured Sharpe was tough, and his suspicions had been proven correct as soon as the detective had arrived at Times Square this morning, in his distinctive black car.

Zaine should have left then, walked away... Sharpe might have seen him last night, could spot Zaine in the crowd now and put two and two together. But Zaine needed to make sure the man was doing okay. Clearly, he was. He stood with another detective, likely his partner, squinting through shades and discussing their dead body. Eric Sharpe was lean but in a strong, wiry way. Not too thin, with enough muscle to make Zaine work when he'd hauled his ass up his apartment stairs last night. Today he was wearing dark blue pants and a shirt under a jacket, and he wore them *fine*. The shades, however, hinted at his rough night. But just a hint, and only because Zaine knew to look for it.

Sharpe had gone from an out cold meat-bag Zaine had carried up to his apartment to the fiercely professional detective who appeared to have his shit together. He knew how to pretend, a skill Zaine approved of.

Eric Sharpe could clearly take care of himself. And he didn't seem the sort to start ranting and raving about vampires in New York.

Zaine threw his hood over his head, swung a leg over his Ducati 950 Sportsbike, started the engine, and sped away, carving through downtown traffic like a knife through butter. The bike's highly tuned engine sang pleasantly between his thighs, eager to race. As soon as he broke from the traffic on the outskirts of the city, he opened the throttle, hunkered down, and raced the bike toward the Atlas compound.

If all went well, he shouldn't have to see Detective Sharpe again.

Better to be a flicker of a memory in someone's mind than leave a mark, Mikalis would say. But not leaving a mark was easier said than done. Zaine was still feeling the repercussions of leaving a mark on a life he should never have touched, a life he'd cut short. That could never happen again.

TWENTY MINUTES LATER, Atlas's sprawling collection of steel and glass buildings stretched over green parklike surroundings. Security gates rumbled open for Zaine as he cruised through on the purring bike. He parked in the sublevel parking lot next to the array of the Brotherhood's blacked-out vans and SUVs, then strode past the collection of European sports cars. A ride for every occasion.

Just like the gates, the glass entrance doors whispered open on Zaine's approach. A pleasant shiver washed over him as soon as he stepped into the air-conditioned foyer. Tinted glass blocked exhausting UV rays, instantly easing the irritating burn trying to turn his bones to dust. He could withstand a few hours of sunlight, more than most of the Brotherhood, but it still ground him down.

Thrusting his hands into his pockets, he quickened his pace. If he could make it to his quarters without being seen, he wouldn't have to explain last night's screwup. He didn't usually come back all beaten-up, but Sharpe had made things complicated, and if Storm noticed—

"Hey, Zaine, back late?"

Zaine winced at the voice behind him and kept right on walking. "Yeah, just gonna crash, Kazi. Catch up later."

He might have gotten away with it if the elevator doors

hadn't dinged, revealing Storm. Storm's real name was so old it was unpronounceable. The nickname Storm had stuck a few hundred years ago, apparently because he'd once been a whirlwind with his blades despite being packed with muscle, making him as immovable as a concrete bunker. Zaine figured the name had more likely stuck because Storm was just as foreboding as his namesake. The big guy took one look at Zaine and his keen blue eyes narrowed. His lips parted, tasting the air, and Zaine knew he was fucked.

He slowed.

Storm stopped, blocking the elevator, and folded his arms. "You have twenty seconds to explain why I smell blood."

Zaine tried a smile, although that had never worked with the Brotherhood and was unlikely to work now. The smile was more of a reflex for when shit hit the fan. "It was just a taste." He glanced back and saw Kazimir closing in, his typically pretty face now all business. "C'mon, guys. We're good, right?"

"We'll see," Storm grumbled. "Hands away from your guns."

The derision in Storm's tone worked its way under Zaine's skin. Storm just had to be so damn righteous. Half the time Storm acted as though *he* was their leader. Zaine didn't have to listen to him, and being frowned at like a freshly turned nyk grated on his sunlight-pricked nerves.

He did, however, lift his hands away from his sides. It would take some creative drawing to free his guns from under his hooded shirt, but it could be done, and he didn't want to ruffle Storm's feathers any more than they already were. Some fights were worth having; this wasn't one of them.

"Shit went down. The nyk was tougher than I expected," he explained. "We got into it. There were a lot of factors—"

"Did you kill the nyktelios?" Kazi asked, stopping just behind Zaine, close enough to get him in an armlock if it came to it. The Brotherhood closed in like hungry sharks when they got like this.

"I maimed him." The nyk had been fast, brutal, and he'd had a few hundred years on Zaine. Intel Zaine could have done with before he'd heard gunshots and plowed into the club's back room to find the nyk about to drain the undercover cop.

"You *maimed* him?" Kazi echoed, shaking his head, sending all those dark, wavy locks tumbling. "He got away?"

These two assholes were getting on Zaine's nerves. He hadn't done anything wrong. Not recently. "Yes, he got away. Which is why you need to get off my back so I can rest up and get back out there."

Storm jerked his thumb over his shoulder. "Get in the elevator, Zaine."

He sighed, lowered his hands, and resigned himself to a day of explanations. Hopefully, Mikalis wasn't here and wouldn't need to get involved. If it was just Storm and Kazi, he might be done in a few hours.

He stepped into the elevator. Kazi entered, folded his arms, and raised an eyebrow. "You reek of blood."

"The murdering happened before I got there."

"Save it," Storm grumbled.

"Or you could just take my word for it?"

"We did that last time, remember?"

"That was fifty fucking years ago, Storm."

Kazi and Storm didn't reply, just flanked him like two prison guards. That was the problem with the Brotherhood. They all had long memories. One screwup, one little altercation, one falling off the wagon fifty years ago, and that shit clung on half a century later.

The elevator pinged and the doors swept open into Atlas's shining underground corridors. "You're lucky Mikalis isn't here," Storm said, leading the way ahead.

Zaine puffed a sigh. At least something had gone right today. This didn't need to get heavy. And had Mikalis been here, shit would have gotten *real* heavy. He followed dutifully behind Storm, passing confinement doors left and right, all but one with a green unlocked light. Confinement was always a last resort for anyone who stepped out of line. The door lock of 3B glowed red. The keypad lock screen read DO NOT ENTER. A tiny hint of music squeezed through the minimal gaps in the heavy reinforced door, the sound soft and haunting. A shiver spilled down Zaine's spine as he passed. If the others reacted, they didn't show it. In all the years the Brotherhood had occupied the Atlas building, Zaine had never once seen inside 3B. As far as he knew, nobody but Mikalis entered. Someone was in there, but the one time he'd asked, he'd been shut down and it had been made clear nobody talked about room 3B.

Storm shoved through an all-glass door and entered one of the labs. Monitoring screens flanked one wall.

Storm switched them on and the instruments blipped and buzzed to life.

"This is a lot of fuss over nothing," Zaine said pointlessly. Once Storm got an idea in his head, he rarely relented.

"Sit," Storm ordered.

Kazi guarded the door, legs spread, arms crossed. He wasn't wearing any weapons but didn't need them. Kazi was the fastest of them all, unbeaten in training. He had the pretty-Instagram-model look down to perfection, all that long hair and pouty lips, but he could also punch your teeth down your throat and pull them out your ass two seconds later.

"Guns."

Zaine glared at Storm.

Storm's thick fingers beckoned.

There was no getting away from this, but Zaine didn't have to like it. He pulled his top over his head and unhitched the shoulder straps on his holster, then laid the pair of guns on a metal table. Storm tensed and Zaine sighed again. "I'm not gonna shoot you, Storm."

"You know it's protocol." Storm wheeled the table away, putting Zaine's guns out of reach. "Wouldn't do much but piss me off anyway." He picked up a penlight and turned back to Zaine.

"Might slow you down a step or two."

Storm shone the light deep into Zaine's eyes.

Pain spiked the back of his skull. "Fuck." He jerked his head away.

"Sit still." Storm's big mitt slammed down on Zaine's head. The light blinded one eye, then the other, scorching his brain matter. Storm straightened, taking a step back, and Zaine blinked hard, refocusing.

"How are you feeling?" Storm asked.

"Great. Thanks for the migraine."

"Uh-huh. Who was the vic?"

A spike of anger tried to derail Zaine's efforts to stay calm. "He wasn't my victim. And I didn't bleed anyone. If you'd listen for a second—"

"So your victim was male. Does he remember anything?"

Zaine huffed and sucked on his tongue, holding a few curse words in. He gripped the examination table, squeezing hard. "One, I'm not new to this. Two, it was nothing, just one hit."

"Because a nyk got the drop on you?"

Zaine narrowed his eyes. "There were extenuating circumstances."

"Uh-huh. Lift your shirt."

He almost quipped about there being other ways to get his clothes off, but Storm clearly was not in the mood for jokes and the quicker they did this, the quicker he could get some rest and get back out there. The nyk was onto him now. Things always got messy once they were outed. Zaine had planned on rattling him loose but hadn't expected the array of punches the nyk had hammered him with.

When he'd burst into that room, the nyk had had Sharpe against the wall, a twitch away from tearing his throat out. Nyks hated losing their marks. He might try to get to Sharpe again.

Zaine unbuttoned his T-shirt and set it aside. "Can we

hurry this up?" He didn't need to look to know his chest was a patchwork of bruises. He'd been on the receiving end of the nyk's punches, punches that would have snapped a normal man's spine. They wouldn't even look that bad now. If he hadn't taken a hit of Sharpe's blood to boost himself, he'd probably be more broken and maybe Storm would be bribing the cops to get him out of custody instead of eyeing up Zaine's abs.

Storm sighed. "You're clearly in pain." To prove his point, his thick finger poked a damaged rib, setting off a firework of pain through Zaine's middle, making him hiss. "How did the nyk get the drop on you? You're usually better than this."

"It's fine." Zaine shrugged. "Nothing I can't handle."

Storm picked up a finger prick kit connected to a tablet and pinched its end on Zaine's finger, taking a blood sample. Zaine hissed again and Kazi snorted.

"Had you gorged yourself on your victim's blood, you'd be halfway to incoherent by now," Storm said. "But you did take blood without consent." Which was one of the big never-to-be-broken rules. They weren't supposed to take blood at all, not from the vein. Storm glowered at his tablet's screen. "There's something else showing up in your blood work."

"That'll be the cocaine."

Kazi snorted again. "Wow. You know how to pick your blood-bags."

Eric *was not* a blood-bag. "Look, you pair of dicks. I walked into a situation that needed to be dealt with fast. The room was already saturated in blood. The nyk had his mark against a wall. I *saved* the vic. Yes, the nyk got away, but I'll get him. I then sampled the vic while he was out cold because I'd just had the crap beaten out of me and the air was full of blood and for a second there, I needed it. If I hadn't acted, the vic would be dead and the nyk stronger for it. Tell me you wouldn't have done exactly the same in that situation?"

"Yeah, no." Kazi smirked.

"Because you're so fucking perfect, Kazi. I fucked up, sure. I took blood without consent. I know it was wrong." Storm was listening. As one of the oldest of the Brotherhood, he understood the need to improvise. There was no way he'd gotten to be a few thousand years old and not fucked up a few times along the way. The fact he didn't say anything meant he agreed. Probably. He was as easy to read as a brick wall.

"I'm going to sleep it off." Zaine hopped off the table and grabbed his shirt. "This doesn't have to go any further. Right?"

Storm's eyes narrowed. "Mikalis will want your report."

"And he'll get it, minus a few... minor details." It wasn't like Zaine hadn't covered for Kazi before. For all his snark, he'd have Zaine's back. But Storm was harder to crack. A stickler for rules and so far up Mikalis's ass he was practically his mouthpiece.

"Sleep it off," Storm grumbled. "Have that report ready. We didn't see you."

Zaine grabbed his guns and headed for the door.

Kazi stepped aside, smirking like Nyx's eternal blessing shone out of his immortal ass.

"And Zaine," Storm said, "it ends there. You don't see the nyk's mark again. It's not worth the risk."

"After a few centuries, I know the rules, Storm."

But Storm was right. It wasn't worth the risk. One taste could be worse than gorging. Because one taste was the appetizer before the main meal—it was never enough. Zaine had to stay away from Sharpe. It was a damn shame because Detective Sharpe was all kinds of intriguing, and these days not much got Zaine's blood flowing. But sinking his teeth into the unconscious Sharpe had lit his heart on fire in more ways than it should have if he was a true, devoted Brotherhood member. Storm didn't need to know how, for a second, back in that room surrounded by blood and expired humans, his fangs deep in Eric's neck, he'd *wanted* to drink the detective down. Just a fleeting desire. It hadn't overruled him but it had been there, that little voice urging him to *kill*. A voice all nyktelios had, even those of the Brotherhood.

He sauntered down the corridor heading toward his quarters. The more he considered the nyk who had gotten the jump on him, the more he wondered if not seeing Sharpe again might be difficult.

He'd suspected Sharpe was tied up in the nyk somehow. He'd seen him at the club a few times, and even before getting up close and personal, something about Eric Sharpe had drawn Zaine's gaze back to him every time. The haunted look in his eyes when he'd sat alone at the bar above that poker room, maybe? The way he could switch on his smile, using it to slam down barriers? As though he had some ghosts in his head. Zaine knew what that felt like too.

Sharpe was all kinds of complicated. *Intriguing* complicated. Alluring complicated.

Maybe their paths wouldn't cross again. But as the detective was working the case of the Times Square body, it seemed likely they would. Especially as Zaine had been the one to prop the body on that bench for the whole of New York to see.

CHAPTER 4

ric

THE VICTIM, Capaldi, had proven to be an "Employee of the Year" type. Everyone had loved the guy. Nobody had had a bad word to say against him. There had been a great deal of tears and hushed murmuring among the staff. Annoyingly, nobody had triggered Sharpe's suspect instincts. No interoffice romance. No vendettas. Not even a jealous colleague.

The next stop had been the man's family. The uniformed cops' family relations staff had already informed the wife of her husband's demise. Nate had gently questioned her while Eric cruised the house looking for anything that might suggest Capaldi wasn't the squeaky-clean banker he appeared to be. The house was as clean as the rest of Capaldi's life.

But something wasn't adding up.

After speaking with the wife, they left the house and Eric dropped behind the wheel of the Charger. "It all feels too damn perfect."

"Meaning?" Nate asked, settling in the passenger seat.

"C'mon." Eric reversed the car out of the driveway and headed back toward the precinct. The sun had finally begun to set, taking his low-level headache with it. He removed his shades and folded them away in the center console. "Nobody is this clean."

Nate sat quietly for a few moments. "Yeah, but we see a lot of shit. It skews our perspective. There aren't always bad guys everywhere."

True. They lived the worst the city had to offer every day. "Right. Except this is New York. Everyone wants something, everyone is hustling, everyone wants a piece of the action. And good people don't get their blood drained and their bodies dumped on a bench in Times Square."

"Yeah," Nate drawled. "Not gonna argue. It does feel contrived."

Eric clicked his fingers. "That's the word. *Contrived.* Capaldi is too good to be true, like a damn cardboard cutout of a nice guy. That tells me he was very good at hiding whatever got him killed. We're missing something, something buried. Forensics might have more."

"In a few days."

They talked some more on the drive back to the precinct. Eric turned over all he knew so far, which wasn't much, and then grabbed a coffee and sat at his desk. Someone had stuck a sticky note to his computer to remind him to put some cash in the pot for Dora's retirement gift.

He yanked the note off and squinted at the screen, then pinched the bridge of his nose. Remnants of the wretched, thumping headache lingered despite popping Tylenol all day.

He dragged a hand down his neck and snagged on a scab. Wet coolness kissed his skin. He dabbed at it, and his fingers came away with a smear of blood. "Shit." He must have caught himself on a nail. He left his desk and entered the men's room. Two uniforms chatting by one of the stalls spotted him and nodded a greeting.

Eric balled up a wad of tissue and dabbed at his neck, then leaned over the basin and turned his head. A yellowish bruise had spread across his neck, and near its center, two small, puckered marks leaked a dribble of blood. What the hell? He pressed the tissue over them. The headache throbbed some more, as if he didn't already have enough to deal with.

He ran the faucet as he set the bloody tissue aside, then splashed his face with the cool water. His reflection blinked at him. He really did look like shit. Pale, and he'd forgotten to shave that morning. He dragged a hand down his shadowed jaw. Jesus, he hadn't felt like himself all day. What was going on with him?

Maybe the reason he looked so wrecked had something to do with executing six men? The Times Square case had kept his mind off it all day, but with tiredness sinking into his bones, the weight of his actions began to push down on him.

What he'd done, it had been right. Every one of those pricks had deserved it. The law would never have touched them. They'd have gone on killing cops and now, thanks to

Eric, that was over. He'd *saved* lives by taking theirs. It was fucking justice.

The man looking back at him from the mirror didn't seem to care, though. He'd killed six people. Shouldn't he be sick about that? "Jesus." He bowed his head and breathed. Maybe he was broken. *Sweet One.* Fuck, the voice chipped off an old memory, the shard digging into his head, making the ache start up again.

"Hey, man, you okay?" one of the officers asked.

"Yeah, good." He smiled, trying to reassure them he wasn't about to have a breakdown in the men's room, and watched them leave, then turned to face his reflection again. At least the weird marks on his neck had stopped bleeding. He leaned in and probed at the bruise. He'd seen marks like those before...

Sweet One.

A wave of sickness rolled over him. He whirled, stumbled into the stall, and heaved up the cheap sandwich he'd eaten for lunch. Cold sweat dampened his face and chilled his neck. He leaned against the stall's flimsy wall and waited for his guts to settle, thoughts whirring.

Old memories fluttered in. The man... The suave man with the stunning eyes... He'd known him. Known his smell, a sickly sweetness like spoiled fruit. Eric's guts made a pathetic attempt at flopping over again. He swallowed, breathed, and pressed his forehead to the cold wall. Was he sick? Or was this some kind of post-traumatic reaction? He didn't feel traumatized. Didn't feel much but satisfaction when he thought about how he'd pulled the trigger on Vergil. A good person would feel remorse. A good person would feel guilty.

He pushed from the stall and stared at himself in the mirrors, with his haunted eyes and sickly pallor.

Nate was right. There were bad guys everywhere. And Eric was one of them.

He had to get his shit together. He ran wet fingers through his hair, straightened his clothes, and returned to his desk. His coffee had gone cold, but it washed away the bitter taste on his tongue.

He searched the precinct call logs for any sign of the multiple homicide from Vergil's club. Nothing. It hadn't been reported. That was a stroke of luck. Someone would have discovered the scene by now so that meant it was being kept away from the cops. As he'd suspected, Vergil's people didn't want the NYPD snooping around their business.

Sweet One.

A shudder ran through him, not quite sickness, something more visceral. An old memory bubbled to the surface and filled his head. Cold, wet grass beneath bare feet. Cold ankles too. He'd forgotten his slippers when he'd run outside, hearing his little sister's screams. He'd gotten his pajamas wet. Ma would be mad.

No, no, no...

He couldn't see what happened next.

That wasn't real. He couldn't relive it, couldn't go back there, to that night... fifteen years ago.

"Fuck." He scrunched up a fist and pressed it against his temple.

All he had to do was squeeze the past out of his head. Sweat dripped down his back. The shrill sound of ringing phones and clattering voices stabbed at his skull. Shit, it was too much. Everything was too much. He couldn't be here at his desk. He needed to move, to get out, to get a drink. He scooped up his jacket and hurried toward the elevator.

"Sharpe, wait," Nate called from the kitchen area.

"I'll be back later." He didn't wait. The elevator swallowed him, took him down to the parking lot where he climbed into the Dodge and gunned her grumbling engine, spinning her tires on the asphalt as he left.

Sweet One.

He knew that man's smell from before, had felt his hands on him then too, sparking forbidden desires. But he couldn't think about it. Those thoughts were dangerous. They tipped him toward a dark place where it would be too easy to fall over the edge and never come back.

The flash of the man's smile. The firm hand on his shoulder. *Come with me.* The memory lashed, tearing Eric's mind open.

Eric slammed on the accelerator, speeding through traffic until the world outside was a blur. He was falling again, falling back into those nightmares. Teeth at his throat, tongue sweeping, and how his body had blazed, so desperate for touch that when it had come, he'd spilled—confused, ablaze, wanting more, so much more. Wanting to drown in the smell of him, even as his thoughts had faded, his head emptied, until all that was left was the suave man, his smooth voice coiling like a snake around Eric's shuddering body.

Blood trickled down his neck. He growled and swept it away. The Charger growled too. He shot through a red light. Horns blared and suddenly reality crashed back in.

What the fuck was he doing? He slammed on the brakes, breathing too hard, heart about to burst, and slowed the car. He was losing his damned mind.

The pressure in his head swelled, threatening to crack him open and spill out all his terrible secrets.

He pulled up outside a bar close enough to his place to walk home later, went straight in, and ordered cheap whiskey. Three glasses went down one after the other, and only then did the sharp angles of the past stop gouging him. His heart slowed, his body checking out, and his mind finally stopped bubbling with insanity.

Jesus, he was a hot mess.

If he didn't get a hold of himself, he'd lose his job, the only damn thing in his life that meant something. He couldn't fuck that up. Just a few more drinks. He'd crash tonight, and tomorrow morning everything would start to look better. It had always worked before.

Three hours later, past midnight, he stumbled out of the bar and squinted at the bright streetlamps illuminating the sidewalk back to his apartment building. Five minutes and he'd be home, back in his own bed, too fucking drunk to remember everything he was trying to forget.

Someone or something kicked a bottle. He lifted his head and peered into the gloomy alley near the back of the bar. Nothing. Just a stray cat maybe.

He staggered and tripped his way back to his apartment building, unlocked the main door, and stomped upstairs. An envelope had been wedged in his apartment door. He fumbled the lock, plucked the envelope free, and stumbled inside, flicking on the lights. After tossing his keys onto the kitchen counter, he tore the envelope open.

Sweet One,

I have something of yours. Something you left behind. Something incriminating.

Come to me at La Dolce Vita.

Don't keep me waiting.

The smell of sweet, ripe fruit wafted from the paper.

Eric dropped onto the couch cushions, buried his face in his hands, and breathed, because breathing was the only damn thing he could control.

He couldn't hide from this. He couldn't push it aside and pretend it didn't exit. The past he'd been running from for fifteen years had caught up to him.

He'd believed the suave man was dead. He'd thought he'd killed him.

Eric had never dreamed he'd come back—no, that was a lie. Until he'd become a cop, he'd dreamed it every night. He used to wake drenched in sweat and semen and tears, afraid the suave man was in the room with him, in his bed, *in his body*.

Sobs bubbled up in his throat. He let them. Because tomorrow, he'd have to face his nightmare and somehow resist him all over again.

CHAPTER 5

aine

THE BAD NYKTELIOS, or nyks as they were known by the Brotherhood, were creatures of habit. Most were ancient, and after living a few thousand years, they got stuck in the same behavioral ruts. The Brotherhood were nyktelios too, but with a thin line of rules separating good from bad. The nyk Zaine had tracked and failed to kill was back at one of his favorite clubs, La Dolce Vita, as though he hadn't brushed up against death in the form of the Brotherhood just two nights before. The arrogance of the nyks had them believing their immortality was a constant, as fixed as the setting sun. Zaine was happy to liberate them from that thinking by turning their bones to ash. He'd killed around thirty in his own extended lifespan. This nyk would be joining his dusty brethren soon.

He'd gotten the drop on Zaine. That wouldn't happen again.

Zaine entered the club sans guns. He'd borrowed some of Kazi's designer clothes. The guy was forever dressing like he had a date with a red carpet. He wouldn't even notice the expensive pants and silk shirt were missing. He and Zaine were roughly the same build, Kazi being slimmer, but a tight shirt never looked bad on a ripped guy. With a suit jacket thrown over it, Zaine knew he turned a few heads.

Music thumped from the club's multiple dance floors. The VIP private lounge was on the second floor, up a flight of open stairs on a suspended mezzanine area, invite only. So Zaine cruised the bars running along the outside of the dance floors, keeping an eye on the smoky glass balustrade above as he watched for the nyk.

This nyk went by the alias of Sebastien Goldman. To most people, Sebastien Goldman was a New York businessman, unmarried, no kids. Nothing that would expose him for the bloodsucker he was. In the last thirty years, hiding in plain sight had gotten a lot more difficult. Cell phones and the internet could see a single image spread around the world in seconds. But Sebastien was smart. He knew how to play at being human.

Every person in the club had a cell phone, a recording device. Every single one was a potential witness and every single one could upload a video and have it go viral. A nyktelios couldn't sink his teeth into all the potential witnesses, making them forget. So they liked to hide behind drugs and alcohol, low lights, large crowds, shadows, and sex. As centuries-old killers, they'd perfected blending in, like snakes in the grass. Nobody believed in vampires, right?

Zaine knew all this because, like them, he was a snake in the grass too.

The Brotherhood were, after all, a few bites of the vein away from the nyks they hunted and killed.

He sat at the bar and ordered a drink, absorbing the club's loud music and the throng of people. An hour later when two young men climbed the stairs—brothers, from the similar bone structure and blond hair—Sebastien emerged at the top and greeted them with his arms spread and his face lit by a charming smile, acting the part of the gracious host.

Sebastien was handsome, Zaine had to give him that. He had exotic good looks, tanned skin, dark hair, and blue eyes that screamed a European heritage, which was pretty damn close to the truth. The goddess Nyx had known exactly what she was doing when she'd crafted her first nyktelios at the dawn of creation. This nyk, Sebastien, was maybe fifth generation, older than Zaine had realized, a mistake that had cost him the element of surprise. Zaine was at least tenth generation, Nyx's blood and power diluted by the time it had gotten to him. But what he lacked in heritage, he made up for with his guns. Storm was fourth gen. Mikalis... shit, nobody knew what Mikalis was. Rumors swirled around him like wildfire. Some even said he wasn't nyktelios at all. But the word was the leader was second gen, sired by one of Nyx's two precious children, his mother so close to the goddess she might as well be a goddess herself. Zaine wasn't sure he believed it. Nyx was a First Order goddess, more monster than god. He figured her Second Order children would be scary fuckers too. Mikalis was scary, but he wasn't a *Second Order pillar of smoke and vengeance* scary, the kind to suck all the blood from your veins from across a room in two seconds flat. Or maybe he was part monster and Zaine just hadn't seen that side of the Brotherhood leader yet. He'd learned in four hundred years that when it came to the Blackrose Brotherhood, anything was possible.

He tapped the bar and got a refill. As he lifted his drink to his lips, he spotted a familiar face coming through the crowd and froze. Detective Eric Sharpe was heading straight for the space at the bar beside Zaine. Storm's warning about staying away flashed through Zaine's thoughts at the same time as his gaze dropped to the Band-Aid on Sharpe's neck. A dart of lust shivered down Zaine's back straight to his cock.

Hello, hunger, my old friend.

"Bourbon," the detective said to the bartender. His gaze skipped over Zaine, just a cursory glance, regrettably without any meaning behind it. The detective's thoughts were clearly elsewhere.

Zaine stared into his drink, skin prickling. There was that damned feeling again, that fluttering rush kick-starting his weary heart. He knew what it was—desire. The violent kind. The kind that had Zaine wanting to throw the detective against a wall and kiss him until he came undone in Zaine's hands. And when Sharpe was out of his fucking mind with want, Zaine would sink his teeth into the detective's neck and drink him down, drink him deep, gorge himself and maybe fuck him too if Sharpe was into it. *Shit*. Those thoughts were dangerous. He needed to unthink them immediately.

"You all right?"

Zaine twitched and cleared his throat. He licked his teeth, slotting the fangs back in their resting position against the roof of his mouth, and smiled. "Good. You?" That came out more aggressively than he'd planned.

"You're breathing pretty fast. You need an inhaler or something?" Sharpe said, eyebrow raised. "A doctor?"

Zaine laughed, his ego dented. "No, I do not need an inhaler. Or a doctor." Christ, Kazi would howl with laughter if he'd heard that.

"Maybe you should look into that?"

Zaine side-eyed the detective. He couldn't tell if the man was serious or deliberately baiting him. He was a little pale under the bar's colored lighting, partly Zaine's fault—Sharpe's body was still trying to repair the blood loss—but his eyes dazzled. Those haunted eyes were what had caught Zaine's attention on first seeing him. So much weight behind them, so many horrors, and a whole lot of strength to survive them.

The detective broke Zaine's gaze by offering his hand. "Eric."

Don't see the mark again. Storm was going to lose his shit.

Zaine wrapped the man's warm hand in his—hot blood, skin on skin, paradoxically soft but firm—and willed his instincts to calm the fuck down. "Thomas," he said, plucking the name out of the air. He'd assumed Sharpe wouldn't remember him. A bite like the one Zaine had given him generally left the mark's thoughts muddled, and then there had been the cocaine screwing up his recall, but he also suspected the detective was keen-eyed. It was equally likely Sharpe remembered something about Zaine from their brief meeting and had decided to approach to see if he could shake anything lose.

Sharpe looked at their hands, still locked together, and Zaine quickly let go, internally kicking himself. He was going to have to be careful. Sharpe was, well, sharp. And Zaine, having tasted the man's blood, wanted more of the good stuff. His body was telling him he *needed* it. Needed to make Sharpe *run*. Needed to *hunt him down, throw him against a wall, and feed and fuck.*

He shifted on the stool, alleviating some of the pressure in his pants. Hell, he hadn't been this aroused in... what felt like forever. Resisting Sharpe was going to be harder than he'd thought.

"You meeting someone?" Zaine asked, hoping Sharpe didn't hear the lower-than-usual timbre of his voice. He could do this. He wasn't some newly turned, rabid nyk. He was a member of the fucking Brotherhood. Better than the leeches he hunted down. He lived and breathed *control.*

"Er, yeah." Eric's gaze flicked up toward the mezzanine lounge.

Was he here for the nyk, Sebastien? He'd be a fool to go up there after what Zaine had seen transpire between them. The nyk had been about to tear into Eric. Unless...

Oh shit.

Was Eric a feeder?

When Zaine had plowed into that poker room, the nyk

might not have been about to kill Eric at all. Maybe he'd been about to *feed.*

Sharpe didn't look like Sebastien's type. Too old, to start with. Zaine had watched the nyk long enough to know he liked his feeders young, verging on pubescent boys. Boys full of raging hormones, the easily seduced. Eric Sharpe didn't look like the type to be easily seduced by a pretty face and a few smooth words. He'd be a more difficult catch.

But as old as the nyk likely was, he'd be extremely persuasive. Almost impossible to refuse, especially if the feeder was attracted to men. Zaine ran his eye over the detective again. He'd rolled his sleeves up, revealing fine forearms, the type ancient Greek sculptors would swoon over. Eric's heart beat slowly, pulsing through his veins, resolute and determined. Zaine could have listened to that soothing sound for hours. Was he into men?

"You know, I feel like we've met before," Eric said, lifting his drink to his lips.

Zaine's heart tripped. "I don't think so. I'd remember a handsome face like yours." He tipped his glass, letting the words slide right off his tongue as a test, a tease, a hook... to see if Eric would bite. Zaine certainly did.

Sharpe smiled his flick-of-a-switch smile. "It's just..." He turned to face Zaine and tucked a hand into his pants pocket. "You weren't at the Collective Club a few nights ago?"

Dammit, he remembered. Not all of it, or he wouldn't be standing so close, but enough to raise the detective's suspicions. If the Brotherhood discovered Zaine had left a loose end behind, he'd end up getting grilled again, and Mikalis would get involved.

"I was... or tried to. Didn't get in. You saw me waiting in the line outside." There was no room for doubt in his words. Eric had to believe him.

Eric's mouth twitched up at one corner. "Yeah... maybe." His gaze drifted over Zaine's shoulder to the stairs and his smile quickly died.

"You should be careful up there. I hear the club owner bites." Warning him was a risk, but one worth taking. Zaine didn't want to see Eric used, not in the way the nyks used their feeders. He likely had no idea what he was about to walk into and sure as hell might not walk out of again, not with his mind intact. Storm's *don't see him again* circled around Zaine's thoughts like water down a drain.

Eric lowered his glass. "Yeah, I heard that too." He left the drink he'd barely touched on the bar and headed for the stairs. "Nice meetin' you, Thomas."

The security guard unhooked the velvet rope and let Sharpe pass. He climbed the stairs. Something like guilt or regret poked around Zaine's determination to back off. It was a damn shame if Eric was a feeder. Maybe if Zaine could end the nyk soon, it would save Eric before he had the chance to become addicted—assuming he wasn't already.

The only problem was, killing a nyk was a whole lot harder to get away with these days than it used to be.

Eric disappeared on the lounge level, and with him out of sight, Zaine frowned into his drink. *Don't get involved.* Another Brotherhood rule. Another way for them to slip unseen between the ages, extracting the nyktelios from humanity like bad apples from the barrel. *Do not get involved.* His fluttering heart was a warning. *Kill the nyk and move on.* Because nobody lived a few hundred years without having their heart broken, and Zaine's heart was already in tatters.

CHAPTER 6

ric

Soft lighting gleamed in the club's upstairs lounge. A few groups gathered around tables, drinking, probably high, the typical VIP crowd. Eric scanned the faces, looking for the one he'd recognize until coming to rest on the man at the back of the room. He reclined in a leather couch, arms spread along the back cushions, bracketed by two young blond men seated on either side of him. They appeared to be laughing and having a great time, but it was the dark-haired man Eric zeroed in on.

His memory flashed. *Come to me, Sweet One.*

The voice from a lifetime ago seeded itself inside his thoughts and tugged on conflicting instincts. Run. Obey. Fuck. His skin tried to squirm off his bones. He swallowed, willed the noise from his head, and made his way over. Fifteen years, the suave man had said, but he didn't look old enough to be the same nightmare from Eric's flimsy memory. This guy was maybe early thirties. He'd been early thirties then too. He *couldn't* be the same man. Was Eric really so fucked up that he was seeing his past everywhere?

But he knew things, and his voice... his smell...

Eric stopped at the table and cleared his throat.

The suave man slid his gaze from his companion. Dark eyes came to rest on Eric, spearing through his heart. Memories simmered like hot poison. Goose bumps shivered across his skin and the fine hairs on his arms lifted. All he had to do was pretend he had his shit together long enough to find out what incriminating evidence this man had on him. If it was the gun, he just had to get it back. And all this would be over.

"I got your note," Eric said, sounding more confident than he felt.

"Detective Sharpe." The suave man's voice unraveled some part of Eric that was wound so tightly he hadn't known it existed. The ghost of this man's touch, the memory of his warm mouth on Eric's, the murmur of his desires and what he was going to do—*Beg, Sweet One, beg me to fill you*. Eric shook the unwanted thoughts from his head. He could not afford to let the past in, couldn't let it distract him.

"Sit."

He caught himself obeying as though it was the most natural thing and straightened instead. "I'll stand, thanks."

The blond twins—they had to be brothers—dragged heavy-lidded gazes over Eric from head to toe and back again. They both had the youthful innocent appearance of kids who shouldn't be in nightclubs. "You two over twenty-one?" Eric glowered.

The one on the left smirked. "What's it to you, Daddy?"

Eric flipped the edge of his shirt up, showing his detective's badge.

The young man tensed and immediately looked to the suave man for reassurance.

"It's fine. The detective has no interest in you." He waved a hand. "Leave us for a moment."

The pair huffed and slunk away, crossing the room to the private bar area and glowering from the shadows.

Eric breathed in, filling his lungs. His blood thumped hot and heavy through his veins. The music throbbed, and the suave man merely smiled, nonthreatening, almost amused. "Do you like to kill, Detective?"

What the hell kind of question was that? "What?"

"I'm going to assume events didn't go to plan two nights ago when you executed six men? Did you enjoy it? Murdering them? It's not the first time you've killed, is it?"

Eric ground his teeth together. He clasped his hands in front of him, stance relaxed. "You have me confused with someone else."

"Hm." The sound rumbled through him like a purr. He leaned back and drew his sultry gaze over Eric, trailing a path as though he remembered Eric's body. "No. You and I... we're connected."

Eric fought to keep the memories buried even as they boiled around his pitiful efforts, desperate to be free. He'd locked all that shit away a long time ago. "I don't know you. You asked me here because you have something of mine. So let's talk."

The suave man's smile spoke of delicious, wicked things. A smile Eric almost *wanted* to see. "I'll return what is yours. But first, I need you to do something for me. There's a man who appears to be making it his mission to make my life difficult. You met him, in fact. Although"—his eyes narrowed—"it appears you're struggling with your memories." The suave man touched his own neck, indicating the marks on Eric's.

He touched his neck, mirroring the gesture, and skimmed the Band-Aid.

The suave man's laugh spilled into Eric's mind, further unraveling all his secrets. The laugh was the same one that had rumbled through him so long ago, the same one that had instantly gotten him hard back then. But that man was dead. Eric had killed him. This man couldn't be him. It was just some mind-fuck, some trick, brought on by stress maybe.

Unease made him squirm, as though he'd been caught doing something wrong, something terrible. A therapist had told him his memories would resurface if he didn't deal with them, but that had been... years ago. Why were they assaulting him all over again now?

The suave man smirked. "After many, *many* years of observation, I've learned the human mind is remarkable. It smothers severe trauma like a coagulating wound. Those memories you're fighting so hard to deny? Your mind is desperately trying to protect you, Detective, from a past we both know to be real."

Eric flashed him a hollow smile. He'd had enough of

this man's superior attitude. "I'm a detective with the NYPD but I also don't fuck around, as you saw in that poker room. You're attempting to blackmail the wrong person. Give me the fucking gun and I'll walk away."

The suave man chuckled again. "You're a homicide detective who killed six men. There's a beautiful irony in that, almost poetry. Don't you think?"

He didn't like any of this, didn't like the way the man peered through his lashes as though he was thinking of all the ways he could pick pieces of Eric apart. Didn't like how he just sat there, so confident and relaxed. Didn't like the heat and the noise, and he didn't like how, deep down, Eric knew he was right. About everything. "You haven't reported the deaths. I assume Vergil was something to you, a grunt, whatever. You no more want the cops snooping around than I want to be here. Give me the gun and back the fuck off."

The man cocked his head. "I regretted letting you go."

Eric swallowed, or tried to, but his heart had pounded its way up his throat and had begun to choke him. Sweat cooled on his back. "You didn't let me go, you fuck," he growled, low and menacing.

The suave man rose, like a panther stretching, and came around the table.

Eric's heart raced, his breaths racing with it. The suave man stepped close, peering into his eyes. Eric had never learned his name all those years ago. He'd been a figment of his imagination, or so the psychiatrists had told him. A way to process grief. He'd witnessed something so terrible, so traumatic, his mind had created a monster to blame it all on. He'd believed them. Until now. Because the monster was looking him in the eyes and dragging Eric back fifteen years.

The suave man skimmed his fingers along Eric's jaw. "I know how you taste, sweeter than all the rest." He tipped Eric's chin up. "I know the soft moan you make when you come." He bowed his head, mouth so close to Eric's that he could already taste the sweetness of his lips. "I know how you feel, trembling in my arms, begging to be fucked *in every way*." Those last words skimmed Eric's mouth.

No... It was lies. It had to be. But the monster was real, and here, and so close, smothering Eric's heart and mind all over again. He feared him, was hard for him, so achingly hard that if the suave man told him to bend over and take his cock right now, he'd let it happen. "Get out of my face."

Something sharp and cold flashed through the suave man's gaze. He laughed and stepped back. "Clear the lounge!"

The guests hurried down the stairs. Even the two blonds left, huffing like spoiled teenagers. And now Eric was alone with the monster, surrounded by thumping music and his thumping heart and the flash of colorful memories scorched into his mind. He wasn't going to be intimidated. He wasn't the victim. Not anymore. This man was just... a man. He could no more hurt Eric than any of the criminal assholes who came at him, fists flying.

"Fate brought you back to me, Eric." He picked up the bottle of wine and poured two glasses. "I see the power of hatred in your eyes." His gaze dropped. "And how your body remembers me."

"You're insane. *This* is insane. Where's the gun?"

"Drink with me?" He raised the glass. "To reunions."

If Eric didn't leave now, he was going to do something he'd regret, like lunge, grab this bastard's arm, twist it behind his back, and fuck him raw exactly as *he'd done to Eric.* "We're done." He turned on his heel. The air shifted, a blast of sickly fruit smell wafting toward him, and the suave man appeared in front of him, blocking the way to the stairs. *Impossible.* Eric reeled. The suave man's hand shot out, locking around Eric's throat, and when the man smiled, his two gleaming canine teeth extended.

"Enough games," the man hissed.

His grip squeezed. The air in Eric's lungs burned. He clawed at the hand on his neck, tried to pry off the fingers and take his eyes from the man's teeth—long and pointed and sharp. He knew what they were. He'd felt them sink into his skin a thousand times.

"You will obey, Sweet One." He yanked Eric close, so close he had no choice but to fall into the silver flooding the man's eyes. This wasn't right. This wasn't normal. But he knew deep down, far down where he'd buried it, how this had all happened before, when he'd stood barefoot on the lawn and seen a monster butcher his family around him. The grass had been cold and wet but not with rain. With blood.

"You will remember." His mouth opened, fangs gleaming. He struck, folding Eric into his steel-like embrace, his body firm and warm and horribly familiar. Jagged heat flashed down Eric's neck, his back, and danced through his chest into his heart. He bucked and opened his mouth to scream but no sound came. Maybe he didn't want to scream at all because this was right, this was how it should

be, this was how it had been before when the monster had taken him into his arms and filled his body with a rush hotter and brighter than any drug. The heat poured through him now, filled his veins, filled him up with lust, and burst all the memories wide open.

They'd told him it wasn't real. They'd told him he'd dreamed it.

But they'd been wrong.

Vampires were real. And Eric was coming undone beneath one.

He fought pathetically, got a fist locked in the vampire's clothes, and managed to wheeze a single word. "Please..." *Please don't, please do, please kill me, fuck me, feed from me, please, please, please...*

He fell now like he'd fallen then. Because it was so much easier *not* to fight, easier to let the monsters win. Exactly as he had before.

CHAPTER 7

aine

Eric wasn't among the people who left the lounge. Neither was Sebastien. That was, in all likelihood, not good.

Whatever was about to happen, Zaine shouldn't get involved. He couldn't, not without things getting very messy and the Brotherhood coming down on him hard.

There were rules. So many rules. Necessary rules to protect the Brotherhood and their work. People died all the time when they could have been saved, to protect the Brotherhood and its cause. *The needs of the many outweighed the few.* They saved more in the long run because of the rules. It was hammered into them over and over, like nails through the hands. *Memento mori. Remember, you must die.* Death was a fact of human life. The Brotherhood circumvented it unseen.

That was all well and good, but if Zaine had acted faster, the nyk would already be dust and Eric wouldn't be suffering—because whether he was a feeder or not, he probably didn't have a choice in it. *Maybe Eric wanted it?* Maybe he was a lovestruck feeder? Zaine wasn't buying it. Not Eric. He didn't know much about the detective, but he knew Eric hadn't gone up to that lounge to have the nyk feed from him and fuck him dry.

Whatever was going on up those stairs, Zaine couldn't sit at the bar and let it happen. He just wasn't made that way. "Ah, fuck."

He eased off the stool and started for the stairs. Every step warned him this was a mistake. He'd pay for it. But his heart, that fleshy, damaged organ behind prisonlike ribs, refused to listen.

"You can't go up there." The security guard thrust out a hand. Twice Zaine's size, the guy was built like an old oak tree and would, for any normal person, be just as immovable. Around them, the music beat and lights flashed. Human eyes weren't designed to see in flickering light or the dark. Most were too drunk or so focused on their own lives, they wouldn't see what was about to happen. The camouflage was almost perfect.

Zaine struck the guard with a precision punch to the chest, just enough—he didn't want to kill the guy—and when he dropped, puffing and wheezing, Zaine caught him. "There ya go. Have a rest, you've earned it." He propped him against the side of the step, patted him on the shoulder, and unhooked the velvet rope. "I was never here."

He climbed the stairs to find the sight he'd feared all

along. The nyk had Eric bent backward in his arms, his teeth deep in Eric's throat, drinking him down. A spike of barbed lust tried to muscle in on Zaine's motives, telling him he wanted a piece of that action, that Eric was *his* and *only his.* He shoved the rabid urges aside. "Hey, man? Any idea where the men's room is?"

The nyk jerked his head up, teeth bared. *"You."*

"Me, asshole." No guns. He'd have to take the nyk down the old-fashioned way. Zaine raised his hands, still approaching.

"You've made a mistake coming here, Brotherhood." Sebastien panted. Aroused and flushed with Eric's blood, he wasn't going to make this easy.

Eric's gasping breaths came too fast, like a fish out of water. Still braced in the nyk's arms, he didn't move, didn't fight. There were a whole lot of reasons for why he wasn't moving, all of them bad. Whatever happened next, Zaine's goal had to be to get Eric to safety.

"Put down the meat-bag and let's do this. You and me."

The nyk snarled, baring fangs. "Mikalis sent you?"

Zaine grinned. "Sweetheart, it's just me. You don't even feature in his footnotes."

Finally, Sebastien stepped back and gently laid Eric on the couch. He took the time to sweep Eric's hair back from his forehead in a curiously tender gesture that set Zaine's teeth on edge. When he straightened, that tenderness vanished.

He strode toward Zaine. "I should have killed you when I had the chance."

"The feeling's mutual."

The nyk shimmered with power. Flushed with fresh

blood, he was high on his own supremacy. Zaine, on the other hand, had downed a Brotherhood blood-bag that had barely touched the sides, was unarmed, and had none of the typical advantages, such as surprise and daylight, he'd planned on using when he confronted this nyk.

This was going to hurt.

He grinned, letting his fangs drop. "Let's see what you've got."

Predatory lust flashed behind the nyk's eyes. He lunged, slammed into Zaine's middle, and scooped him off his feet. He had a second to realize he was airborne before the nyk's hands yanked him down through a table and *into* the floor, jarring his teeth and rattling his bones. The nyk —fangs fully extended—struck at his throat.

Zaine thrust an arm up. Pain slashed through his muscles as teeth sank in and tore free again, taking a chunk of flesh with them.

Fury set the nyk ablaze, stripping him of all that smooth charm, revealing the real beast just beneath his sophisticated surface. Silver eyes swam with primordial magic. Chaos and darkness, gifts from the goddess. He tore at Zaine like a whirlwind, teeth snapping, fingernails ripping his clothes, trying to tear away strips of skin.

The mental chains Zaine kept in place to control the beast inside broke free, and with a roar, he bucked, kicking upward, and flipped the nyk overhead, slamming him down behind Zaine. But the nyk flipped to his feet, grabbed a nearby chair, and swung it, narrowly missing taking Zaine's head off. The force of the throw exploded the chair against the far wall.

Fuck...

Sebastien smiled. "Pathetic weakling." His eyes flared, teeth flashing. "Who are you to try and stop me? You are nothing but a child—"

Three gunshots blasted in quick succession. The rounds punched into the nyk's chest, each one rocking him backward. He stumbled and growled, more pissed off than hurt, then jerked his head up and glared past Zaine to Eric and his smoking gun.

"My sweet one—"

Eric pulled the trigger again. The fourth round struck Sebastien between his eyes, flinging him backward through the glass balustrade and right over the edge. Panicked screams erupted from the dance floor below, a sound that meant witnesses. Zaine turned, smiled at Eric for saving his ass, and faced down the barrel of Eric's gun, so close he tasted hot gun oil.

"What *the fuck* are you?" The detective panted.

Zaine raised his hands. A shot to the head wouldn't kill him, the same as it hadn't killed the nyk, but it would bring an abrupt end to this fight and make things extremely complicated. "Eric, wait, listen. Sebastien's not dead. He's either on his way back up here to finish us off or he's already gone, and we have about eight minutes until your colleagues at the NYPD arrive."

Eric's brow furrowed. He staggered on the spot and dabbed at his bloody neck with his free hand. His gaze wavered, losing focus. "I keep killing him," he muttered. "Why won't he die?" He wobbled and dropped to his knees.

Zaine swooped in.

Eric jolted at the contact, shoved at Zaine, and scrabbled backward, trying to scoot away. "Don't touch me. Get the fuck off!"

Zaine relented, hands up. "I need to leave. Now. I'd prefer it if you came with me."

Eric panted or maybe choked on a sob. As gray as an old sheet, he wasn't going to last much longer. He needed treatment. He needed a hospital or the Brotherhood. Shit, shit, shit. "Eric, listen to me." Zaine knelt and fixed him with his stare. He didn't have the hypnotic ability Storm was rumored to have, but sometimes the right words were enough. "I'm not here to hurt you. I just want to see you safe. If you stay, there will be questions. Questions I don't think you want to answer anytime soon."

Eric doubled over, clutching his chest. "It's fucked. Everything is fucked... He's under my skin. I feel him." He gasped, mumbled some more, then clawed at his forearms, scratching at himself.

Zaine couldn't leave him like this. Fuck the rules. He reached out a hand. Eric jerked, nostrils flaring, but when Zaine gently touched his face, he stilled, calming. His eyes widened, seeking something in Zaine's gaze. Hopefully, the truth. Zaine would *never* hurt him. Those old wounds in Eric's eyes, they spoke of terrible things and made Zaine want to tear down the club if it meant he could take Eric's pain away. "You can trust me. I promise. I will never hurt you, Eric."

He blinked. His breathing calmed. He'd clearly needed to hear those words.

"Never," Zaine said again. "Nyx as my witness." He meant it, vowed it with his heart.

Eric nodded tightly. Zaine carefully got an arm under

him, propping him against his side. His trembling made Zaine's teeth ache to sink into something or someone, to make the nyk pay.

Together they staggered from the club, pretending to be panicked members of the crowd. Chaos made the deception easier, and in the furor, they snuck out of sight of security. Any camera footage the Brotherhood would track down and *disappear* later. Zaine walked Eric farther from the club, away from the frantic noise, keeping a watchful eye out for the nyk. There had been enough blood to suggest Sebastien would need to be holed up for a few days to heal. He wouldn't attack again anytime soon.

Eric had fallen quiet, probably clinging to consciousness out of pure stubbornness.

"We can go back to my place—" Zaine began.

"No," Eric mumbled. "I just want to go home."

Zaine pulled his phone from his pocket and reluctantly called Kazi's number.

"Sup, Z?" Kazi drawled.

"Hey, Kazi, need a pickup. On the quiet. Don't tell the others."

"Dammit, Zaine. This had better not be connected to that mark."

"Lay into me later." He hung up, sent Kazi the pin of their location, then propped Eric on a low wall. Eric shivered and sweated. He didn't need his bed; he needed a hospital.

"Listen, you've lost a lot of blood—"

"Uh-huh." Eric chuckled.

And delirious too. "I can take you somewhere. Not a

hospital, we don't need the questions. Somewhere... safe. They'll help—"

"No."

"At best, you need a transfusion—"

"Hey," Eric snapped. "Don't think I didn't see what you did—think I don't remember." He waved a hand at the mess that was his bloody neck. "You're like him. I'm not going '*somewhere safe*' with you. The only reason I haven't shot you is I need answers. And you have them."

He was barely conscious, but that mind of his was still ruthlessly churning on. "All right," Zaine said, relenting. He backed off, giving Eric space, and paced the spot near the edge of the sidewalk. He couldn't tell Eric anything. He should leave him here, call Kazi off, and walk away. But Eric would never let this go. He was onto Zaine now, onto their world. The detective's entire career was based on digging up secrets people had tried to bury. He'd never drop it. Shit, if Mikalis learned about this, he'd go straight to the nuclear option and have Eric disappeared and Zaine tossed into confinement for a few years to cool off. That could not happen.

The headlights of a sleek silver sports car swept over Zaine. The Jaguar pulled to the curb and its passenger window rolled down.

Kazi frowned from behind the wheel. "Are those my clothes?"

"What? No." Zaine sighed through his nose and stepped aside, revealing Eric slumped on the wall. He was gray and sickly and breathing fast, with blood drying on his neck.

Kazi rolled his eyes. "You found a stray?"

"It's not like that."

"Whatever. It's your funeral. Put him in the back."

Zaine opened the rear door and collected Eric. "Who is he?" Eric mumbled.

"A friend... sometimes."

Eric slumped into the back of the car, and despite being close to passing out, he eyed Kazi hard. "Don't fuck with me, guys. I will shoot you."

Kazi adjusted the rearview mirror, getting a long look at Eric, and smiled. "You aren't my type."

Zaine climbed into the passenger side and slammed the door. "Kazi, just drive."

CHAPTER 8

ric

HE HAD TO STAY CONSCIOUS. Getting into cars with strangers was right up there on the Top Five Things Not To Do To Avoid Being Murdered. Eric had closed enough cases featuring victims just like him. *Not a victim.* Not anymore. He shivered, his head throbbing. His veins burned. He wanted to crawl out of his own skin and hide in a hole. He wanted to scream. To smash something. His mind was shredded, his memories in the gutter, swirling down a drain. He might even be insane, or halfway to it.

The two strangers walked him to his apartment. The tall black-haired Italian-model-looking guy who had turned up in the sleek sports car kept side-eyeing him and smirking, as though all of this was a joke. The other guy, Thomas, wasn't smiling now like he had at the bar. He'd been the one who had fought the suave man in the poker room—Eric remembered that now. What was Thomas's place in all of this? Good, bad, friend, enemy?

Eric's thoughts were full of fog, his body like lead. He didn't even feel like himself anymore. Some fragile part of him had cracked open and spilled out. A small quiet part wanted to fold himself into a corner and hide. Another part wanted to rage and set the world on fire. But most of him just felt... empty.

Thomas flicked on Eric's lights, leading the way inside as though he'd been here before, and Kazi followed behind Eric. That one moved differently too. Slowly, carefully, with an eerie kind of grace, part sensual, part predatory. They reminded him of...

"He needs to leave," Eric said, nodding at the one named Kazi.

Kazi's gaze flicked to Thomas's and the pair left the living room to mutter quietly in the hall. Eric dropped onto the couch, slumped back, and closed his eyes. He could just... rest a while.

A few minutes later the door clunked closed and Thomas returned. "Kazi's gone. He's going to scout the neighborhood—check the nyk isn't watching."

The nyk? Eric groaned and slid sideways, sprawling on the couch with his head on a cushion. None of this was real. That was the only explanation. He was trapped in one of his nightmares. He'd wake up soon. "Your name isn't Thomas, is it?" he mumbled, eyes still closed.

"No. It's Zaine."

"Huh." Zaine... The Z from the text messages? That would mean he'd been here, in Eric's apartment, before. He'd brought him home, undressed him, left out the glass of water and the painkillers. And in the morning, he'd vanished like smoke. Poof. Maybe he'd be gone tomorrow too, which would be a shame because despite the fangs, the strength, the blurred speed, and the fact Zaine definitely wasn't human, Eric didn't feel like he was falling into the darkness when Zaine was close.

"Not even the goddess herself will get past me tonight," Zaine said.

Eric had no idea what that meant, but he liked the sound of his gravelly voice, chasing him down into an exhausted, dreamless sleep.

ERIC GROANED AWAKE, light-headed, his thoughts full of fluff. When he laid eyes on the sleeping blond male sprawled in the armchair by the window, one leg thrown over the chair's armrest, his eyes closed and face relaxed and his floppy hair messily strewn about his face, a whole lot of clear, sharp thoughts rushed at Eric. Zaine's tight shirt was askew and missing buttons, making the ruffled picture somehow *more* enticing. Eric swallowed. All the noise from last night tried to muscle into his head, but he kept it back in favor of admiring Zaine instead.

The blinds behind him were closed, as were all the blinds in the apartment, but some smaller blades of sunlight peeked through, landing on Zaine. He breathed softly, the rise and fall of his chest almost too slight to see.

Last night Eric had seen Zaine and the suave man trade blows, both moving like liquid, exchanging attacks that shook the air they blurred through. He'd seen one pick up the other as though he were a doll. It defied physics and reason.

But he wasn't thinking about that.

He *was* thinking about Zaine's soft lips. Even in his sleep, they wore a hint of a smile. What would they feel like on Eric's? He hadn't noticed the man's body much last night, too preoccupied with staying alive, but he recalled now exactly how firm and corded with muscle it had felt with Eric tucked close.

Eric turned his face away and squeezed his eyes closed. All right. He really did have to think about last night and what had happened at La Dolce Vita. Clearly, he'd hit his head or something... But first, he needed to get the sweet rotting fruit smell off him. He rose from the couch slowly, stumbling a bit, but made it to the bathroom without falling on his ass. He'd seen better-looking reheated pizzas than his reflection in the mirror. Crusted blood flaked down his collar, making his neck itch. Downing a few pills, he stripped and stepped under the shower's jets.

Hot water pounded over his shoulders and down his back, thawing some of the ice in his veins. He had to think slowly, to gently turn over last night's revelations so they didn't all tumble down and bury him. Softly, softly, like picking off a scab.

He turned the shower off, stepped from the rolling steam, grabbed a fluffy towel—

"You all right?"

"Fuck!"

Zaine leaned against the bathroom doorframe, apparently comfortable. The smirk on his lips suggested he'd been there a while.

"What the hell, man!" Eric clutched the towel to himself. "You ever heard of privacy?"

"Just checking you were alive. I wouldn't be much use as a bodyguard if you'd slipped and cracked your head open in the shower." Zaine arched an eyebrow. "By the way, I wasn't sleeping while you were eye-fucking me. Just resting. I don't sleep." His gaze slipped down Eric's chest with enough heat in it to shorten Eric's breath, and then he was gone again, the bathroom door closing behind him.

"Fuck." Eric swore again, grabbing the edge of the basin. Clearly, Zaine had zero personal boundaries and didn't care for privacy. But he had kept his promise. He hadn't hurt Eric and he'd had the opportunity to.

There was no denying Zaine was mixed up in all this. But why and how? What did he want? Who even were he and his supermodel friend from last night?

What were they?

He exhaled and stared at his reflection, ignoring the small voice in his head screaming for him to run far, far away. He had to get his shit together. He was a grown man with a career, a life. He did *not* believe in vampires. There would be an explanation for all of this. Zaine had the answers. He'd have answers about the suave man too, like how he'd survived a knife to the heart all those years ago.

The smell of freshly brewed coffee roused his senses. He opened the door, ducked into his room to throw on a T-shirt and pants, then hurried into the living room slash kitchen. Zaine was leaning against the counter sipping coffee, perfectly at home, like a stray cat who had waltzed in off the streets and declared himself king of this new domain.

"I need answers, but first I have to make a call." Eric grabbed his phone off the counter and dialed Nate's number, but voice mail picked up. He ended the call and tapped out a quick message to Nate that he was sick—again. It was past ten. That his partner wasn't already banging on the door was a miracle.

Zaine's eyes tracked him back and forth. Crystal blue eyes. Kazi, his friend, had the same startling blue eyes. Were they related? Apart from the eyes, he and Kazi couldn't have been more different. Kazi had been lean, his sharp lines striking, whereas Zaine was heavier and shorter than Kazi, although almost the same height as Eric. Very different bone structures. Not brothers, but close—lovers? No, that didn't feel right either, although Zaine's interested gaze last night at the bar had suggested he might be into men.

Eric tried Nate's number again. Why wasn't he answering?

Zaine slid a mug of coffee across the counter. "Will you slow down before you fall down? You've been through a lot. You *should* be in the hospital. Drink the coffee."

Eric picked it up, needing the caffeine hit, but eyed it suspiciously. Zaine wasn't here to hurt him. If anything, he was trying to take care of Eric. It was a strange feeling, having someone *care*. He sipped, sighed, and closed his eyes, clearing his head by sliding the nightmares sideways like he'd learned to do years ago.

When he opened his eyes, Zaine was still gazing at him without blinking, eyes soft and lips softer. There was a great deal happening in Eric's life right now without adding sex to the mix, but the way Zaine admired him, it made it difficult *not* to think about it. Eric noticed Zaine's tight shirt was all wrinkled, the sleeve bloodstained. "You hurt?"

"Huh? Oh this?" He lifted his arm and frowned at the purple bruise on his forearm. "It's nothing. Mostly healed."

Mostly healed... right. Because that was a thing people did overnight. He wanted to ask but didn't know where to start, or even if he should. He'd seen things he'd been told in the past were insane. What if he *was* insane?

Zaine must have seen the confusion on Eric's face because he sighed and said, "Before I try and explain everything, I need to know one thing. Are you Sebastien's feeder?"

"Sebastien?"

"The guy who owns that club. He owns a few, actually. They're a nyk's typical hunting ground—" Zaine cut himself off. "Are you his feeder?" His eyes narrowed. "You let him feed from you in a symbiotic relationship? He gets your blood, you get off?"

Eric blinked, frozen between two moments. The now, when he wanted to rage at Zaine and throw him out, and the past, where he'd been a kid seduced by a man who had fucked him. He had let him... take his blood and body and his mind somewhere far away, where reality couldn't touch him.

Zaine's narrowed eyes softened, the accusations in them lifting. "What did he do to you?"

Eric didn't have to tell him anything, just that he had to leave. Zaine would go, Eric knew that about him. He'd walk away, and there was a chance Eric might never see him again. That last thought made his heart flutter with panic. If Zaine left, Eric would never get the answers he needed. Answers that had been kept from him for a large chunk of his life.

"I was fifteen," he heard himself say, and now he'd begun, he didn't dare stop. "Home invasion turned triple homicide. I don't know why he chose our house, or why he chose me." There. It was said. It was out there, made real. "At that age, you think you're strong, that nothing can stop you. But I… I just… I watched as he slaughtered my family, my sister. She was, er… she was only eight." Eric's voice cracked. He coughed to clear it. "He… Anyway, he didn't kill me…" The words did get stuck in his throat now. He couldn't speak them. Couldn't breathe life into the strange desire-soaked waking dreams. "A cop found me two years later wandering an Atlanta highway. I went into care but not for long. The cop who found me, Grahams, he took me under his wing, and here I am. Fifteen years later. Living the fuckin' dream, right?" He chuckled thinly, sounding more than a little unhinged.

Zaine dropped his gaze, closed his eyes, and froze, just for a few seconds. "You survived a nyktelios for two years?" he asked, keeping his eyes closed. The fingers of his left hand curled into a fist.

Was he mad? Was Zaine connected to *Sebastien* in some way? "I… A what?"

He opened his eyes. Their gemlike sparkle shone a little brighter. "Sebastien is a nyktelios—a nyks. Greek word, loosely means darkness. He's not human. He doesn't age. He's been around a lot longer than you or I. He's a predator. And you and others like you, mostly young boys from what I know of him, are his prey."

Eric had known all that. Most of it at least—not the name for what he was but the rest. Always known it, no matter how hard he'd tried to deny it or the times people had tried to tell him it was all made-up nonsense from a traumatized mind. He'd known monsters were real. But when they'd been in his head, he could keep them there. Now they were out, and Zaine was speaking about them. It was all horribly real.

Eric lowered himself to the edge of the couch. "So what are *you*?"

"I'm nyktelios. The same." Zaine smiled but there was no humor in it now. "But different. We've been called Guardians of Night, Lords of Shadow... The primordial being Nyx made two nyktelios to protect her from her handsy counterpart, Erebus, after he started getting frisky, right?"

"Wait." He rubbed his forehead. "Ere—who?"

"Primordial being. A god before there were gods?"

This was a lot. But so was everything Eric had witnessed. "I'll get it. Keep going."

"Nyx made two warriors. Stronger, faster, vicious, and she made them hungry. So they would never stop hunting. The problems started when the two nyktelios warriors figured out they could make more of their kind without Nyx getting involved. Two became four, became eight... They spread like a disease. Shit got real for a while, and then a few of the nyktelios realized chaos was a terrible endgame. They saw where it was going, i.e. more killing until there was nothing left—Nyx is the mother of chaos, it's in our genes—and they broke from the rest and turned on their own kind, cleaning house. The Blackrose Brotherhood was born. And they—*we* have been trying to control the nyks—the bad guys—ever since." Zaine spread his hands and tipped his head in a small bow. "I know, I'm in great shape for a four-hundred-year-old."

Eric laughed. The sound just fell out of him. He wasn't even sure why he was laughing. It wasn't that he didn't believe Zaine. Shit, he'd had Sebastien feed from him and make him feel things that had messed him up for life. He'd stabbed the monster in the heart when he was seventeen and shot him four times last night, and he'd still come back.

He laughed until the laughter turned to gulps, and then he rubbed both hands over his face. "You're four centuries old?" His voice was pitched way too high.

"Give or take a few decades."

"You, er... you're right. You don't look it." Four centuries. Four hundred years. What was that... the time of... He couldn't think. Before electricity, before the British had colonized America, before the known world?

"I'm the young one," Zaine said. "The rest of my kind are older than dirt."

"Your kind. The Brotherhood? How many of you are there?"

Zaine hesitated. "Everything I'm telling you, you have to keep to yourself. If word gets out I talked, it won't end well for either of us."

Eric almost laughed again. "Who would believe me?"

"You'd be surprised."

"So why tell me at all?"

"Because you're the kind who'll never let it rest. You will poke and prod and the Brotherhood will know you're digging around. They do not look kindly on people who know too much."

Zaine was right. He wouldn't ever let this rest. He couldn't. His whole damn life was a lie, more than Eric had even understood.

"There are eleven of us in the US. More in Europe and Asia," Zaine said, answering his earlier question.

Eric got to his feet. He needed to move, to shake out the anxiety making his veins itch. He paced a while, his thoughts running in a loop. The whole world was still ticking along outside his window, nobody aware they had bloodsucking *beings* among them?

Zaine watched, his face patient, because he had all the time in the world. He didn't age. Four hundred years... and Sebastien was older.

Leaning against the counter, he absorbed the information, surprised to find it helped calm his mind. He wasn't insane. This shit was real. And now he knew, for sure, he could climb over that hurdle and move on. Or try to. "How many *nike-tell-os*—Wait, I got this. *Nike-tell-eh-os*—the bad types, are there?"

"Good question, and one we're trying to figure out. The last estimate was between three and six hundred. Down from several thousand a few centuries ago. But they reproduce, so six hundred could be double that in a few years." Zaine's brow pinched in a troubled frown.

"Don't the Brotherhood reproduce?"

Zaine winced. "Not really. We recruit. It's complicated."

Eric spread his hands. "I'm not going anywhere."

Zaine breathed in and sighed hard. "All right. I guess

I'm all in now anyway. So here goes. We abstain from taking blood from the vein. We still have to consume blood but we get it bagged from donors, which keeps us controlled and less blood-hungry. To make more of us, we'd have to go back to drinking from the vein, and that's a slippery slope none of us want to ride."

Eric held Zaine's gaze. He remembered the feel of Sebastien's teeth sliding into his skin—a brief spark of pain that had rapidly numbed, turning into throbbing waves of heat, hardening his cock and making his body sing for more. "What happens when you drink from the vein?"

He didn't wince, not this time, but his eyes darkened. "Inside every single one of us there's an ancient being, a seed of Nyx. It isn't human and it's hungry—all the time. Deny it fuel, and it's controllable. But feed it, and it consumes everything."

"You lose control?"

Zaine nodded. Had Zaine ever lost control? He seemed perfectly in control now. So... normal. Just a guy. A hot guy, in a bloody shirt, but just a guy. But, deep down, he was the same as Sebastien.

"All right, so let me see if I've got this," Eric said. "Vampires are real. The one who killed my family is back. You're a good one, trying to stop him from hurting more people?"

"That's about it." He smiled.

"So where the fuck were you fifteen years ago?"

And the smile vanished. "I wasn't on the East Coast then, and even if I was, we don't... we don't save individuals. We kill nyks. There's a difference."

"You don't *save* people?" Eric sighed. "Jesus." He shook his head with a shallow, sharp smile. "Then why do you keep saving me?"

For the first time since meeting Zaine, the lighthearted gleam in his eyes vanished. "Because Sebastien should be dust already. If I'd stopped him before now, you wouldn't..." He cleared his throat and his stonelike stance shifted. "You wouldn't have had to deal with him again."

At least he was honest. "I want to help. I need to—"

Zaine began shaking his head. "I get that. I do. But a feeder's relationship with their nyk is complicated. You hate him, I'm not questioning that, but nyktelios saliva alters the brain's chemical composition. The short of it is, every time he bites you, you get off on it, on all levels. He's like the best drug and sex all mixed up in one euphoric hit. You want him dead, but you also can't help wanting him too. Desire makes people unpredictable. Don't get me wrong, I don't doubt your passion to kill him. But if he orders you to take a shot at me, you'd probably do it."

Eric winced and pushed away from the counter, needing to move again. He couldn't even deny it. All he had to do was think about Sebastien's touch and his damn cock swelled. "Shit." He paced. This was a lot. But it was good. It gave meaning to all the insanity he'd been carrying for years. He'd been so convinced he was out of his mind that he'd locked it all away, forbidden himself to go there. But to hear it was real, and to know his memory was wrong and he hadn't loved the psycho who had killed his family, that he wasn't that fucked up after all—that knowledge set his soul free.

"Are you all right?" Zaine asked. "Apart from the obvious."

"I just... need a minute." His voice wavered. He sat on the edge of the couch again. Yes, this was good. A lot, but good.

"I have to get to Sebastien before he goes underground, and he will," Zaine said. "If I lose his trail, he'll keep killing elsewhere. I was hoping I could finish him alone, but I've failed twice. Mikalis would have my ass if he knew. And not in the good way. Unfortunately, I need help."

"Mikalis?"

"Mikalis—badass Brotherhood leader. Scary on a good day. Hope you never meet him."

A few knocks sounded at the apartment door. "Hey, Eric, open up."

Eric froze, then caught Zaine's raised eyebrow. "Shit, it's my partner..." he whispered, lurching to his feet. "Detective partner, not the other type." Zaine's eyebrows rose. Why he'd said that, he had no idea. "You have to hide,"

"Hide?" Zaine snorted.

"In the bathroom. Go."

Zaine frowned, once again reminding Eric of a stubborn alley cat, the kind that could turn deadly in the blink of an eye but right now preferred stubbornness.

Eric spread his hands. "You said you're good at hiding? So go hide."

"Or you could tell him you've got company and send him away?"

"That's not how this works," Eric whispered sharply. "I

can't lie and let him think I skipped work because I got laid, okay?"

Zaine's lascivious smile grew. He sauntered out from behind the counter, crossed the floor, and glanced over his shoulder. "Then next time we'll make it true." He smirked and headed toward the bathroom.

Eric's mind shuffled around all the thoughts of things he could do with Zaine between the sheets, his gaze dropping to Zaine's pants-clad ass. The pants hugged just enough to give his ass that perfect curve. Eric already knew he had a body that wouldn't quit and he was *clearly* into men.

No, he couldn't go there. Zaine was the same as Sebastien. Different, according to Zaine, but the same too.

Nyktelios was just a fancy word for vampire.

He had a hot four-hundred-year-old vampire in his bathroom.

Knocking sounded on the door again. "Eric? C'mon, man, I hear you in there. You okay, huh?"

He ran a hand through his hair. "Yeah, I'm coming."

CHAPTER 9

ric

NATE TOOK one look at Eric and frowned. "Man, you *are* sick."

Eric dragged a hand through his hair and stepped back from the door, letting his partner in. "Rough night. I don't know. I'm all right, just drained." Literally. He drifted into the living room, noticed the blinds were still closed, and opened them, letting the sunlight flood back in.

"Hey, I was passing by and wanted to check that you were okay." Nate took a seat on the stool at the breakfast counter looking as fresh and bright as a daisy, like always. "Glad I did. You need anything? Like a ride to the ER?"

"No, I'm fine, really." Eric managed a genuine smile. "I just need a day, that's all."

"While I'm here, you wanna hear about work?"

"Sure." He approached the counter. "Hit me with it."

The two used coffee cups sat on the countertop between them like neon signs. Eric scooped them up and dumped out the coffee. Nate's gaze rode his back. It didn't take a detective to figure out Eric hadn't been alone.

What he did in his spare time wasn't any of Nate's business. He could have had a friend around, just like Nate was here now. It didn't have to mean anything. It certainly didn't mean he had a vampire in his bathroom. Shit, he needed to get rid of Nate. "You know, maybe we should do this later—"

"We got another body, male, around twenty," Nate said. "Exsanguination, just like Capaldi. No ID yet."

"Shit. Where?"

"West Forty-Ninth."

Not far from La Dolce Vita. Drained of blood. Was Sebastien the one killing these men? Someone drained of blood was a damn obvious way of leaving a vampire calling card, but why now? Zaine had said Sebastien had been killing people for hundreds of years. Bodies drained of blood weren't common. So why was the nyktelios getting sloppy now? It couldn't be anything to do with Eric personally, could it?

"You good?"

"Huh?"

"You zoned out there. You sure you don't need a doctor or something?"

"Sorry. You, er... you want coffee?"

His partner brightened, forgot about calling a doctor, and continued on with a description of the new victim. Eric poured Nate his coffee, only half listening, and glanced toward the bathroom door. Zaine could probably hear everything. He might know if Capaldi was linked to Sebastien. And if it was all connected, where did that leave the case? Eric couldn't start ranting about vampires. He'd made that mistake in his teens and earned himself a small trip to a psych ward for his trouble. He needed more information from Zaine, maybe from the Brotherhood too.

"There's something else," Nate said as he sipped his coffee, eyebrows raised. "You're not gonna like it."

"Jesus, what?"

"The remains of five of Vergil Sonneman's known associates were discovered at a waste transfer station where they sort trash."

Eric had been drinking his own coffee and it got stuck in his throat. He spluttered, almost choked, and took a few seconds to *breathe*, all while Nate's gaze was getting more concerned.

"I figured you'd want to know."

"Any leads?" Eric croaked out.

"Wounds were consistent with an execution style. Intergang violence, probably. I doubt it'll go much further unless Vergil resurfaces or the murder weapon is found."

Murder weapon. The same gun Sebastien had. "Vergil's missing?"

"Seems that way. Our CIs can't find him."

Eric stared into his mug while he gathered his composure back together, then looked up at Nate.

"Sorry, man," Nate said. "I know you wanted to see them behind bars. Fate got to them first."

"Yeah, fate. Looks that way."

"Anyway... I've taken up enough of your time. Take the

day, huh? You look as though you need it." He downed the coffee. "Better get back. May I use your bathroom?"

"Sure."

If Vergil's body hadn't surfaced, did that mean Sebastien had it? If the body turned up with the gun, Forensics just had to match the round to the gun and dust for prints, and Eric would be behind bars for multiple homicides.

Nate opened the bathroom door.

Shit, Zaine! "Nate, wait! I..."

Nate froze, glancing back, the door wide open in front of him with nobody inside. No six feet of blond vampire. But Zaine *had* been in there.

Nate shrugged.

"Sorry, I just... thought... Never mind, you're fine. Yeah, go right ahead."

Nate frowned and disappeared inside the bathroom, probably thinking Eric was losing his mind.

Eric checked the bedroom and the closet, but there was no sign of Zaine. He'd vanished. Could he do that? He had crept out of Eric's apartment before.

Nate reappeared. "You'll be back tomorrow, right?"

"Sure. I'll be there."

Nate finally left and with a groan Eric slumped onto the couch. Nate clearly suspected Eric of something, probably having a secret lover. It could be worse. At least he didn't suspect Eric of murdering Vergil's men.

He dropped his head back and closed his eyes, exhaustion tugging at his mind.

The Brotherhood.

Vampires.

It was all real. All the nightmares were true—the man from his deepest, darkest dreams existed. He was out there, walking free, with the blood of Eric's family all over his hands.

Eric snapped open his eyes, grabbed his laptop, and got to work.

CHAPTER 10

aine

ZAINE EASED through Eric's apartment window, dropped down the fire escape, and strolled away, leaving Sharpe to go over the truths he should have been told years ago. Secrets like those he'd been carrying could rot a mind like cancer.

Brotherhood rules be damned. Telling Eric had been worth it, just to see the weight of his horrible past lift off his shoulders.

Zaine had done the right thing.

Fifteen years old and abused by a nyktelios for two years. Jesus. A nyk could break a mortal in a few months, leaving them raving mad. Eric had lasted *two years* and he'd still had the presence of mind to escape. Then he'd gone on to qualify as a detective and right wrongs. Eric Sharpe was a modern legend. Zaine had no right to be proud, they barely knew each other, but he admired Sharpe. He was resilient. Brave. Strong. A born survivor.

Sometimes, living the life he did, it became too easy to forget how remarkable humans could be.

A black van cruised around a corner up ahead. Its engines roared, the van lurching ahead faster.

Zaine's grin wilted. "Ah, fuck."

Kazi had told the others where to find him.

Zaine was so screwed.

He took his hands from his pockets, letting the driver see he wasn't armed, so they didn't need to do anything drastic. Who was behind that wheel? Not Kazi, he didn't like to get his pretty hands dirty. Storm, probably. And maybe Octavius, if the ice-cold prick was back from upstate.

Zaine wasn't supposed to be here. And he definitely wasn't supposed to go back to Sharpe's apartment. They'd take Zaine off Sebastien's case. Eric would get forgotten, written off as a feeder too far gone to save. Eric would get himself killed trying to right the wrongs of his past. The thought of a world without him in it was not a good one. *Mine*. The primordial part of him demanded he go back, gather Eric up, and take him away. And that was because Zaine had tasted him. Something else he shouldn't have done.

Shit.

A shadowy alleyway caught Zaine's eye. It was to his left, too narrow for the van. Storm wouldn't pursue on foot. He was fast for a big guy, but he hated daylight. But if

Octavius was in that van, he'd hunt Zaine down like a dog, daylight or no.

But what choice did he have? They were going to haul his ass in, lock him up, and put one of the others on the case to get it done. Zaine was about to be benched. He'd probably never see Eric again.

Mikalis would say it was for the best. But if the old vampire even had a heart, it hadn't beat in centuries.

Screw him.

Zaine bolted down the alleyway. He dashed between dumpsters, climbed a fence, and vaulted over the top, landing in a crouch on the other side. The screech of tires rang out like an alarm.

He sprinted across a street, through a gate, over another fence, and slipped into a stream of pedestrians, head down, hands in his pockets.

Storm would think he'd gone rogue. At best, he'd think Zaine was close to turning. At worst, they'd think him a vein away from going full nyk. But Zaine would get it all worked out eventually, after Sebastien was dead and Eric was safe.

Until then, Zaine had to do this alone. For Eric's sake.

He kept moving and sent a text to Kazi to call off the dogs, letting him know everything was fine; he just wasn't going to be pulled off Sebastien. The prick didn't reply. The only way to stop the Brotherhood coming after him was to speak with Mikalis directly. That was what he *should* do, but if Mikalis wasn't yet involved, Zaine wanted to keep it that way.

He ducked into a clothes shop, ditched Kazi's tattered

designer labels, and bought some jeans and a branded T-shirt. Then he hunkered down in a nearby diner, keeping an eye on the big window overlooking the busy street for any conspicuous black vans. He'd given them the slip, and they had better things to do than chase his ass all over New York. Still, he wasn't going to risk emerging too soon.

His phone pinged. He dragged it from his pocket, expecting Kazi. The name Sharpe showed on-screen. With a smile, he swiped up and opened the chat.

Sharpe: *I need to deal with S. With or without you.*

And this was exactly what Zaine had feared.

Z: *No. You. Don't. Leave it to me.*

Sharpe: *How do I kill him? I can't believe I'm typing this but... stakes?*

Zaine snorted.

Z: *Forget the horror movie crap. You can't kill him. Only another nyk—*

Zaine deleted the last part. He was giving away too much and didn't want sensitive information sent in a text message.

Sharpe: *Crosses?*

Grinning, he replied.

Z: *We predate religion.*

Sharpe: *Garlic?*

He had to be joking. Zaine chuckled.

Z: *Love it.*

The dots rippled, Eric typing... for a while. Finally, his next message came back.

Sharpe: *Dinner? We can talk some more.*

Zaine hadn't expected that. But his ego wasn't so

bloated that he couldn't see what the invite was really for. Sharpe wanted to know *everything*. It was his nature. If Zaine didn't give him the information, he'd get it elsewhere. He'd turn over every rock he could find, start asking questions, and he'd get flagged by the Brotherhood's algorithms as a security threat. Zaine had begun this; he had to tell him everything.

Z: *Stop Googling us and we can do dinner.*

Sharpe: *How do you know I am?*

Z: *You're too curious not to.*

Sharpe: *How did you escape my apartment?*

Zaine smirked.

Z: *Bats.*

The messages stopped for a while. Ten minutes later, when Zaine thought Eric had moved on from the chat, his phone pinged.

Sharpe: *Thank you.*

Zaine's heart swelled in a way he hadn't ever expected to feel again. He sent the address for a restaurant where he was a regular and told Eric to meet him there at nine. A thumbs-up came back a few moments later.

Zaine set the phone aside and peered out the diner's window.

He couldn't get involved with him, not least because Eric was vulnerable. He'd been abused by a monster, a monster Zaine was only separated from by the Brotherhood's principles. Still, having dinner with Eric wasn't going to hurt anyone. The detective was intelligent, and he had a dry wit and a body Zaine wouldn't mind getting more familiar with after carrying the man home twice and having his warmth tucked close—although that last fantasy had to be off the table. He knew his limits, and fucking a guy he'd recently bled was a one-way ticket to hurting Eric and getting himself thrown in Brotherhood confinement for a few years to cool down.

Just dinner. Nothing else. Eric wanted answers. Zaine could keep him out of trouble. There didn't have to be any more to it than that.

He was going to need dinner clothes.

ZAINE SPENT the day bouncing from diners to park benches, then stopped to change into more new clothes in the restroom of a bar. He took a cab to the parking lot near La Dolce Vita, retrieved his bike and, careful to check he wasn't being tailed, rode to the restaurant. He'd messaged Eric earlier in the day suggesting he might want to circle the block a few times and check for tails.

The restaurant was glitzy but cozy, not too expensive but with just enough sparkle to feel special. Which had nothing to do with why he'd chosen it. This wasn't *a date.* This was an exchange of information.

A balcony clung to the back of the building with a panoramic view of downtown. Multiple exits made for an easy escape, should the Brotherhood make an appearance. He didn't think they would—they had other problems to deal with besides chasing Zaine down—but it paid to be careful. Mikalis liked to spring surprises.

When Zaine arrived, he spotted Eric waiting at the bar, a half empty glass of wine in front of him. Zaine took a few extra seconds to drink the man in without him knowing. Ruffled chestnut hair lay in short floppy locks on top, even shorter at the sides, hinting at a curl if he'd let it grow long. He'd shaved, which was a shame. Zaine had enjoyed the roughness of those whiskers brushing his cheek when he'd helped prop Eric up.

He wore a dark blue suit and looked so like a cop, it was almost comical. He'd probably deny it. He was a good man who'd done bad things, and Zaine knew what that felt like. Besides, he'd been around long enough to know nobody was all good or all bad. Despite what the detective thought of himself, Eric was one of the good ones.

"Hey," Zaine said, ignoring his racing heart and his body's desire to have Sharpe in his arms again.

Eric's smile lit up his face. There was color in it too. He'd recovered fast.

"Hey," Eric said. His gaze dropped, slipping appreciatively over Zaine. He'd picked up a smart gunmetal gray suit and dressed it down, sans tie and with a few shirt buttons undone.

"How you feeling?" Zaine raised a hand, catching the bartender's eye for his order.

"Fine. Slept most of the day. Starving, though."

Eric chuckled and the light, easy sound squeezed Zaine's heart some more.

"That's good. It means your body is working properly, able to repair itself. What are you drinking?"

Eric told him his preferred wine and Zaine ordered a refill for him, enjoying the weight of the detective's gaze. Their drinks arrived, and Eric shared some small talk about traffic that Zaine had trouble following with the man's hot, wiry body so close. He had the kind of body built for stamina, not strength. Not muscular but fast.

Eric's smile danced. "So, I looked you up."

"What did you discover?"

"Not much. Zaine *Hanson* is on Facebook. Nice photo, by the way. That's how I knew it was you. Apparently, you're employed at the tech company Atlas near Spring Valley." He frowned playfully. "You don't seem the type for IT."

"Don't I?"

"Yeah, you're more of a hands-on, in-the-field kinda guy."

I'd let you get your hands on me. Zaine refrained from making the quip resting on his tongue and let his smile twitch. "I work in security. The tech-heads need a guard."

"Right." Eric smirked.

"Tell me more about myself."

"You have an Instagram account with some nice stock photos. It's all just enough to be present, but it's flimsy. And none of it is you. I doubt you've ever posted there?"

He was right. "We have people who create social media footprints for us. They switch it up every few years."

"Hm." Eric sipped his drink, and Zaine tried not to stare too hard at how the man's tongue swept across his lips. "Your profile won't stand up to much scrutiny. You should get that looked at. Kazi, though, he does his own social media?"

Zaine rolled his eyes. "What gave it away? The thousand selfies on Instagram? What's he got now, fifty thousand followers?"

"More." Eric laughed and the soft sound of it, the *true*

sound of it, did something strange to Zaine's chest, like give his heart an extra beat. He could blame it on the bite, on having gotten too close, but it felt like more than that. He knew what it was. He *cared.* And that was the opposite of not getting involved.

"Don't take this the wrong way—" Zaine sighed. "—but don't dig any more. We have means of tracking down people who know too much. I'd hate for you to *disappear*."

Eric sipped his drink, thinking the threat over. "Aren't you the good guys?"

"Depends who you ask." Zaine raised his glass and tilted it toward Eric for a toast. "To being good?"

Eric chinked his glass with Zaine's, raised it to his lips, and swallowed, his throat moving. Zaine could imagine how sweet he'd taste if he just leaned in and kissed him there on the neck. A soft sweep of the lips. He'd touch his chin, peer into his eyes.

He turned his face away and willed his needs to cool the fuck off. "Listen, if Kazi contacts you, you don't know anything and you don't know where I am. Okay?"

Eric's smile twitched again. "You in trouble?"

"Something like that." Zaine lifted his gaze. His skin tingled, warming with anticipation for things he couldn't have. It didn't hurt to soak up Eric's allure and the tingling sensation of needing him close, just so long as he didn't take it too far. "Shall we eat?"

Eric's shifting smile grew. He held Zaine's gaze, and there was definitely hunger in the man's eyes for something other than the meal they were about to share. His attention fell to Zaine's mouth. Zaine wet his lips, acutely aware of the heat Eric's gaze ignited. Maybe they could forgo the meal, head out to the balcony, and Zaine would show the detective all the ways he could undo him with his tongue—which definitely could not happen.

He looked away and collected his drink. "Let's find our table."

THE RESTAURANT HUMMED with the warmth of good company and good times. They ordered food and wine, and he watched closely as Eric talked about an old partner who had been killed. He didn't say it, but from the way Eric's voice lifted, Zaine suspected the old partner had been the same man who'd picked Eric up on that highway all those years ago. They'd been close, and his death must have been a terrible blow. Eric's life had been a string of tragedies. He didn't speak of a boyfriend, a girlfriend, a lover, or anyone. Eric's work was his life.

"What about you?" Eric asked.

"Me?"

"I mean, you know... do you have someone? Or are there Brotherhood rules about that too?" He smirked, that sly humor sparking in his eyes.

Zaine smiled, as he seemed to do a lot around Eric, and sipped his wine, wondering how much to reveal. "We learn to give up the things we care about the most."

Eric's grin faded. "You don't have anyone?"

"No, but don't feel bad. It's not... It's just... When you've lived as long as some of the Brotherhood have, you know how every story ends. After a while, it's just easier not to begin one."

Eric's fingers stroked his wine glass, but all his attention sizzled on Zaine. "What about you, though?"

What was he asking exactly? Zaine had had lovers. Most had been fleeting but some had lasted, only for Zaine to walk away in the end heartbroken and alone, every damn time. After a while, it was easier not to love, not to get involved. The Brotherhood had that rule right. "We keep our distance. It's better for everyone in the long run." He sounded like Mikalis. The old guy was right in some things. "We live a long time."

"You don't... get involved with each other?"

"Fuck, no." Zaine laughed. "They're all assholes."

Eric nodded slowly and stroked the glass some more, sweeping his fingertips down its smooth stem. He lost himself in his thoughts and Zaine lost himself in watching him. The soft quiet peppered by the tinkle of laughter and the sounds of cutlery from the other tables was a delight. Zaine folded his arms on the table and leaned in, and Eric's eyes flicked up. Zaine wanted to tell him he'd rarely met a braver man, tell him he was one in a million who had caught Zaine's eye, tell him he was strong and wonderful, that he made Zaine want to bundle him up and squirrel him away somewhere tragedy couldn't touch him.

"You wanna get out of here?" Eric asked, voice hitching.

"Sure." Zaine's heart leaped. "I'll get the check. Meet me on the balcony."

Eric downed the last of his wine and meandered through the tables toward the balcony doors. Zaine raised his hand for the server, and while waiting for the check, he watched Eric step outside. Had there ever been a finer view? It was a crime, Eric being alone. He needed someone to make him smile more, someone to show him the world wasn't the dark place he'd survived.

But that person could not be Zaine. Despite his heart, body, and mind aching for it.

CHAPTER 11

ric

He leaned against the balcony rail and admired the sparkling city spread in front of him. Traffic honked below. The wind whipped up the sound and teased through Eric's hair, mussing it. He sighed, feeling... content for the first time in a long time. Zaine did that. With him nearby, the lights shone brighter and the colors all seemed more vibrant.

He'd been fighting to keep his head above water for much of his life. Zaine being close felt like a hand finally holding him afloat—allowing him to take a breath.

The door behind him opened and clicked closed, and then there he was, the man who wasn't a man at all, with his golden hair and clear blue eyes, his permanent smirk, and the way he made Eric feel... good, just by being close. Eric had moved through his own life like a ghost until

Zaine had told him the truth. Now everything was in full color, even his own pounding heart. He'd come alive.

Eric straightened. Zaine leaned a hip against the balcony, gazing at him. Not speaking, not needing to. His lips twitched up at one corner.

"So why am I supposed to lie to your brother and tell him I haven't seen you?"

Zaine raised a finger. "One, Kazi is not my actual brother." A second finger went up. "Two, because I'm not supposed to see you again. It's against the rules."

"Oh?" Eric arched an eyebrow. "What rule?"

"It's..."

"Complicated?"

"Yeah."

Eric laughed softly, barely a noise at all. Zaine's eyes shone, sparkling under the city lights. His smile demanded to be kissed in all the ways Eric had been imagining during their meal. He'd suggested dinner so he could have all his questions answered. But now that he had him here, this powerful man who wasn't a man at all, Eric's mind was half distracted by wondering what he'd taste like. He stepped closer, forcing Zaine to straighten to meet his gaze. "You don't get involved. None of you."

"Right," Zaine said, his face turning serious. His fingertips touched Eric's neck. An electric shiver spilled down Eric's spine, waking his cock. "We do not get involved," Zaine echoed, closing the last few inches between them until his heat pressed against Eric. "It's a rule."

Zaine was clearly the type to bend the rules, maybe even break them. Eric lifted his gaze, meeting the vampire's eyes. That was what he was. A vampire. A monster. A killer. A creature he'd always known had existed, even when the world told him he was insane for thinking it.

Zaine's warm fingertips skimmed up his neck, along his jaw, and Eric almost moaned at the thrill spilling into his veins. Zaine hadn't moved in for the kiss. Maybe those rules were holding him back. "Does it help if I break the rules for you?" He plastered himself against the firm heat of Zaine's body, opening his thighs to slot him close, and ran a hand up his neck, fingers diving into his hair.

Something inside Zaine must have broken open. His mouth crashed into Eric's, hot and devastating, turning Eric's skin molten. He rocked with the weight of Zaine's body on his, needing him closer, needing to crawl under his skin. A fire had started in his head and heart, burning up his veins.

He broke the kiss to breathe. Zaine's cheek brushed his, his breath panting across Eric's ear. The man was hard—the press of his cock dug into Eric's hip, Zaine's hand on his ass. What would it be like to have Zaine inside of him, his hands scorching his skin, his teeth...

That last thought glitched Eric's desire. He turned his head, meeting Zaine's dazzling eyes, now a molten silver. *Wait...* A hint of sharp, curved teeth shimmered between his lips. Eric's instincts shriveled, fear and lust twisting together. He didn't want this, but he *did* want it. He wanted Zaine to take him right now against the balcony, fuck him hard from behind and bury his cock in him and his teeth in his neck at the same time, because Eric knew exactly how that felt and he needed it again. Needed it so badly that his hard, aching cock wept for it.

Zaine's eyes narrowed. He swallowed and growled, "You don't want me."

Eric laughed, taking Zaine's hand from his ass and pressing it to the bulge in his pants, barely restraining himself from rubbing into his touch. "Tell me again how I don't want you."

"No, I mean, you can't— Fuck it." Zaine growled and kissed him again, tongue thrusting in, sweeping against his. Eric surrendered right there with the vampire's tongue deep in his mouth and his cock grinding. He wanted to fuck, to be fucked, to lose himself in the feel of Zaine's body sliding over his.

The balcony door opened and a laughing couple spilled outside. Zaine broke the kiss, smiling, his gaze falling into Eric's, and it was all Eric could do not to tilt his hips and slide his cock against Zaine's leg. He'd never wanted someone so viciously, not since...

The unwanted memory assaulted him like a slap to the face.

He swallowed and stilled. Zaine was... so like *Sebastien*. He smelled different, of something warm and spicy, felt different too, less like stone, more strength in motion. But this was... too similar to how it had been with *him*. "I, er..." He stepped back. "I think maybe you're right. I don't want you." He couldn't do this. Not because he didn't want Zaine, because he *did*, but it was all mixed up with the past, with Sebastien, and what those teeth sinking into his neck would mean. His body wanted any cock, any fangs, and Zaine was just the easiest route to his fix. His body knew what Zaine could do and desired it over and over again. *Bite me. Fuck me. Bleed me*. Sebastien had taught him that. He heard himself begging for it, all over again.

Eric stumbled away. He couldn't let Zaine see his thoughts on his face. "I have to go."

"Eric, wait."

"No, I think your Brotherhood has it right. We can't..." He opened the balcony door. "We shouldn't... Don't come by my place again."

He heard Zaine swear before the balcony door closed on him, sealing the vampire outside. Eric left the restaurant. He couldn't be the victim again. Not for Zaine. Not for anything. *Bite me. Fuck me. Bleed me.*

He marched down the sidewalk, keeping his head down, letting the cold air chill the lust from his head. He didn't know what was real around Zaine. He might be everything he'd said he was, but he could just as easily be as bad as Sebastien. How was Eric supposed to separate them?

He couldn't go there. He couldn't be that person again. He had to get his life back in order, get control of himself, and get that gun from Sebastien before it implicated him in multiple murders. Afterward, he'd kill Sebastien, somehow.

He looked up to find he'd walked two blocks and found himself outside some kind of half-constructed office building near the waterfront. Plastic sheeting fluttered in the wind. He turned on his heel, heading toward more familiar territory, and saw the car parked against the opposite curb, headlights low, engine idling.

He picked up his pace, senses prickling. Just a car. He

strode by, catching a glimpse of his own ghostly reflection in the tinted glass.

The car's door opened behind him.

Eric glanced over his shoulder.

Sebastien climbed from the car. "Please, do run, my sweet one."

Eric dropped his hand to where his firearm would usually be. He hadn't brought it. Not on a date. It wouldn't matter anyway. Four rounds hadn't killed him.

Run! His thoughts screamed. But that was exactly what the vampire wanted. If he ran, Sebastien would catch him.

The vampire leaned an arm on the open car door, waiting.

Eric stood his ground. "I'm not who I was."

"Oh, I know." Sebastien opened the car's rear door. "Which is why I'm going to enjoy breaking you so much more now. You know I will. You *want* me to. You can't deny it." The man's eyes flashed silver. "I smell desire on you."

No! Eric bolted, running like the fucking wind down the nearest side street, legs pumping, heart racing. Laughter bubbled through the air behind him, bounding off the brownstone walls. The rows of houses were all residential. A few lights glowed from inside. Someone had to see this; someone would call the cops.

The wind switched direction, blasting him from behind—and that smell, so sickly sweet. A smell that tangled around his soul. Eric's shoes pounded the sidewalk. He pried his phone from his pocket and hit call on Zaine's number.

Something hard hit him from behind. He slammed

against one of the brownstone's front walls. His head smacked brick, his ears ringing. His phone—gone—slipped from his fingers. Something wet trickled down his forehead.

Sebastien loomed. He raised Eric's phone. "Hello, Brotherhood."

Eric couldn't hear Zaine's response, not over the ringing in his ears and the pounding of his own panicked heart.

"I have your man. If you want him back, you'd better come for him. Alone." Sebastien ended the call. "You want to play games with me, Sweet One?" He leaned in, his weight and smell smothering Eric, suffocating him. He cocked his head and nipped at Eric's bottom lip, drawing blood. "I play by my own rules."

CHAPTER 12

aine

ZAINE SEARCHED the street outside the restaurant, then doubled back and searched another block, then another. Searching on foot while keeping his stride relatively slow to avoid alerting the public they had a primordial being in their midst was both killing him and taking too long. He returned to his bike, revved her up, and sped down the street. But there was no sign of Eric. Or Sebastien.

He pulled to a halt outside a row of brownstone terraces, braced the bike between his legs, and *breathed*, filtering New York's air deep inside. His senses picked a myriad of scents apart until finally, buried under the smells of hot asphalt and baked stone, he caught Eric's scent nearby. A few hundred yards down the same street brought him to a phone discarded on the ground, its screen smashed. Eric's phone.

Ice filled Zaine's veins, holding him motionless, the broken phone groaning in his fist.

The nyk's call from Eric's phone had made his demands very clear.

Sebastien had Eric. And as strong as Eric was, the nyk would break him. It was just a matter of time.

"Fuck!"

He couldn't do this alone, despite what Sebastien wanted. He had to get the Brotherhood involved or Eric would suffer. *Memento mori. Remember, you must die.* Fuck that. Zaine would give up everything for Eric, even his freedom.

He spun the bike around in the street, squealing the rear tire, and launched into the night.

THE RIDE back to Atlas passed in a blur. He ran red lights, broke a dozen traffic laws, and didn't care. After screeching to a halt outside the main Atlas doors, he abandoned the bike and raced into the building. The elevator doors slowly rumbled closed, taking too damn long, and the car finally moved downward, heading below ground level. He braced an arm against the wall. He had to handle this carefully. If he lost control, ranted in any way, Storm would reel him in and the Brotherhood would go nuclear on Sebastien. Eric could get hurt, or worse. At best, they'd sideline Zaine and forget about Eric, writing him off as a victim.

No way.

Zaine ground his teeth. After all the shit Eric had been through, he deserved better.

The elevator doors opened and Zaine breezed toward the common room. The TV sounded from inside, and Storm's voice rumbled. As he shoved through the door, three faces looked up at him. Kazi, the prick, stood by the pool table, cue in hand, frowning. Octavius was at the far desk, papers spread out in front of him, his shock of long white hair a beacon to nyks everywhere to kill him before he killed them. Storm, to Zaine's left, had stopped talking into his phone the moment Zaine had entered.

"Zaine." Storm's voice rumbled like thunder.

Zaine swallowed. "I need to speak with you. Privately."

Octavius glanced at Kazi, the pair of them sharing a look suggesting they knew Zaine was about to have his ass handed to him. And they wouldn't lift a finger to intervene.

"I'll call you back," Storm said into his phone, probably to Mikalis, and hung up. "Give us the room," he told the others.

"No need." Zaine raised a hand. "Let's take this somewhere else." More glances were exchanged. Zaine didn't care. They could believe whatever they wanted about him —let them think he was losing his control over a sip from a vein. He didn't give a shit.

Storm agreed with a nod and led the way back through the door. Zaine followed, right after seeing Kazi shake his head and carry on playing pool.

Picking one of the comfy side lounges, Storm flicked on the lights and gestured for him to sit.

Zaine sat, then sprang to his feet again. "I need your help, and I need it on the quiet."

Storm folded his muscular arms and grumbled, "Zaine—"

That disapproving tone would follow Zaine until the end of his days. But he had nobody else to ask. "If the others get involved, then so will Mikalis, and he'll... I don't want to risk it."

"Explain everything."

"There's not much time. The nyk has his mark. He's going to kill him unless I get to them first. If I go alone... The nyk is tough. Strong. Fast. I've fought him twice and barely scratched him. I need your help in this, Storm, but Eric can't get hurt."

Storm listened like he always did, patiently, face expressionless, keen eyes observing. "Eric is a feeder?"

"Yes and no. He was. But not now."

"Saving a single feeder makes things a lot more complicated. He's going to be traumatized. He'll have questions we can't answer. Sometimes it's better for everyone if—"

"Don't feed me the party line. He's not traumatized—well, he is from before, but that's not the point. He's a good guy who got caught up in our shit years ago and was left to figure it all out himself. He's done a damn fine job of it until now, until I screwed up and the nyk got his claws in him again." Zaine stopped, afraid he was coming on too strong. "I just need you to get access to the traffic cams," he added softly. "Find out what vehicle the nyk is using, and you and I will track down the registered address and deal with it. On the quiet. Mikalis can't know. Which means the others can't know."

"He'll never approve it."

"Exactly."

"I know for a fact he'll mobilize us all, attack the nyk's nest, and have it over with in a few hours."

And that was exactly what *couldn't* happen. "And Eric will get killed. I can't..." Zaine stopped himself as his anger boiled. He couldn't lose his calm in front of Storm. Eric was too damn important. "Storm, just... this once?"

"But it's not this once, is it? You're walking a fine line, Z."

Zaine closed his eyes. They just couldn't forget what he'd done fifty years ago. "This isn't like Albuquerque, okay?"

"Sure."

When he opened his eyes, Storm glared, unconvinced. "Traffic cams. Address. Then you and I deal with the nyk. And that's it. Easy."

"And what happens to the feeder?"

"I'll deal with him. It'll be fine. He doesn't know anything." The lie might have been the first he'd told to the Brotherhood for... fifty years. Since Albuquerque. But he wasn't thinking about that. This was very different.

"You had better, or it'll be my ass on the line too."

"You're in?"

"Fine," he grumbled.

Zaine tried and failed not to grin. "I knew I was your favorite."

"I don't have favorites, and if I did, it wouldn't be you. C'mon..." Storm headed for the door. "Let's get to the Ops Room. Show me the nyk's file, everything you have on him."

Zaine followed. *Hold on, Eric. We're coming for you.* The detective was tough. The fact he and the nyk were familiar might even be a positive. Eric knew what he was dealing with. Before, he'd been young, blindsided, and abused. He was older, wiser, and stronger now. He'd be okay... for a while. But the nyk knew him too. Knew his desires. Knew what made Eric tick. Feeder and sire was a tough bond to break. Zaine didn't know of a single feeder who had escaped it once they'd been pulled under. But if anyone could, it'd be Eric.

THE SUB-LEVEL OPS Room's enormous domed ceiling arched over a central table. The table, when not activated, appeared to be a normal boardroom table. But as soon as Storm approached, multiple screens unfolded from its middle, and behind those, holo-technology hovered. The Brotherhood's international operating system fed into the room from around the globe. Each cell was connected, like spokes on a wheel, with Atlas at its center.

Zaine grabbed a seat at the table, keyed in his code and fingerprint ID, and pinged Sebastien's files up on the holo-screens. Swiping the files sent them to Storm's view and he immediately scanned the information.

"He's good at covering his tracks," Zaine began, skimming the files again. "I found old references to Sebastos going back to seventeenth-century France. He's used various aliases but more recently returned to using Sebastien. Like they do." Most nyks preferred to keep their original names or some form of it. Their name was often the only thing that stayed with them in a world forever evolving. "His front is the CEO of an investment banking firm here in New York," Zaine explained.

"Bad luck for him, landing in our city," Storm grumbled.

Zaine said, wondering aloud, "He mentioned Mikalis. Seemed put out that Mikalis wasn't on this case personally."

Storm's right eyebrow lifted. "You think they've crossed paths?"

"Could be. But Mikalis has crossed paths with a shit ton of nyks over the years. They all want a piece of the Brotherhood. He's probably name-dropping."

Storm finished skimming the information. "There's not a lot here, Zaine."

"It's all Atlas could find."

Growling low in his throat, Storm said, "I'm not comfortable doing this without Mikalis's approval, especially if they are familiar."

Of course Storm would get cold feet. Zaine sighed through his nose. "All right, look." He inserted himself between the big guy and Atlas's table, forcing Storm to peer down his nose. "We have one swing at this. Just you and me. If we fail, which we won't, but if we do, then we go to Mikalis."

"You'll go to Mikalis. On your knees, if you don't want him to nail your balls to the wall."

"It won't come to that." Zaine chuckled nervously. "Sebastien is overconfident, shortsighted, and a dick. You and I can handle him."

"You know who else is overconfident, shortsighted, and a dick?"

"Well, not me, because I'm definitely your favorite." Zaine grinned.

Storm's glower shifted to an expression that looked a lot like disdain.

The Atlas System flashed, zooming in on a map of New York and then focusing on an address in leafy Stamford, northeast of the city. Atlas also opened a previous realtor listing for the property with a helpful floor plan of the interior.

"Nice. The car seen cruising the area within the time Eric was taken is registered to a Sebastien Lawson. Sunset Court, Stamford." Zaine zoomed in on the satellite image of the house and the street. "And we have our target."

Storm made some more grumbling sounds, generally unhappy ones. "It's too convenient."

"No, it's Atlas at work. C'mon, we hit him now, we'll get there before dawn, right when he's settling in for the day." Eric had already been with Sebastien for too many hours. It had to be now. Zaine swiped the information away so nobody else could see what they had been researching and got to his feet. "Let's go."

Storm, though, hesitated. If he said one more word about telling Mikalis...

With a resigned huff, he lifted his gaze to Zaine. "Tell me one thing straight. Do you care for the feeder?"

Caring for a feeder was high up there on the hell-no list. The reflex to deny it teetered on Zaine's lips, but Storm would know the lie. Just like he already knew the answer. "Yeah, I do. And if that means I get to spend a few months in confinement to cool off, I'll take it. Eric is brilliant. He's intelligent, funny. He's the bravest person I've met in..." *Don't say fifty years.* "Well, a while. He's not a feeder. He was, but not anymore. He's a fighter, and he's had to fight this alone for fifteen years. I'm not walking away. I just can't. Tell Mikalis that, I don't care. But tell him when Eric is safe."

Storm pursed his lips and sighed. "All right. What are we waiting for?"

CHAPTER 13

ric

Being bound with a rope at his wrists and gagged with some kind of cloth was better than the alternative of having Sebastien drain him dry and leave his body on a Times Square bench, assuming Capaldi was Sebastien's victim, as all evidence suggested.

A burlap sack had been removed from his head a few hours ago, revealing he'd been tied to the pipes of a free-standing bath in the corner of a nicely decorated bedroom. Sebastien had manhandled him in here, sat him down, fixed his ropes, and left without saying a word. An unsettled, squirming, half-forgotten part of Eric knew he'd displeased Sebastien—his *master*—but that was the kid from Eric's past, the kid who'd been desperately eager to please so he'd be rewarded with a hand on his cock and teeth at his throat.

Eric was no longer that kid.

And nothing about this fucked-up situation was pleasing.

Zaine would come for him; he knew it as certainly as the sun would rise. He would know it was a trap too. Sebastien had baited him on the phone, but this wasn't Zaine's first rodeo. Maybe he'd bring the Brotherhood?

A Brotherhood that Eric couldn't find a damn thing about online and who Zaine seemed to consider questionably *good*. But anything was better than Sebastien and everything that cocksucking bastard wanted from Eric. Blood. Sex. Submission. He remembered it all now. Remembered it like he'd watched it happen to someone else, because he *had* been someone else back then. Detective Eric Sharpe was not a vampire's slave. He couldn't be. Never again.

He stretched out an aching leg, changing position to alleviate the pins and needles numbing his ass. The ropes chaffed his wrists, rubbing them raw, and the gag between his teeth had soaked through, cracking his lips. His mind raced, his body vibrating with tension. He couldn't think about the past, only how to escape when the time came.

A thump sounded in the house, then footfalls on floorboards, a door opening and closing. Eric's heart fluttered. The footfalls drew closer, up a set of stairs, then along a landing. The bedroom door opened and Sebastien approached. Eric glared. It was all he could do. Sebastien's dark hair and blue eyes triggered all of Eric's instincts telling him he desired this man, this creature. His heart pounded, blood racing. His thoughts swam, fogging over, muddying everything he'd been so damn sure of moments ago.

Crouching just out of reach of Eric's legs, Sebastien smirked. Zaine had said something about the nyktelios bite being poisonous, altering their feeders' brains, reconditioning them to desire. Eric hadn't been bitten today, but his body hadn't forgotten. He fought it, breathing hard through his nose. Fought the lust flushing his senses and hardening his cock while Sebastien just gazed unblinking, blue eyes as mesmerizing as precious gems.

Eric shoved harder against the bath's pipes, holding himself as far away as he could get. Minutes passed. His body burned with want. His dick was as hard as it had ever been, obvious now from the bulge in his pants, but he glared right back, putting all his hate into it. He could want to fuck Sebastien and despise him too.

"If I let you go now: you won't run like you ran then," Sebastien said, his voice so smooth it stroked through Eric. "You've changed. I see that in you. I admire it." His heavy gaze drank him in some more. "I don't have to be your enemy, Eric. We both know you want what I can give." He lowered his hand.

The touch at Eric's ankle lit him up like a firework. Desire sparked down his spine, making him moan. He kicked Sebastien's hand away and cursed through the gag.

Sebastien's soft laugh coiled around Eric's heart and squeezed. When his hand came down a second time, the touch burned like a brand, like he owned Eric. His hand roamed higher, up Eric's calf, over his knee, touching his sensitive spot at his thigh through his pants. Eric moaned, hating himself, hating how he needed this, how his cock pulsed and Sebastien's smile grew.

Come closer, you son of a bitch. Come so fucking close and see in my eyes all the ways I want to kill you.

Sebastien purred low in his throat then stood. "Not yet, my sweet one. It's been a long time since I've tasted blood like yours. I will not be rushed. The anticipation of our reunion will make our eventual coupling all the more gratifying."

Eric glared until Sebastien left, then slumped against the wall, his body a trembling, sweating wreck of want and sickness, his skin writhing, his cock aching for relief—and he was trapped inside it all.

He closed his eyes, focusing on breathing and calming his heart.

He had to get out of here. He could resist Sebastien for a while, but he was right about one thing—the second he let Eric go, he'd lunge for him, *fuck him,* try and kill him *while he fucked him.* He wanted to fuck him so much it hurt to think about it. His cock was a goddamned iron rod straight from the fire. He'd hold Sebastien down and fuck his every hole, get his hands around his throat and squeeze. He wasn't that submissive, pathetic creature he'd been before.

Maybe... just maybe that would be the way to get to Sebastien. To give him exactly what he wanted, and make it the last thing he ever felt.

CHAPTER 14

aine

DAWN THREATENED the horizon with a red hue behind Sebastien's million-dollar house on Sunset Court. It had taken too long to drive out here, and now they only had half an hour before that red glow turned into bright sunshine and Storm began to suffer. He already wore a permanent frown behind the van's wheel.

"We should try again tonight," he said.

"No." Zaine scanned the front of the house. The blinds were drawn in all the windows. A car was parked out front in the driveway. This was the place. Eric was in there; Zaine could feel it. He wasn't leaving without him.

"This is a mistake. Once that sun rises, I'll be working at half my strength."

"Sebastien is old, like you," Zaine said. Storm's eyebrow

arched. "No offense—he'll be feeling the lethargy too. It's an advantage."

Storm glowered. "As your *elder*, I'm telling you this is foolish."

Maybe. But it wasn't wrong. "Eric is in there. You know damn well what Sebastien will do to him if he hasn't already. I'm going in with or without you."

"Every damn rule says you shouldn't!" Storm started the van. He was just going to pull away and abandon Eric, as easy as that. Just leave? No way, the man wasn't that cold.

Zaine grabbed Storm's thick arm. "This isn't about the rules, Storm. I can't fucking leave him. I just can't. Tell me you've never done something you know you shouldn't because everything inside tells you it has to happen."

Storm huffed. "We have rules for this exact reason. You're too emotional. He knows we're coming. We're not prepared. We should be here with a team—with Mikalis."

"Fuck this." Zaine opened the van door. "And fuck the rules. We're on the clock here. I'm not waiting another second."

"Damn you," Storm snapped.

"Yeah, well. Already there." Zaine climbed from the van. He'd let Storm leave if he wanted to. Although he'd thought more of the big guy, thought he'd have his back in this. But he should have known better. The Brotherhood got *colder* with time. The engine died, and a few seconds later, Storm joined him near the van's front fender. Zaine checked his twin holstered guns and raised his gaze to Storm's glower. "We good?"

"I'm here, aren't I?"

He knew Zaine was right.

Hiding his smirk, Zaine took a few steps toward the house, but Storm's heavy hand landed on his shoulder, hauling him back. Storm had twice Zaine's strength. If he really didn't want him doing this, he'd throw Zaine over his shoulder and toss him into the back of the van. It wouldn't be pretty, but it would work. Instead, though, Storm held Zaine's glare. Sharp, cold blue eyes chilled Zaine's veins, reminding him he was dealing with an ancient being. But there was more in Storm's eyes than ancient threat. Old understanding softened the glare, and there was concern too. "Listen, Zaine, and listen good. Don't think for a second none of the Brotherhood have never wanted to intervene. We've all cared, and we've all suffered for it. The rules *protect us* and the people we save in the long term. You will come to understand this."

Zaine understood it all right, but perhaps being the youngest gave him a different perspective. "Just because you've been doing something the same way for thousands of years doesn't make it right." He shrugged Storm's hand off. "C'mon, big guy, before you wilt in the daylight."

On approaching the house, they split up, Storm going east and Zaine west in a typical pincer movement. The house was alarmed according to the stickers on the windows. But all new alarms had kill switches that alarm companies used to disable a faulty alarm remotely before engineers arrived to fix it. Zaine pinged Atlas, typed in the address and the alarm make and model, and voilà, Atlas kindly temporarily disabled it, the little blinking light under the outside siren turning red.

He grabbed the back doorknob and gave the door an

inhuman shove, dislodging it from its hinges. The kitchen sprawled across the rear of the house, all shiny and new and dark. There were no lights on and all the window blinds were drawn. Only the refrigerator hummed, the rest of the house silent.

Storm appeared like a damned ghost in the doorway, his movement impossibly quiet on those tree-trunk legs of his.

"Feels wrong," Storm whispered.

"Hm."

The kitchen was spotless, not a used cup, plate, or bowl, and nothing on the countertops. No coats on the hooks. No photos on the refrigerator. The house was staged, somewhere Sebastien didn't use but kept up the pretense of having for his home address. That didn't mean Eric wasn't here, though.

"You do the basement," Zaine whispered. "I'll take the upstairs."

Sebastien would have heard the door frame fracture. He'd know they were here.

Storm vanished again, heading deeper into the house, and Zaine climbed the stairs. There was a high chance he'd find Eric on the bed, spent and used—if he walked in on that, he might lose his fucking mind to rage. But it hadn't been long since Sebastien had taken him, not long enough to really get into it with Eric. Zaine hoped.

He pushed open the first door. Bathroom. Then the next. Small bedroom. The main suite was ahead, door closed. Nothing sounded from inside. No panting breaths, no begging, no smell of blood. Zaine's heart sank. He'd fucked up. Eric *wasn't* here. The house was a dummy.

Resigned, Zaine twisted the final door's handle and pushed. A sheet hung from the end posts of a large four-poster bed. On it, someone had used a Sharpie to draw a dagger behind a stylized shield, the Blackrose Brotherhood emblem. The words *memento mori* had been scrawled over it in... red paint? *Remember, you must die.*

The smell of old blood tugged on Zaine's instincts.

Not paint.

His phone rang.

He stepped forward, felt a tug on his boot, and looked down. A slim wire tugged at a blinking white box fixed to the wall. Its little green light turned red.

"Shit."

"Get out!" Storm's yell rolled up the stairs. "There's a—"

A blast of noise and heat barreled over Zaine like a freight train, and then the heat scorched the world white, boiling skin and hair, melting fabric. He gasped, swallowed fire, and drowned in agony.

CHAPTER 15

ric

Sebastien had come in the dark, pulled the bag down over Eric's head again, and walked him from the room, down the stairs, then along a corridor with soft carpet—Eric had caught glimpses of it through the bag's seams—and into a warm, snug space where the sound was muffled. Maybe a lounge? He heard blinds being lifted, felt the shift in the air.

"Sit," Sebastien said.

If Eric ran, he wouldn't get far with the ropes around his wrists. There wasn't much point in fighting either, not yet. Sebastien was stronger, faster. He held all the cards in this game. Eric could only listen and learn and buy time until Sebastien made a mistake.

He knelt, then quickly shifted to a sitting position. Sebastien adjusted Eric's wrist ties, fixing them tightly to something in front of him, then yanked the bag from Eric's head.

He blinked into bright morning light spilling in from all four sides of the glass room. A conservatory. Outside, green bushes blocked any chance he might have had at getting a look at the neighborhood.

Sebastien reached toward him and untied the gag, bringing himself so close that the rotting fruit smell of him dizzied Eric's head. The gag loosened and finally Sebastien plucked it from Eric's dry lips. Working his tongue around his mouth, he spat out threads and fluff.

"Better?"

"Fuck you," he croaked.

Delight sparkled in Sebastien's eyes. "You have more fire in you now, Eric. I like to credit myself with some of that fierceness."

He couldn't tell Sebastien to go fuck himself without sounding like an unimaginative idiot, so he pinched his lips together and glowered instead as he got a good look at the glass-walled surroundings. Two buckets sat conspicuously to either side of the door, one red, one black. Eric's wrists were tied with rope and fixed to a metal eyebolt cemented into the floor. The floor itself sloped toward a central drain hole. This was not a normal conservatory, more like a wet room. Like a butcher's workshop.

"Don't worry, company is on its way." Sebastien headed for the door.

"Why are you doing this?"

Sebastien stopped but didn't turn. "Because I can. Because you are mine and will always be mine until the day you die. Because the Brotherhood have no idea what's coming for them." He chuckled to himself and left, closing the door behind him and turning the lock.

He couldn't hear Sebastien leave. Was the door soundproofed? Eric shuffled, getting comfortable. Why the change of scenery? Why not just keep him in the bedroom? What was the point of all the glass?

Above the door, a camera peered down, its little light blinking.

Eric shifted again and got his knees under him, but the ropes were too short to give any more than a few inches of movement. He bent double and picked at the rope knots with his teeth. They weren't going to fray easily, but if he had a few hours, he might be able to work something loose. Sebastien was watching. He wouldn't let Eric get free, but he had to try.

SUNLIGHT POURED into the greenhouse with no letup. Sweat dripped down Eric's back, sticking his shirt to his skin. He'd taken a break from chewing the ropes when his cracked lips had begun to bleed.

The heat pushed out all thoughts from his head and baked the strength from his bones.

Sebastien arrived, bottle of water in hand, and when he knelt and raised the uncapped lid to Eric's lips, he wasn't fool enough to turn his head away. He drank long and deep, ignoring Sebastien's gaze on his throat, and when Sebastien pulled the bottle away, Eric felt his thumb sweep a dribble of water from his chin.

Sebastien lifted his thumb to his own lips and licked the water away, blue eyes flashing with hunger.

"You can do whatever you want to me, but I'll never be yours again. Not like... *before*."

"Hm... I'm afraid, Sweet One, you have little choice in the matter. Love is nothing more than a chemical reaction in the brain, a chemical I control. You will love me again soon."

A crackling fury sizzled through Eric. He hadn't *loved* him before. He'd been a boy. He hadn't even known what love was.

He gathered a small amount of saliva around his tongue and spat in Sebastien's face—the vampire moved with whiplike speed and slammed Eric to the floor. Cold, hard fingers squeezed his throat, holding him pinned. Eric gasped, or tried to, but Sebastien's grip closed in. He tried to buck, but the vampire's weight was too vast, too visceral. His strength was a mountain bearing down on him.

The vampire's eyes blazed, crackling with ice-white power. "*You will love and worship and respect me as befits my kind. I will fuck you and feed from you, and you will thank me for the pleasure of it.* Don't think I cannot crush your heart and mind, child. I have done crueler things to stronger men than you."

He let go, moving so fast the absence of his grip left a burn behind, and slammed the door, leaving Eric on his back panting and blinking hard. Cold tears left tracks down his hot face.

He didn't want to move or breathe or face any of this. Only yesterday he'd been doing just fine at the precinct, solving homicides and righting some of the wrongs in the world. Even though it had been a drop in the ocean, it had felt like he'd been doing some good. But now... He wasn't even sure who he was anymore. Wasn't even sure any of this was real. Was he a cop? Had the last fifteen years been a dream? Had he ever truly escaped Sebastien, or was it like the vampire said, that Eric's life had never been his own, not since that moment on his front lawn with the blood soaking between his toes.

Heat made some part of the conservatory frame creak. He couldn't lie there. He had to move, to get back control.

He propped himself up on his elbows and flipped Sebastien the bird. The asshole probably wasn't watching, but it felt good. The door rattled a second later. Eric tensed for a second round of abuse, then froze at the unexpected sight of Sebastien with an unconscious blond-haired man slung over his shoulder. A waft of smoky air came with them. Sebastien knelt, flopped the man onto his back on the floor—

Zaine.

His eyes were closed, his face all cut up and scabbed. Scorch marks stained his clothes, and in some places the fabric had melted. He smelled of burned oil, of melted plastic and hair.

Eric watched, pulse thumping hard in his throat, as Sebastien cuffed Zaine's limp wrists to a similar eyebolt as his, using a padlock to fix them in place. His cuffs were metal, not ropes like Eric's.

"What did you do to him?"

Ignoring Eric, Sebastien straightened and admired his catch.

"You know the Brotherhood will kill you for this, right?"

Sebastien's icy glare flicked to Eric. "You know nothing of the Brotherhood and their true purpose. This young one is as much a puppet as the rest." Sebastien collected the buckets and brought one to Eric, then left the second for Zaine. He placed a bottle of water in front of Eric and tapped its lid. "Focus on keeping yourself hydrated, hm? We can't have you passing out."

"You sick psycho—what is this? What's the point, huh?" Eric lunged, snapping his ropes tight. "They'll come for you!"

Sebastien left and Eric slumped, his rage boiling him further. He tried to shuffle toward Zaine, but with his hands bound, all he could do was poke Zaine's elbow with his shoe. "Zaine? Hey?"

Zaine's chest rose and fell enough to indicate he was alive, but he didn't wake. Not a scrap of clothing had escaped the fire damage. His face didn't look so bad, though. Just paler than usual.

"Jesus, what did he do to you?" Eric could only sit and watch and wait as the sun beat in through the glass panels. Sunlight. It lay like a blanket over Zaine's body. Zaine had said he could resist it, but for how long?

The reason for the change of scenery became clear. A glass room, trapping in sunlight. This was torture—for Zaine.

CHAPTER 16

aine

THE SECOND HEARTBEAT in the room thumped in his head like a drum or a homing beacon. Blood. Hot and fresh and close. The single thing he needed to repair himself. His whole body sizzled, every inch of his skin hypersensitive to every piece of fabric, every tiny pinprick of grit between him and the ground. His jaw throbbed, fangs extended and aching to sink into the source of all that thudding, arousing *noise*.

"Hey... Zaine?"

Zaine squeezed his eyes closed, willing the voice away. Because if Eric was here, they were both fucked. He swallowed, ran his tongue over his teeth, and parted his lips, tasting Eric's soapy, sweat-soaked scent. He was damn close. He could reach out and—

He groaned and rolled onto his back. Every muscle

throbbed and burned. Shit, he hadn't felt like this since... he'd been turned. Like he was one rogue thought away from blacking out and letting his instincts take over. It was easier that way; just let the urges satisfy themselves and he wouldn't have to fight anymore. He'd survive. But Eric wouldn't.

"Hey, Zaine, you with me?"

To make it worse, Zaine *knew* exactly how sweet Eric's blood tasted. Metallic, obviously, but like nectar too. Without coke, it'd be less bitter, almost smooth when it flowed over Zaine's tongue and down his throat. *"Jesus,"* he hissed, raising an arm to cover his eyes. A chain rattled and it took him a few moments after opening his eyes to realize the chain was attached to his wrists, and his wrists were padlocked to the floor.

Sighing hard through his nose, he shuffled his thoughts into some kind of order and squinted into the gray scale surroundings, finding Eric layered in shadows and kneeling way closer than was safe. His scent saturated the air: sweat, sweetness, and Eric.

But it was night. Which was probably why Zaine was conscious.

He closed his eyes and swallowed *again*. He could do this. He wasn't too far gone, not yet. But he had to act fast. He couldn't last like this for long. Rolling onto his side, he blinked at Eric, saw the man's soft smile and the way his hair half-covered his eyes and how he'd gasp the moment Zaine's teeth pierced the skin at his throat and drank him down—which hadn't happened. He shook his head and with a growl got a hand under him, levering himself into a sitting position.

"Hey. Are you okay? Talk to me."

"Just..." He growled. Were the sounds he'd made even words?

"Is this going to kill you?" Eric asked. "The sun, I mean?"

He looked around them. Glass walls. Glass roof. "We'd better hope it does." Zaine ground the words out, making sure to enunciate. He wasn't an animal. He wasn't a nyktelios. Not anymore. He was fucking Brotherhood, built for this shit. Except Sebastien knew exactly what he was doing in chaining Zaine inside with Eric, like chaining a rabid dog inside its kennel with a docile rabbit. The outcome was inevitable. He'd snap, and the part of him that wanted Eric, wanted to keep him and care for him, also wanted to fuck and feed and ruin him by bathing in his blood.

"Shit." Zaine dragged a hand down his face and managed to retract his fangs. He had enough control left for that but not much else. His body was fucked, burned and broken. He'd rested, repaired much of the central damage, but there was a long way to go, and he needed blood or his body would tear itself apart again, his mind too. The beast in him would go rabid if he didn't get blood soon.

"Zaine?"

"Eric, just..." He held up a hand. "Okay, rules. Number-fucking-one, stay over there. Do not, under any circumstances, come closer. Do you understand?"

Eric tugged at his wrists near the floor, and the reason for him having not moved became clear. He was restrained. That might just save his life. "Stuck here."

"All right, good." Eric's frown said he didn't understand. Zaine winced. What to tell him? *You're trapped in a glass room with a starving vampire who needs your blood to survive, and at some point, the nice guy you think you know will vacate the building, leaving just the monster behind. Good luck surviving that.*

Zaine's chains were looser than Eric's. He could get to his feet and move his arms. The chains weren't long enough for him to reach Eric's ropes, and that would mean getting close to Eric anyway, which was off the table. But he had some freedom. Probably just enough to attack Eric, which was exactly what Sebastien wanted.

"What are you thinking?" Eric asked. Sweat had soaked through his shirt, making it cling to his chest.

"How to keep you alive."

"He won't kill me. He wants me as a feeder, like you said."

"It's not him I'm worried about."

There. Eric's eyes widened and he drew his knees in, consciously or subconsciously moving farther from Zaine. "You need blood."

Zaine smiled, still fighting to hide his retracted fangs. "You recall the fight in the poker room? I was drained then, and took some of your blood to bolster me so I could get us both out of there. This is like that, but a thousand times worse."

Eric nodded. "I get it."

"I don't think you do. Sebastien isn't the worst thing that can happen to you. What he does to you, it fucks you up but it's designed to keep you alive. What I'll do—"

"I said I get it."

He didn't. Not really. He looked at Zaine and saw a four-hundred-year-old guy who happened to look pretty hot, came armed with some quips, and could handle a gun and himself in a fight. He had no idea of the primordial monster lurking beneath all that. He'd seen some of it in Sebastien, the refined version. But he could bet Sebastien wouldn't have risked a feeder in his presence if he'd been half-starved. Feeders were too precious.

"It's a defense mechanism," Zaine said, half-focused on keeping his breathing slow and calm. It helped to focus on himself and not the hot blood-bag in the corner ripe for biting. "If we're newly turned or close to being drained, conscious thought checks out. We will stop at nothing to feed. Doesn't matter that I..."

"That you what?"

He might as well tell him. They might not have long left. "That I care about you. I'll kill you just as quickly as any other random person who happens to have a heartbeat."

Eric smiled for the first time since Zaine had woken and he rolled his eyes. "*That's* what you hear? Not the *I'm going to kill you* part?"

"I thought the Brotherhood didn't do feelings?" Eric smirked. Zaine loved that smirk. Loved the way it played on his lips and lit up his eyes.

"Yeah, tell me about it. If we get out of this, Mikalis is gonna bitch-slap me back to the sixteenth century." Mikalis had been right. Storm had been right too. Had he followed the rules, he wouldn't even be here in this situation, with the reason he was fucked sitting right across from him all tousled and cute looking.

Had Storm escaped that house before the explosion? He better have. Storm would for sure mobilize the Brotherhood, just maybe not in time to save Eric. Eric, who still smirked, was still hung up on the "care" part. A small bead of sweat ran down Eric's face to his jaw. He wiped it on his shoulder, extending his neck, and Zaine's teeth throbbed to sink in, *to drink*.

"Did he hurt you?" Zaine growled. If Sebastien had laid a hand on Eric—Zaine's heart raced, his breaths quickening. *Shit, shit, shit...* He squeezed his eyes closed and *breathed*. Eric said something, but it was lost in the thickening fog descending over Zaine's thoughts.

"Hey, man. Did I tell you about the time the office pranked me with an alien autopsy?"

The words *alien* and *autopsy* filtered through the fog. "What?" A smile tugged at Zaine's lips.

"Right?" Eric loosed a soft chuckle and that small sound chased the fog away. "The bastards. They had me go down to the precinct basement on some excuse, I forget what it was, and had the whole thing set up with floodlights, doctors in gowns, the works. It should have looked fake. I don't know what I was thinking..."

"What did you do?"

"I've seen a lot of bodies, but Pat, the forensic investigator—she's a beast and she doesn't joke, so when I saw her standing over this alien, I thought it was real. I really did." He laughed. "Then one of the assholes watching from a side office couldn't stay quiet and laughed, ruining the whole thing, and the squad appeared, howling with laughter. So yeah... Those are the idiots I work with."

They sounded like good people. The Brotherhood

wouldn't know fun if it bit them on their asses. "Respect to them."

"Right? They're good..." Eric's smile faded some.

"So are you."

"Yeah, no, not me." Eric shook his head.

"Good people sometimes do bad things. The bad shit isn't who you are."

"Isn't it?" There were parts of Eric's past... Parts he couldn't face, even now.

"Most people don't kill a whole bunch of drug dealers, but yeah, nobody is all good."

"You knew I killed them?"

"Yeah. Saw the headshots. Guns aren't Sebastien's style and you were the sole survivor of that poker game. Ipso facto..."

"If I were good, I'd regret that."

"Nah... You know what I see? Someone who isn't afraid to do the right thing despite the rules."

"Sounds familiar."

Zaine snorted. "You 'n' me, huh. Fightin' the good fight with a bit of morally gray on the side."

Quiet settled, like the welcome quiet in Zaine's head. Eric had deliberately distracted him, they both knew it, and he was grateful. But soon distraction wouldn't be enough.

"For what it's worth, I enjoyed our dinner and I'm sorry I ran out on you at the end there. I have some—" He flicked his fingers toward his head. "—hang-ups when it comes to hot guys with sharp teeth."

"I get that. It's a lot." He'd promised he'd never hurt Eric. Shit, he was going to break that promise if they stayed in this conservatory much longer. He had to get them out. There was no other option.

Gathering both chains in his hands, he twisted and pulled. The links groaned but stayed stubbornly fixed to the floor. He heaved again, getting his feet under him and his weight into it—heaved until his arms shook and the cuffs cut into his wrist. "Shit!" He was too weak. He wasn't going to be able to break the chains or the bolt.

Exertion made his chest and head throb. He dropped back onto his ass and rested his arms over his bent knees. "We have to get out of here."

"He didn't hurt me..." Eric said. A complicated array of emotions touched his face, each one just a twitch or a glimmer, too fast for Zaine to read. "He's not interested in my pain. He wants me devoted to him... the way it was before. I remember feeling... for him before. I would have... I *did* do anything he asked."

Zaine held Eric's gaze. "You have power over him, remember that. You're probably the only one who does."

"I won't be his victim again."

He was so goddamn fierce in the face of impossible odds, like the warriors of old, charging an opposing force. He couldn't damn well die here, and Zaine couldn't be the one to kill him. It would destroy Zaine. He'd never come back from that. The Brotherhood would have to kill him. "This is my fuckup. If I'd just got the job done—"

"No, if it weren't for you, I'd never have learned the truth." He leaned back, resting against the side of the conservatory, and stretched out a leg. The reclining angle was ruined by having to keep his wrists close to the hook in the floor. "Whatever happens, I needed to know."

"Yeah." Eric was so damned strong. Zaine could resist going feral for a while, maybe a whole day in the sun, but already wounded, he couldn't last much longer and he wasn't likely to be coherent at the end of it.

"You can't turn into bats then?" Eric asked with a smile.

Zaine snorted. "That would be useful about now, huh?"

"Yeah. And you can't break those chains?"

"Not unless you have a few blood-bags up your sleeve?" He regretted it as soon as he'd said it and Eric's expression turned serious. "No."

"You could take some?"

"No. No. Not going to happen."

"It would help, though, right?"

"Don't even think it. I can't..." Zaine blew out a sigh. "I'm too hungry for you—for that—shit, just no." One bite, one sip, would tip him over the edge and flip the nyk switch. He'd wake up with a dead Eric in his arms.

Eric sighed and after a few minutes of silence said, "Too bad we didn't fuck when we had the chance."

"Sleeping with a feeder..." Zaine chuckled. "That would earn me maybe two years in a cell."

"They'd lock you up for that?"

Running his tongue across his teeth, Zaine dragged his gaze over the disheveled man. The things he could do for him, how he could make him moan for more, erasing Sebastien's awful, manipulative touch and replacing it with unfettered, true want and desire. "Worth it."

The detective laughed. "If we get out of this, I'll hold you to that."

The lock snicked and the door opened. Zaine lifted his head, automatically baring his teeth in a sneer.

Sebastien took a few steps inside the conservatory and threw a manila folder to the floor, fanning sheets of paper toward Zaine. "You cover your tracks well, almost as well as I do. But not well enough. Not enough to hide what happened in Albuquerque." He left, and Zaine stared at the images of a butchered body strewn across the floor. He'd seen it before. Witnessed it firsthand. But that wasn't the worst of it. The fact Sebastien had the images meant he had the unthinkable—someone working for him *inside* the Brotherhood.

"What happened in Albuquerque?" Eric asked. One of the images had slid toward him, close enough to reveal a dead man's face and the horror frozen there forever.

Zaine wanted to look away, to deny it had ever happened, but that would be an injustice. "The same thing that's happening now," Zaine said, tone flat, heart hollow. "I butchered the man I loved."

CHAPTER 17

ric

THE SITUATION WAS RAPIDLY TURNING into a ticking time bomb. Once the sun rose, Zaine would suffer in ways Eric didn't fully understand but figured would be bad for the both of them. Zaine was already trying to hide his pain, but Eric saw it in his stillness, the glimpse of fangs, his ragged breaths. As he understood it, when Zaine snapped, the man took a back seat and the *thing*... whatever it was inside of him... took over. He'd seen snippets of it when Zaine had fought Sebastien—the viciousness behind his brilliant eyes and savage strength.

Damn, Eric wasn't ready to die here, and he wasn't ready to have Zaine suffer for something he clearly had no control over.

His gaze fell to the crime scene photographs strewn

across the floor and the reason Zaine had fallen quiet. "Who was he?"

A muscle in Zaine's cheek twitched. "Just a normal guy. If we hadn't met, he'd still be out there having a life." Zaine's heavy sigh spoke of all the things he couldn't or wouldn't say. "The Brotherhood look like you, talk like you, breathe and eat and fuck like you, but we aren't human. It's easy to forget, for everyone. Charles was a guy trying to better himself. I derailed all that. I thought I could be a part of his life—thought we could have something." His voice creaked under the weight of too much emotion. "I forgot the rules. Actually, no, that's bullshit. I ignored the rules. I did it all on the quiet, kept it from the Brotherhood. It was selfish, stupid, and it cost him his life."

"I'm sorry that happened." Words didn't seem like enough. He'd said the Brotherhood knew how every story ended. That had come from a place of sorrow. Zaine had made mistakes. Hadn't everyone? But there was more to Zaine than his mistakes. He could have left Eric behind to deal with Sebastien alone. Could have walked away, like he should have. But he hadn't. "The bad isn't who you are."

Zaine lifted his gaze. "Yeah?"

"Isn't that what you said to me? I don't see a bad guy. Badass maybe... but not bad."

He chuckled. "You don't know me, Eric."

"You don't know me, but you still think I'm good?"

"Because I've seen bad, I've seen genuine evil, and it's not you."

"Do you think you're evil?" Eric asked quietly.

"I think what's inside of me could be the primordial, nonreligious version of it, yeah."

"But that piece of you... That's not who you are." Eric smiled, knowing he'd talked the big bad vampire around in circles.

Zaine chuckled again. "Man, you're stubborn."

"Because I'm right."

"Whatever, Detective." He chuckled some more, and when his soft laughter died, he smiled, his pale eyes now warm. "You know, we pretend not to feel. Storm, Octavius, all of them, even Mikalis, but we've just gotten real good at hiding it. Some more than others."

"Because you know how every story ends."

He nodded but held on to his smile. "I'll hold out as long as I can. You'll see... things about me. Probably hate me, definitely fear me. Just know I'll do everything in my power not to hurt you." His gaze fell to the photographs. "That can never happen again."

It wasn't going to come to that. Eric nodded and listened to Zaine's relieved sigh. It wouldn't come to that because Eric had power over Sebastien. He just had to figure out how to use it before it was too late for him and Zaine.

USING the bucket to relieve himself was an embarrassing escapade with his damn hands tied, but Eric managed it, then drank some of the water and rolled the bottle to Zaine. Sebastien returned not long after to collect the bucket.

"Hey," Eric said, pulling Sebastien up short as he was about to leave. He swallowed, throat suddenly tight. Zaine's torture wasn't right. And what did it cost Eric, really? "Let Zaine go and I'll do everything you want."

Sebastien's eyes narrowed some more, and when he turned back to face Eric, reading him, his own face remained neutral.

A few hours of hell? It wouldn't be anything Eric hadn't done before with Sebastien. Pleasuring him, being pleasured. Some part of him even *wanted* it to happen. His stomach turned. But it could save Zaine.

"No, Eric," Zaine snapped. "Don't—"

"I won't fight you," Eric told Sebastien, ignoring Zaine's fraught expression. "If that's what you want. It'll be just like before. Just you and me. If you let him go."

"No," Zaine said again, with more force behind it, and when he didn't get a reply from Eric, he pleaded with Sebastien. "No, he doesn't know what he's saying."

Sebastien tilted his head and glanced at Zaine, triggering his denials again, then fixed his gaze back on Eric. Would it be so terrible? Eric already knew his body wanted Sebastien. He could do this, do whatever Sebastien wanted, and he'd get over it, like he had before. But Zaine... The way he'd talked about his own mistakes, how he'd killed someone he'd clearly cared for. He acted the immortal, unstoppable vampire, but there was a vulnerability to him too. He'd never forgive himself if he killed again.

Sebastien considered the idea for too many minutes, then took a step toward Eric and crouched, bringing himself to eye level. "You'd like that." He smiled. "Sacrificing yourself for him? Make yourself a hero, Eric? Do you care that much for this Brotherhood puppet?"

"No, I'm just bored of this greenhouse and I've remembered what it was like, being yours. I want that again." The words almost choked him, but they sounded smooth and convincing.

"Hm." Sebastien pinched Eric's chin between his finger and thumb, preventing him from looking away. "You believe you can escape. You think that once untied, you'll find a way to overpower me. That won't happen, Sweet One." Eric's heart thumped. "You walked away before because I allowed it—"

"Sebastien," Zaine growled, his voice lower and as broken as Eric had ever heard it. "You touch him and I'll rip your goddamned balls off. You wanna fuck with someone? Fuck with me, huh? Or don't you think you can handle one of your own?"

Sebastien's smile turned toxic. He withdrew his hand, freeing Eric, and snarled at Zaine. "There is no outcome that ends well for you, Brotherhood."

"Please," Eric heard himself say, heard how he begged, and heard the boy in his voice begging his master for more. "Don't do this. Take me."

With a dry snort, Sebastien stood, retrieved the bucket, and backed away. "I already have you both exactly where I want you. You have nothing to bargain with."

"The Brotherhood will come!" Zaine yanked on his chains, rattling them.

Sebastien's luscious laugh filled the conservatory. "I do hope so. And when they do, they will find you as rabid as the day you were turned. Enjoy your last coherent moments. When the sun rises, you won't have many more."

"I'll kill Eric!" Zaine yelled. "You know this!" He kicked at the spilled photos. "That's what this is all about. I'll fucking kill him. Is that what you want? Huh, your precious sweet one dead? You want me to drain him dry and fuck his corpse?"

Sebastien suddenly launched at Zaine. He picked him up and threw him against the wall. Glass exploded, raining jagged fragments, but instead of Zaine flying through, his chains snapped, jerking him back, straight into Sebastien's arms. Rage contorted Zaine's expression. He got a hand on Sebastien's face, jerked his head to the side, and bared gleaming fangs, about to drive them deep. Some kind of liquid gleamed at their shining tips. Eric watched it all in horrible clarity. He'd have him, sink his teeth in and tear out his throat. But Sebastien flung Zaine to the floor, brutally overpowering him. Zaine slammed down so hard, something snapped, and his eyes shone silver and inhuman. Sebastien's foot came down on his throat, forcing Zaine's jaw closed and his head back.

"Stop!" Eric pulled pathetically on the ropes. "Don't!"

Sebastien leaned all his weight on one knee, through his leg, and onto Zaine's neck. Zaine choked in silence and clawed at Sebastien's leg, but after the sun had beaten him down and with his earlier wounds yet to heal, he was too weak to free himself.

Sebastien folded his forearms on his bent knee and smiled at Zaine. "If you care for Eric so much, perhaps I'll allow you to watch as I consume his heart, body, and mind. I think you'd like that. I think, deep down, you want to do the same. We are born of the same Mother of Chaos. Nyx's hunger runs through your veins, the same as it does mine."

Trapped under Sebastien's foot, Zaine couldn't reply, just glare with full murderous force. There was nothing Eric could say or do to stop this. Sebastien was winning. But he hadn't already won, not while Zaine still had his control, and perhaps that was the key.

Eric shuffled backward, and when Sebastien straightened and lifted his foot off Zaine's neck, Eric turned his face away, not giving him the satisfaction of seeing his disgust and anger. The door clicked closed, leaving him and Zaine alone again.

Shattered glass glistened on the floor, a small piece lying beside his bound hands. Eric scooped up the small sharp piece and cradled it in his fingers, unseen by Zaine.

Zaine lay on his back still gasping, arms spread as much as his chains allowed, a knee bent. His breathing slowed. He occasionally blinked. He was hurting in multiple ways and there was one way Eric could fix some of that. "Hey, Zaine?"

Just a blink.

"You need blood."

Zaine growled. Low. Deadly. Definitely not a human noise.

A sudden dryness in Eric's throat made him swallow. "You took some before, and it helped. So, maybe you should take some now?"

Zaine's eyes fluttered closed. "Not so simple," he croaked. "Too hungry."

He would always refuse because he feared he'd lose

control, but that was going to happen eventually, so what did they have to lose? A few extra hours trapped in a sunroom together? Eric turned the jagged fragment between his fingers and poked it against his palm until the skin gave and blood welled.

Zaine didn't react. Eric wouldn't have expected him to, not immediately. Blood trailed down his little finger and dropped to the floor.

Zaine's eyes snapped open. His breathing turned saw-like. "Shit, you stubborn fool."

Fear kicked Eric's heart up a gear. He brought his hands around, showing Zaine the trickle of blood. It wasn't even a lot. A few drops. "You need this."

Zaine rolled onto his front, and even that small motion seemed different somehow. More liquid, as though all his body's broken pieces no longer mattered. His eyes had turned silver in the dark. "It won't make a difference." He pushed onto a hand, levering himself to his knees. "It won't be enough." He breathed faster, and Eric glimpsed his fangs behind parted lips.

What or who was Eric dealing with now? Still Zaine, or something else usually buried under his skin? Even his face seemed different, sharper. There was nothing human in that grin.

A shimmer—that was all the warning Eric had—and Zaine lunged. Eric jerked back. He'd calculated the distance he'd need, and luckily he'd calculated right. Zaine's chains snapped tight, his arms yanked taut behind him as he strained hard to reach his prey.

Eric stayed kneeling—he couldn't do much else with his wrists stuck so close to the floor—keeping just a few inches out of reach. Zaine dropped to his knees, his gaze falling to Eric's bloodied hand. He laughed. *"Tease."* No, the word, the voice, it wasn't all Zaine. There was something else behind his eyes now, something eternally hungry and devastatingly cruel. The primordial part of him.

"Here's how it's going to be," Eric said. "I can move a little closer, and you'll get down low. I'll be in control."

Zaine's gaze flicked up to Eric's face and back to his hand. "I'm going to need more than a few drops."

"We'll get to that. Now get down low."

Zaine immediately laid himself down over the glass, arms still stretched behind him, and blinked silver eyes up at Eric. The angle was awkward, but that was good. It meant Zaine couldn't launch himself at Eric.

Eric's heart thumped some more, his veins hot. Some primal part inside of him felt good at the sight of Zaine prone in front of him, looking up with begging eyes. He ignored those thoughts and the curious sensation that came with them, and shifted, stretching his bound hands toward Zaine. Blood dripped on the filthy floor. Just a few drops, but Zaine's eyes widened at the loss.

Zaine stretched forward, tilting his head at just the right angle, and licked up Eric's palm. His warm, wet tongue pushed, eager to clean a path, and then swirled over the small cut. Zaine's lashes fluttered down over his silvery eyes. He lapped at the cut, and Eric's curious sensation was back—power. Over Zaine. Power over the predator. He adjusted his hand, and Zaine's tongue swept in, aiding the blood flow.

Maybe it was some fucked-up thing left over from Sebastien, or maybe Eric had always been this way, but the lap of Zaine's tongue on his skin viscerally aroused him, sending heat to his cock. As soon as Zaine opened his eyes and fixed them on Eric's, the lust doubled down. His whole body tingled, coming alive despite the circumstances. Or maybe because of them.

Zaine dragged his tongue over the wound and withdrew. "More," he growled.

Eric breathed hard too. He wanted to give him more but was that the venom in his head or his own thoughts? Zaine hadn't bitten him, but he wasn't sure how everything worked. Dammit, he didn't care. It felt good to give Zaine what he needed.

He twisted his wrists, angling his elbows down. Zaine struck viper-fast. Eric barely felt the teeth sink into his wrist—knife wounds never hurt straight away and apparently it was the same with fangs. And when a sharp heat began to throb outward, the action of Zaine's jaw undulating, his tongue massaging, mouth sucking, it overrode what could have been pain. It had to be the venom or some kind of magic because Eric's body burned with desire. His cock throbbed in time with each of Zaine's firm sucks, turning into an aching weight trapped in his pants. Yes... this felt good, this felt right, this felt like it had before, only better, so much better, because he could pull away at any moment and stop it. And he'd need to, soon. The shadows in the corners of his vision were growing, and with each of Zaine's drags on his vein, tiredness washed in.

"Stop," Eric said. He pulled, trying to free his wrist from Zaine's mouth. He tugged again. Zaine growled and drew harder on the vein. When Eric looked up, there was nothing human in his eyes at all, just a viciously cold, primordial hunger.

Fear fluttered through Eric's desire, quenching it. "Stop, Zaine."

A territorial growl rumbled through him, and his teeth clamped harder.

Eric had made a terrible mistake.

CHAPTER 18

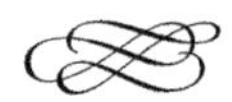

aine

HE'D BEEN STARVED and beaten, exhausted and burned, and all of that had weighed on him like a mountain, but the moment Eric's blood had touched his lips, flowed over his tongue, that enormous weight evaporated. The world outside no longer mattered, just the beat of Eric's heart and its rhythmic thumping pushing life and heat and energy into Zaine. He drifted away, feeding, resting, rebuilding—but that blissful sensation was a lie. Or more accurately, it covered up the fact that he was killing Eric one rapturous gulp at a time.

"Stop!"

Eric's frantic cry cut through the head rush and landed like a slap to his face. Zaine withdrew, sweeping his tongue over Eric's wrist and excreting the enzymes that would rapidly clot the blood, stopping Eric from bleeding out.

The man tore free and scurried away as far as his tied wrists allowed, eyes wide, clearly terrified *and* furious. An intoxicating combination. Eric was hard too, Zaine noticed.

Shit.

Way to fuck him up, Zaine. He locked his jaw closed and turned his face away. He'd warned Eric. He'd told him this would happen. And he'd just had to go and cut himself, then offer a vein. Jesus, he was lucky Zaine had heard his shout. A few seconds later, he wouldn't have cared.

Eric was cursing him out. The words flowed over Zaine as though through water. He let his eyes fall closed, his body shutting down to repair. His thoughts drifted, most of them furious at Eric. If he knew how damn close he'd come to having his veins bled dry and then torn out... The goddamned idiot. Zaine had nearly killed him!

Zaine would tell him, frighten the fuck out of him, so he wouldn't do something so stupid again. As soon as he woke from resting. Because damn, he'd needed that blood and right now it was pouring through him, lighting him up, rebuilding his body and mind.

Eric's foolishness might have just saved both their lives.

ERIC'S SHIVERING dragged Zaine from his healing state. The sun sizzled where it touched any patch of exposed skin, and it wasn't yet late morning. The bushes filtered the worst of the sunlight but it still beat down, gradually wearing on him.

Eric's ragged breaths and shivering were more of a concern.

Zaine had taken too much. "Goddammit. What were you thinking?"

"I was thinking..." His teeth chattered. "We have to get out of here."

He had pulled himself into a tight ball, but the cold was clearly bone-deep, and Zaine couldn't damn well get to him to even try and bundle him close. "I took too much." The fury he felt was more at himself than Eric. He shouldn't have taken from the vein—he could have *killed him.* He still wanted more, always fucking more...

But he was stronger. There was no denying Eric's offering had worked.

Careful to keep his face angled away from the camera's single-eyed glare, he said, "This is what we're going to do. Sebastien would have seen what happened. He's watching. If he sees you're sick, he'll come. Convince him to take you out of here and care for you—" Eric made a grumbling noise, coming from a place of pride, but it was too late for that. "Rest, eat, recover. Do you understand?"

"What about you?"

"I'll be fine." Having Eric removed from his side was the best possible outcome. Without him close, a constant temptation, Zaine could focus on escape, maybe work the chains loose or buy more time for the Brotherhood to find them. It would at least mean Eric was safer, although he'd be with Sebastien, so how safe was questionable. But definitely alive. And alive was better than the husk Zaine would have left him as and still could.

"How do I kill h-him?" he asked, trembling.

"You can't. Only nyktelios can kill their own." He turned his head and found Eric's eyes on him, still fierce and bright despite his sickness. "Our venom. It's the only way."

Eric's brow tightened. He had every right to be angry; he hadn't deserved any of this. The nyk had fucked his life and Zaine couldn't help feeling responsible. He hadn't been there to stop Sebastien all those years ago, and he was doing a piss-poor job of it now. Nobody had saved Eric. He'd had to save himself over and over again. Even now.

A swell of emotion clogged Zaine's throat. "Go with him."

"I'd prefer to die here with you."

Shit, this man. "I know you feel that way, but please... Let him care for you. Or you will die here, and Eric... damn you... You can't. You have to hold on."

A nasty ray of sunlight stabbed through his eyes to the back of his skull. He winced, gritted his teeth, and willed the pain away. Eric couldn't die. Not like Charles had. Not for Zaine. Zaine wasn't worth the man's sacrifice.

"You have to live," he whispered.

"Why?" Eric sneered. "What fucking difference do I make?" A barrage of shivers hit him. He groaned and buried his head against his pulled-up knees, hiding his face.

Zaine couldn't watch him suffer a second longer. "Hey!" he shouted at the camera. "Your feeder is sick! I told you this would happen. Get in here, Sebastien, or he'll die."

"I don't want this," Eric grumbled.

"I don't care. You're surviving."

"Fuckin' asshole."

Zaine chuckled. "I've been called worse. *Hey!*" he yelled again. "You just gonna let him die after you've gone to all this effort? C'mon, he needs you."

The door opened and Sebastien appeared, dressed in pressed pants and a white shirt, as though he'd been about to head to the office for the day. He knelt by Eric, made quick work of the knot in the ropes, and scooped Eric into his arms, ignoring Zaine's glare.

The door closed, and Eric was gone.

If there was any doubt of the depths of his feelings for the man, it quickly vanished the moment that door closed. Regret, guilt, fear—they poured through Zaine, choking him, making him want to rip out his own heart just to make the pain stop.

He sighed through his nose. It didn't matter what happened to Zaine. Eric had to live. He'd damn well make sure of it, even if the stubborn fool didn't want to.

Looping the chains around his wrists, he pulled, straining against their hold. Had Eric's blood been enough? If he didn't escape soon, the sun would beat him back down. Sebastien would be distracted caring for Eric.

Now was the time to escape.

CHAPTER 19

ric

SEBASTIEN'S FIRM, careful hands sat Eric down on the edge of a bed. He carefully unbuttoned Eric's shirt. Eric didn't dare look at his face. The triumph there would be too much. So he sat and shivered and let Sebastien do whatever he wanted.

Sebastien vanished for a moment, and Eric heard the sounds of a shower. When Sebastien returned, he finished methodically undressing him, then guided him naked into the shower.

Eric leaned against the cool tiles, letting the hot water wash him clean and warm him through. None of this was real. It didn't feel real. Sebastien watched, oddly quiet. He didn't gloat, didn't come on to him, didn't try and *do anything.*

Eric pressed both hands to the tiles and bowed his

head. He had to cling to the pieces of himself, he had to be strong, but in this moment, drained and naked and shivering, he didn't feel strong; he just felt so damn tired.

When Eric stepped from the shower, Sebastien wrapped him in a warm, fluffy towel, and he almost groaned from the comfort of it wrapped around his prickly, flushed skin. Sebastien walked him back to the bed and sat him down on the edge, then handed over a glass of water. He left and moments later reappeared with a plate of toast. Eric drank and ate mechanically, detached from it all.

Sebastien reclined in a nearby armchair, the weight of his gaze a constant presence, like a hand on his shoulder.

This was too close to how it had been between them before. It would be so easy to fall back into that, to choose to let Sebastien control him again.

But there was Zaine to think of.

Was Zaine suffering? Was he hurting? Eric had said some things back there, things he hadn't meant, but he'd been scared. Scared of himself mostly, and of how Zaine made him feel. How he'd offered his wrist and enjoyed having Zaine feed from him. Did that make him a feeder?

Around and around his thoughts went, swinging wildly from self-hatred to self-preservation.

"He almost killed me," Eric said. Almost being the operative word. Zaine *had* pulled back eventually. Eric had seen the truth inside him, but it was also one part of what made Zaine who he was. A terrifying part, but still just a small piece of who he was. Not the whole.

"Yes."

Eric licked his lips. His body was thawing, warming,

feeling better with every passing second. The ropes were gone. He was naked, but all things considered, sitting on the bed, his situation was much improved. Sebastien was relaxed and not trying to fuck him over, not yet anyway. And now Eric's head was clearer. This could be the opportunity he'd been waiting for. "If he's your enemy, why don't you kill him?"

Sebastien's soft lips twitched up into a half smile. "I'd prefer his kind find him broken. The Brotherhood are far from invulnerable. It's time Mikalis learned that lesson."

"Mikalis?" Eric asked, playing dumb. He reached for his glass of water on the bedside table and sipped.

Sebastien's lazy gaze rested on Eric. "How much has that one told you?"

Did it make any difference if Eric knew more than he should? "I know about the Brotherhood. How they kill your kind."

Sebastien leaned forward, and when he spoke, curiosity ladened his voice. "And why is that?"

"They believe the nyktelios, left uncontrolled, will eventually slaughter everyone."

Sebastien's confident smirk grew. "The Brotherhood consider themselves our rule-makers," he explained. "They've taken it upon themselves to hunt us down as though we are in the wrong. We're not wrong, Eric. Nyx needs us. We're her apex predators. Nyx created us to restore the balance. And now our numbers have dwindled, the world burns. It is the Brotherhood who are wrong. They are the ones who must be eradicated. We are merely the messengers of chaos, of the Divine Being Nyx herself."

Eric might have sympathized more with Sebastien and

his cause if he hadn't slaughtered Eric's family in front of him, then kidnapped and fucked Eric for two years. But he could play at being on Sebastien's side. That might even be the route to surviving this. "But it's more than that," Eric suggested. "You and this Mikalis have a history?"

Sebastien's lips twitched. "Something like that."

"You want him to know you can get to him and his Brotherhood?"

Sebastien's eyes sparkled with that predatory sheen. He leaned forward. "Mikalis is not who or what his Brotherhood believe him to be."

Eric cradled his glass in his lap. Both wrists were bruised from the ropes, but his right wrist sported a mottled ring of bruises where Zaine's teeth had sunk in. The top fangs had left twin pricks, but there were smaller bottom marks too from a lower set of fangs. Eric suspected the nyktelios injected venom to subdue their targets, to make them believe they wanted to be bled dry. The lower fangs had been the ones to pierce the vein, freeing blood. In the past, Sebastien had bitten Eric a thousand times. He'd fed him, made him feel safe and warm in a bed just like the one he sat on now—venom had taken away his will to fight. Sebastien had killed Eric's sister, his parents, butchered them in front of his eyes, and then swooped in and turned Eric's mind over, exposing everything, and seduced him time and time again. And he'd kept him that way, like a pet, for two years. A feeder. Addicted to the pleasure a monster gave him, a monster that had taken everything from him.

Even worse than that, there were others that had entered Sebastien's bed—other feeders. Eric didn't remember their faces, just the feel of them writhing against him in love and in death. *Kill them*, Sebastien had ordered, and like a good pet, Eric had. Their blood was on Eric's hands.

Maybe the nyktelios were right. Maybe they were the predators designed to control human beings, because the world was a pretty fucked-up place now, but that didn't explain why Sebastien had taken and abused Eric like he had. Why he'd taken a boy and turned him into a murderer.

Sebastien could burn for an eternity in hell, if there was a hell, or some nyktelios version of it.

If only his own kind could kill him, then Eric needed to get Sebastien close enough to Zaine to give him that opportunity while he was bolstered with Eric's blood.

"You should make him suffer," Eric said, lifting his gaze to meet Sebastien's hypnotically beautiful gaze. "Zaine, I mean. For this." He showed Sebastien his wrist. "He tried to take what's yours. Make him pay."

"He already suffers. These things cannot be rushed."

"No." Eric replaced his glass on the bedside table and stood up. The towel slipped from his waist and pooled around his bare feet. "What you said, about fucking me in front of him. That will hurt him more than anything." His insides knotted, but that ingrained part of him attuned to Sebastien wanted this, and that desire set his heart racing. "Do this... like we used to. You and me, and others... we killed."

Sebastien's right eyebrow lifted. He could probably hear Eric's racing heartbeat.

Eric approached the vampire as naked as the day he

was born. He didn't even care, perhaps even liked it... Liked the way Sebastien's gaze roamed, drinking him in, warming his skin. Eric's cock began to fill, hardening with a broken, savage lust. "He cares for me, like he cared for that man he killed." *Like you care for the boy you broke all those years ago.* "Break his heart, then his mind. Drive him mad, make his soul fucking burn." Eric approached the reclining vampire, and when Sebastien parted his knees, he slotted himself between them and peered down at the monster who had ruined his life. He trembled with a new need now, his cock hard, his body so fucking alive he burned. "Show the Brotherhood how powerful you are." Eric leaned forward, braced himself on the chair arms, and peered into Sebastien's silvery eyes. He was clearly trying to hide how much he wanted him, trying to pretend none of this mattered. But just like with Zaine, Sebastien's breathing quickened, and behind his smile, Eric knew his fangs were extended, as obvious as Eric's erection.

He took Sebastien's chin between his finger and thumb, just as Sebastien had done with him. "Do it for me."

Sebastien's lips parted, and there, a glint of fang showed behind his lip's pink wetness.

Zaine had been right. Eric had the power here. Perhaps he always had, and he was only now just realizing it. Sebastien's violent desire controlled him. And Eric controlled that desire.

He could take Sebastien now, and the vampire would let it happen, let him kiss him, mount him, fuck him. His need was as plain as day on his face, in his shortened breaths, his stonelike stillness. And if Eric looked down, he knew Sebastien would be hard too.

He let go and straightened, his body burning for touch, his cock demanding. Whether it was old desire or new didn't matter. It was a weapon.

Sebastien's throat moved as he swallowed. His gaze flicked down. He leaned forward and a flash of lust had Eric's breath catching. Sebastien slid his hand up Eric's thigh, cupped his ass, and licked from the base of Eric's cock up its flushed length, then circled the head. His lips sealed over it and pleasure trilled through Eric's veins. In his head, behind his closed eyes, he imagined it was Zaine licking him from balls to tip, Zaine sealing his lips around him, Zaine's fangs his thick cock slid between.

Sebastien lifted off before Eric could fully lose himself in the delicious sensation. "Wait here," he growled, then left the room... and the door wide open.

Eric swayed on his feet, staggered, grabbed the bed, and sank to its edge. Damn, with Zaine in his head, a few tugs on his cock now would probably finish him off. He had to clear his head, to think straight. The open door beckoned, but running ended nothing. And this had to end for Eric's sanity.

He needed Sebastien high on lust, distracted by feeding, so that Zaine had his chance to attack. In the throes of feeding, Sebastien would be at his most vulnerable to Zaine's bite.

Thumping footfalls sounded down the hallway. Eric clambered onto the bed, still flushed and hard and trembling from *everything*. Zaine would see him naked and splayed for Sebastien—shame tried to douse his desire—but Zaine would understand.

Sebastien dragged Zaine in by the chains. He struggled, teeth snapping, growls simmering, until he saw Eric on the bed. His blue eyes danced all over Eric, reading him, the room, the bed, Eric's nakedness, his hard cock jutting.

"What is this?"

"A lesson in what the Brotherhood are missing," Sebastien said. He searched for something to fix the chains to and settled on latching them around the foot of a heavy-looking set of drawers. The length of chain gave Zaine enough room to stay standing.

"Eric, don't. You don't have to do this."

He couldn't reply, not without Sebastien hearing the tremor in his voice. But he could try and make Zaine see him, make him *understand*. He glared, willing Zaine to see the truth. If he knew Eric at all, he would know this was a play. But his eyes spoke of hurt and confusion and pity.

Sebastien turned toward the bed and Eric, his fingers quickly opening his shirt buttons.

Zaine's growls filled the room. "Eric... You don't know what you're doing. Sebastien, wait—"

Eric straightened onto his knees, facing Sebastien as the master vampire approached. *I control this. I control him.* Sebastien's hungry glare burned into him, burrowing deep to uproot old memories of times just like this one. His mouth crashed into Eric's, rocking him back. His tongue thrust in. In Eric's mind, the kiss was Zaine's, the same as they'd shared on the restaurant balcony. It was Zaine Eric's body burned for, Zaine's kiss that lit him on fire, Zaine in his head, smirking about some smart comment he'd made.

Eric opened his eyes, still engaged in Sebastien's kiss, and locked Zaine in his sights over Sebastien's shoulder. Zaine's fraught expression widened some more, turning stricken, and Eric's heart tried to leap from his chest. No, Zaine had to understand. He had to see this moment for what it was: their chance to escape. The drawers couldn't hold Zaine for long. He just had to realize it and stop fucking looking at Eric and start looking for a way out.

Eric lowered his hand behind Sebastien's back and pointed to the dresser. But Zaine wasn't damn well watching. Silver had spilled into his eyes.

Sebastien's fingers skimmed down Eric's chest, grazing a nipple, and a new kind of fire lit up Eric's body. Then the vampire's hand was lower still, skimming his hip. Eric gasped as Sebastien's fingers wrapped around his cock. Zaine... It was Zaine's hand, Zaine's panting in his ear, Zaine's teeth at his throat... "*Yes.*" Eric gasped.

Zaine roared.

CHAPTER 20

aine

THE DRAWER UNIT behind Zaine squealed, and it was that sound, its legs scraping across the floor, that startled Zaine from the spiraling madness in his head. Eric. Beautiful Eric, brave Eric, was doing this for him, and it couldn't happen. Zaine roared his frustration at seeing Eric so used, seeing everything he wanted to do with him and having it all denied.

Then Sebastien's teeth opened a vein. The scent of Eric's sweet blood filled the air, and Zaine's humanity slid sideways, surrendering to the beast inside. Zaine knew only that he had to get Sebastien away from Eric, because Eric belonged to Zaine.

The dresser's feet squealed across the floor again. Zaine pulled harder, fighting the chains, the clips used to secure them, and the drawers holding him down. Eric's gasp lit him up. Sebastien rocked with him and latched on, feeding, his hand pumping on Eric's cock as his teeth pierced his neck.

The roar that tore from Zaine was something from before time, some dark, primordial piece of him he always knew was there but rarely saw. Wood shattered, the drawers splintering apart and the chains scattering as links exploded. Zaine flew at Sebastien's back, gripped the back of his skull and shoulder, and opened his mouth wide to plunge in for the fatal bite. But Sebastien twisted as he tore free of Eric's neck, ripping open a savage wound.

Eric's eyes blew wide.

The part of Zaine that cared watched in horror as blood splattered far and wide. But that part was no longer in control. All Zaine cared about was killing Sebastien, ripping his fucking head off if he could. Sebastien twisted again and thrust an elbow back with the force of a sledgehammer, slamming into him. Zaine rocked on his feet. Sebastien's teeth snapped together too close to his neck. *Oh, fuck no.* With a right hook, Zaine hit that son of a bitch so hard his face buckled. Sebastien flew sideways, slamming against the wall.

Zaine went for his throat again—teeth bared, dripping venom—but Sebastien moved, and his bite sank deep into Sebastien's shoulder. Venom flowed, pumping not into a vein but inside flesh. Madness and bloodlust blinded Zaine to everything but the desire to kill.

Sebastien let loose, roaring and bucking, desperate to shake Zaine off. He spun, then flung them both to the floor, tangled, crushing Zaine under him. Fireworks of pain danced through Zaine's body, bones breaking, but his teeth stayed fixed, venom pumping deep into Sebastien.

The killing rush consumed everything. Zaine's every heartbeat, his every breath, every working muscle, beat and pumped and pushed to *end Sebastien.*

That was until he caught a glimpse of Eric sprawled on his back on the bed. Just a glimmer in the corner of Zaine's eye, but a flicker of panic hooked in.

Eric was in trouble.

Zaine tore free of Sebastien—the vampire lay beneath him breathing fast, his struggles fading, venom running free through his body. It would have to be enough.

Zaine scrambled off him and dashed for the bed. "Eric... fuck, no."

He lay naked on his back. Blood drenched the sheets, pulsing from the exposed artery at his neck.

"No, no, no..." Zaine clambered onto the bed. Eric's face was blue, his breaths coming too fast, too irregularly. He was dying. Bleeding out. He'd be dead in minutes. Zaine touched his face, turned it to look at him, but Eric's eyes were beyond seeing, gazing at nothing, almost too far gone. Zaine had to stop his blood from spilling.

Zaine bowed his head and smothered the wound beneath his mouth and tongue. He drank fast to clear the blood, then swept his tongue over the terrible wound, delivering the coagulant needed to heal. He swallowed and swept his tongue again, clearing blood and healing. But Eric had lost so much...

"Eric?" Zaine cupped his cool face in his palm.

"Please... no." Eric's open eyes didn't see. Zaine's touch smeared scarlet blood across his cheek. No... This wasn't right. This wasn't how it ended. Not again. He pressed his forehead to Eric's. "Damn you, Nyx. Not him. Take me —*not him*!"

"Zaine!" Storm roared.

Zaine didn't get a chance to look up. Two battering rams hit him from either side, tearing him off the bed and pinning him to a wall. He roared, fought, bucked to get back to Eric, knowing it was too late.

"Check the feeder," Storm barked. Octavius approached Eric's unmoving body on the bed.

"Don't touch him!" Zaine bucked and heaved. "Don't you touch him!"

The Brotherhood were here. Too fucking late.

"Zaine, *stop*," Kazi growled in his ear, pinning his right arm and shoulder to the wall. Thebeus held his other arm. "Stop fighting us."

No, he needed to get free, to get to Eric. He bared his teeth and hissed at them, beyond words. Fresh blood made his body burn with strength. He could tear through them all. He almost broke free, but then Octavius moved in and thrust an arm under Zaine's chin. "Control yourself," the white-haired bastard commanded. *"Control yourself,"* he said again, this time without moving his lips. The order pierced, needlelike, into Zaine's thoughts, instantly stealing his will.

Octavius glanced back at Storm. "We need to get Zaine out of here. He's too close to turning."

Storm's black-clad bulk loomed beside the bed. He

reached out, checked Eric's pulse, and then... dragged a hand down Eric's face, closing his eyes.

Zaine's fractured heart shattered into a million pieces. Inside, he screamed and howled and tore himself apart, but outside he just saw the blood, the body, and Storm's glare accusing him of murder.

Control yourself. Octavius's order reverberated through his soul, trapping him inside a mental glass cage.

Sebastien...

Zaine looked for him on the floor, where his pile of ashes should be had the venom worked. But there was no sign of ash and no sign of him, just an open window, drapes billowing.

Blood coated Zaine. Tainted the air.

Blood had dried on Zaine's face.

On his lips.

Storm approached and fixed Zaine with his heavy glare. "I trusted you, Zaine. I cannot save you from this."

They thought he'd killed Eric.

They'd charged in, seen him crouched over Eric, teeth at his throat, covered in his blood. They thought he'd gone nyk.

And maybe they were right.

Maybe he had. He should have saved Eric sooner. Now it was forever too late.

Storm's grimace turned to a growl. "Get him out of here."

Zaine couldn't even speak to deny it, the words choking him. And as Kazi, Thebeus, and Octavius dragged him from the room, he got one last look at Eric's body splayed on the bloody bed and prayed to the goddess Nyx to bring him back. Because Zaine didn't want to live or fight in a world where good men died and monsters like him went on.

Nyx didn't answer.

CHAPTER 21

ric

MACHINES BEEPED AND PINGED. Eric had woken up in a few hospital beds over the years. As a cop he'd made an easy target and had the scars to prove it. But this wasn't like any hospital room he'd been in before. The quiet—outside of the beeping—was a thick, underground type. No traffic noise, no windows. Definitely underground.

A bag of IV fluids hung from a pole beside the bed and fed something into the back of his hand. Hydrating him, maybe. He needed it. He ached and his joints were stiff, like he'd gone a few rounds with someone a lot bigger than him.

Maybe the guy who had just walked in. He was so big, Eric couldn't imagine they made them any bigger. He had a barrel chest his black T-shirt barely squeezed around, and his short sleeves made a pathetic effort to ring his enormous biceps.

But it was the eyes that both scared Eric and entranced him. A strange glistening pale blue with flecks of silver, they mesmerized.

"You undoubtedly have questions," the big guy man said. "The less you know, the better it is for everyone."

Eric swallowed and attempted to shuffle himself up the mountain of pillows. He opened his mouth to ask who the big guy was but his throat croaked out a sound that wasn't anything like words. He touched his neck and found a thick bandage there. Shit, he couldn't speak?

"Breathe," the big guy growled—probably meaning to sound comforting and failing—and handed him a glass of water from the bedside table. "You sustained substantial damage to your neck muscles."

Eric grabbed the glass with trembling hands and drank the whole thing in a few gulps.

"My advice, Detective? Rest. Take as long as you want. Then you walk away and you do not look back."

Eric handed him the glass and swallowed again, trying to smooth out the soreness. "Zaine?" he croaked.

The big guy pursed his lips. "Forget about Zaine and everything he told you."

Forget? Just like that? Eric frowned. No fucking way that was happening. And who the hell did this guy think he was, telling Eric what he could and could not do. This room, the state-of-the-art machines, this was the Brotherhood. It had to be. So did that make this guy Mikalis? No... that didn't feel right. Zaine had mentioned a second-in-command... *Storm.* Yeah, that checked out. Storm looked like the kind of man the boss used as an enforcer. The muscle.

"The precinct..." Eric rasped. "My partner. They'll be looking for me—"

"It's taken care of. You had an unexpected death in the family. You won't be back to work for at least two weeks. Your captain has been informed."

Eric smiled thinly at the sheer balls of these people. "Appreciate all this... But I don't want it."

Storm's eyes turned cold. "It's not optional."

Right, so that was how it was going to be. They'd patch him up and shove him on his way and everything would be right with the world. No way. Eric wasn't ever walking away from this. He flicked his fingers at his neck. "Sebastien did this," he whispered. "Where is he?"

Storm's big arms unfolded and the man seemed to grow a foot from menace alone. "This is not your fight. Get in the way, and we won't save you again."

"Fuck you. This is *my* fight." His raspy, croaking voice held none of the threat he'd hoped for. He sounded like a mouse squeaking at a lion, but he wouldn't damn well sit back and let this go.

Storm's hard exterior cracked some when the man smiled. "You're not the first to get caught up in all this and you won't be the last, but you can still survive it. If you walk away."

"Zaine was right." Eric swallowed. "You're assholes."

"Yeah, well, as far as Zaine knows, you're dead, and we're going to keep it that way. Or this friendly chat we're having gets real nasty, Detective Sharpe. You won't like me then."

"I don't like you now."

Storm huffed a laugh. "Get well."

Storm left, and Eric frowned at the door as it closed behind him. Zaine thought he was dead? What kind of fucked-up psychos told their friend someone they cared about was dead? For what? The greater good? Eric cleared his throat again and touched the bandage at his neck. The IV tube dangled from his arm and trailed up to the suspended bag. The machines blinked and buzzed. Dizziness spun his thoughts. He slumped against the pillows and closed his eyes. If the Brotherhood thought they could bully him into silence, they'd better think again.

As soon as he was strong enough, he was finding Zaine.

CHAPTER 22

aine

The Brotherhood's confinement cells were the type of high-tech glass-and-steel rooms the US government got hard over. A larger room housed the monitoring equipment and a double layer of security, and inside that room, Zaine paced a second room made of toughened glass. Fifteen paces by fifteen, with a frosted glass bathroom at the back where he showered and took care of the necessities. Animals in a zoo had more space to roam and more privacy.

The whole setup was impregnable. Mikalis had made it that way. Made it so strong and so badass it could hold himself, so all the Brotherhood knew there was no getting out once those doors locked.

This was the second time Zaine had spent an extended period *on vacation.* At least the first time, he'd deserved it.

He paced. One, two, three, four... Maybe if he could talk to Storm, or Mikalis, make them see he hadn't done anything wrong... seven, eight, nine, ten...

The antechamber's door opened and Kazi came into the room on the other side of the glass. He approached the glass door, his usually pouty face severe.

Zaine stopped pacing.

"Step back," Kazi said, adjusting the bag tucked under his arm.

Zaine could grab Kazi the second that door opened, beat him almost unconscious, demand the outer door lock code, and get the hell out of there. Of course, it was a nice fantasy, but it wouldn't work. Cameras in every corner would alert Mikalis. If any of the glass was broken, the outside door automatically locked. There was no getting out of this room until Mikalis ordered it.

"I can shove the bag through the slot and leave," Kazi said. "Is that what you want?"

Zaine backed up.

"Don't be a dick." Kazi unlocked the door and stepped inside. The door automatically closed behind him, locking him in.

Kazi set the bag down on the bed and opened it. "E-reader, not Wi-Fi connected. You'll have to read whatever Octavius loaded, probably erotic tentacle novels or some shit."

Zaine snorted a laugh despite his mood. Octavius barely had a heartbeat and the jury was out on whether he even had a cock. The idea he read anything spicy was ludicrous. "Oculus Rift," Kazi continued. "Also not Wi-Fi connected. You can play Beat Saber to your heart's content and pretend we're the blocks."

Despite the shitty circumstances, the fact Kazi was here, and was the first to come, actually meant a lot. He'd expected Storm to be the first, but the big guy was probably still pissed at him.

He approached Kazi's side and investigated the contents of the bag. "You brought me a care package?"

"Be grateful. Saint doesn't get any of this."

"Saint, who?"

Kazi's expression closed off and he stepped back. "Never mind... How you feeling?"

"Fine. Like I told Storm, I didn't kill Eric." He tried to read Kazi's face, to unpick that wry semi-smile and Instagram eyes. It was like staring into the face of a model with a law degree. Distractingly pretty and way too easily underestimated. "You don't believe me."

Kazi shrugged. "What I think doesn't matter. But Storm and the big man think you partook in the sweet stuff and lost your shit, so..."

"I wouldn't be this coherent if I'd turned."

Kazi drifted about the glass room. "You were in a bad way when we brought you in. In took three of us to hold you."

He had been mostly rabid because he'd been pissed and hungry and sitting in the sun for the better part of a day, and because he'd tried to bring Eric back, to fix him, and it hadn't been enough. "I'd just watched a man die."

"We've seen countless men die."

Zaine filled his lungs and stared at the contents of the

bag. He was facing years inside this room, these walls, but he'd get out eventually, and he'd have to carry on like nothing had happened. Like a good man hadn't bled out beneath his hands. He could have saved Eric if he hadn't been so focused on killing Sebastien.

It hurt to think about it. Hurt so much it was a good thing he was locked away or he'd do something stupid... like deliberately go full nyk so he didn't have to pretend he didn't feel anything anymore.

Zaine hadn't done anything wrong. He'd tried to do the right thing. None of it had mattered. "What are they going to do?"

"You'll probably get ten years, maybe eight for good behavior."

He was so tired of this shit. So tired of trying to follow the rules, trying to be everything the Brotherhood wanted him to be, tried to turn him into. Maybe he wasn't meant to be one of them. "They might as well fucking kill me."

Kazi casually leaned against the glass wall. "You're angry. You'll get over it."

Zaine picked up one of the Oculus controllers and fit it snugly in his hand. What he really wanted to do was pick up his guns and go after the wretched bloodsucker who had killed Eric—make him feel what Eric had felt. "Sebastien is still out there."

"There's no evidence he was in that house. Just you, the dead guy, and a whole lot of blood."

"For fuck's sake, he had—" Zaine whirled on Kazi, making the older vampire tense and straighten. "He had photos of before—" He didn't want to bring Albuquerque into this, but it was never too far away. He rushed on. "I had my teeth in Sebastien. He got a decent dose of venom. He's out there, hurting. I should be tracking him down and finishing him off, not bouncing off the walls in here. Is anyone looking for him? Or are you all just getting off on the fact you have me in a box again?"

"He's not your concern." Kazi glared. "Your bite missed the nyks artery, huh? Sloppy. Storm taught you better than that. Never miss the artery. It just pisses them off. Your whole operation has been a shit show. And you're surprised you're in here?"

"Fuck you, Kazi."

Kazi dropped his cocky smirk and some of the real predator showed on his straight face. "Whatever did or didn't happen, it was a mess, Zaine. That's why you're in here. Quit complaining. They'll let you out in a few years. It's not like you haven't been here before."

The controller creaked in Zaine's tightening grip. "I cared for Eric. Really cared for him." What was the point of all this if they couldn't actually save the people who mattered? Eric had survived so much shit, just to die like Sebastien's discarded trash. Zaine rubbed at his forehead, willing the throbbing ache away.

"Yeah, but you have a track record of this shit, so..."

"Jesus. Albuquerque *wasn't this*."

"You'll get over it. We always do. And we learn not to care. You'll get there, Z."

They were all so patronizing. They talked as though they were untouchable machines. They killed nyktelios and everything was right with the world. That had to be bullshit. In his short four centuries, Zaine had seen the others suffer too. He'd seen Octavius lose his mind from grief, turning himself into little more than a silent statue, his voice gone for at least a century. He'd seen Kazi go off the rails a few times. He'd even seen Storm lose his shit. None of them were perfect. Not even Mikalis.

"What if I don't want that?" Zaine asked. "What if I want to care? I don't want to be a heartless prick like the rest of you. What kind of life is that, huh?"

Kazi came at him, stopping with one stride left between them. "A life serving the Brotherhood because the alternative is you turn into the enemy. Is that what you want? To go back to fucking and feeding from humans, leaving a trail of dead behind you, just like Eric. Because you sure as Nyx's tits keep trying to go back to that, Zaine." Kazi sneered, getting all up in Zaine's face. "Follow the damn rules or I'll put you down myself."

"Fuck the rules. A man died—"

"And whose fucking fault was that?"

Zaine almost hit him. He itched to. His fangs extended, aching to sink into Kazi's neck and finish him off. Kazi glared back, waiting for the second Zaine lashed out. Zaine could take him. Maybe. Kazi was older, and while Zaine couldn't see any blades on him, he'd have them stashed somewhere. Up his ass, probably. Zaine would have fought him once, a long time ago. But he didn't have any fight left in him for this ages-old argument.

He huffed through his nose and turned his back on Kazi. "Thanks for the care package."

Kazi's hand landed on his shoulder and squeezed. "I get it. We all do. We're on your side. Don't forget that, eh."

He left, and the doors locked, and the silence washed back in, broken only by the humming lights and air conditioning. When it all came down to the wire, he didn't have a choice. This had to be his life. The alternative was death by the Brotherhood's hands.

CHAPTER 23

ric

SOMEONE WAS in Eric's room. The lights were low and the glow from the machines cast shadows. Something beeped quietly. And he wasn't alone. He couldn't hear them or see them, but his skin prickled and the fine hairs on the back of his neck had lifted.

"Who's there?"

"A verbal warning will not be enough for you," a male voice said.

Eric peered into the gloom behind the bank of machines and saw him, just the outline of a man. Any distinguishing features were obscured by darkness.

"Allow me to be clear regarding a few things." His voice was cultured and deep, crisp, possibly English, with a hint of some other foreign accent. "You will not pursue any investigations into the Brotherhood or related matters."

"I have a case. A body drained of blood—"

"It's already closed."

"You can't—"

The figure moved like Zaine moved, and the shadow at the back of the room suddenly appeared at Eric's bedside like a glitched movie jumping from scene to scene. Blue eyes so bright and fierce they were like twin stars. Bronze skin, charcoal hair that flopped in messy curls but was mostly tied back with a simple leather band. He looked Italian or Greek, but also nothing like either of those, as though Eric's mind couldn't reconcile the man with the *thing* he knew to be here too. He should have been gorgeous, but something ancient and oppressive stood in the exact same space as the man, and that creature filled the room, its weight suffocating.

"You know who I am."

"Mikalis," Eric whispered.

"Good." Mikalis's penetrating gaze held Eric captive, like a moth drawn toward the flame. "Then know I have protected your world for more years than your human mind can comprehend. In that time, I've seen an ocean of dead, of which you are a single drop. Jeopardize my Brotherhood in any way and you'll disappear into that ocean, Mr. Sharpe. You have no recourse. No human law can save you. Walk away and survive."

Eric blinked and Mikalis was gone as though he'd never been there. The machines continued to blip and the lights were still low, but the smothering weight had lifted. Had he dreamed him up? No, it had felt real. He could still hear the man's words reverberating through his thoughts, as though seeding the command inside his mind. Could the Brotherhood do that, get into his head?

He had to get out of here.

They'd cared for him, fed him, patched him up. And he'd played at being the perfect patient. But he was done. Mikalis's visit proved it. But first, he had one very important thing to do.

He carefully removed the IV from his hand—acutely aware that any fresh blood would pinpoint his location like chum in the water—and grabbed a Band-Aid from the medical drawers. His clothes, brought here from his apartment, sat in a neat pile on a nearby chair. He threw the T-shirt on and fumbled with the jeans fly, tugged on the sneakers, and headed out the door.

Vital to not getting caught was confidence and looking as though he belonged, like he had every right to be sauntering down the corridor. Overhead lights blinked on as he passed under them. Eric hurried on, passing strange unlit office-like rooms he could see through the big glass walls. He turned the corner, spotted the elevator, and stepped inside. If you were a secret society of vampires, where would you keep your secrets? As far away from the normals as possible. He hit SB9—all the way down—and hoped he had it right.

He had to be quick. If Mikalis learned he was sneaking around, he'd no doubt make good on his threat, and Eric really didn't want to incite him any more than he already had. But he had to let Zaine know he was okay.

The doors opened onto another level that looked almost identical to the one he'd left. He strode down the hallway. The doors on either side had high-tech locks on them. All glowed green. Then he spotted a red lock and stopped outside the door. Classical music filtered from inside. Zaine wasn't into classical, was he? He could be. What was a four-hundred-year-old vampire into?

Eric glared at the lock. He hadn't thought this through. Zaine had said he'd be shut away, which meant locked up. Eric had assumed that meant behind bars, like a county jail, not a damn sci-fi movie. He couldn't get through these doors without the code or a thumbprint.

But he wasn't leaving without Zaine knowing he was all right.

He pressed a hand to the door's cool metal panel.

The music stopped.

Was Zaine back there? Could he sense Eric outside?

"Hey!"

The black-haired pretty vampire who had picked Eric and Zaine up from the club rounded the corner. *Kazi*. Eric stepped back from the door and lifted his hands. "I was... looking for the bathroom?"

"Well." Kazi smiled, fangs glinting, "It ain't in there, that's for sure."

Shit. He'd been caught. They'd throw him out and he'd never get to see Zaine again.

Eric bolted back the way he'd come, toward the elevator. He made it four steps before Kazi shimmered in front of him—moving so damn fast Eric had no chance to avoid him. He shoved Eric in the chest. Eric reeled, and Kazi caught his arm, twisted, and slammed him face-first against the wall in a classic move, pinning him there like countless perps Eric had manhandled into cuffs. "Hey!" Eric barked. "Easy, I haven't done anything."

"Hm," the male purred against the back of Eric's neck. "I do like it when they run. Feisty one, aren't you? Hold still. I'm not going to hurt you."

"Having just had one of your kind tear my throat out, I don't much feel like believing you."

Kazi chuckled and backed off, letting go. "If you run, I'll have to chase you, and while you may not be my type, I can make an exception."

Eric turned and scowled at the sassy model. "Zaine... Where is he?"

Kazi's right eyebrow arched. "You can't visit him."

Eric sighed and held the vampire's gaze. "You're really going to let him think he killed me?"

Kazi shrugged. "Not my call."

"After what happened in Albuquerque?"

Some of the snark fell from his face. "You know about that, huh?"

"He told me. Yeah. And if you care at all for Zaine, you'll let me see him. Because if he thinks he killed me, he's never going to stop punishing himself."

"Yeah, you see, that's where your argument falls down. We don't care."

Eric straightened and stepped closer. "Bull. Shit."

"It's true."

"I don't believe you."

"Yeah." Kazi huffed a laugh. "I'm getting that."

"You're going to lock him up for killing me when I'm right here? How is that going to solve anything?"

"That's how it has to be."

Eric met the tall vampire face-to-face in the middle of the corridor. Kazi had a few inches on him, but what

Eric lacked in height, he made up for by not letting his dick get the better of him. "You pretend not to care because it makes your lives easier. I know all about lying to yourself to survive. I had a vampire murder my family in front of me and kidnap me, turning me into his personal chew toy for two years, and to make all that worse, when I spoke about what happened, nobody believed me. So yeah, I get it. I haven't felt much of anything since then. But you know what? That's no way to live. And if you truly don't feel a damn thing, then I'm sorry you have to live like that. But Zaine isn't like you. Let me see him."

Kazi swallowed. And for all his talk about not caring, his eyes weren't cold. He'd felt every word somewhere in that cold, dead heart of his.

"Take me to him."

"I can't."

"You know what I just said, about not feeling much of anything? That isn't strictly true. Zaine is the first person who has treated me like I deserve to know the truth, like I wasn't fucking insane. He made a whole lot of things make sense in my head. You lying to him, telling him I'm dead? That's bullshit and you know it. I'm not leaving until I see him. Drag me out of here and I'll tell everyone about the Brotherhood. So what if they call me crazy? I'll know I'm right. Maybe you'll get rid of me, but not before I've made a whole lot of noise. So take me to him."

Kazi glared, his cheek twitching. All the pretty boy snark and smooth charm had vanished.

"You're his friend, right? Or do bloodsuckers not have friends?"

"Wow." Kazi blinked. "You don't know when to quit, do you?"

"Not for Zaine. Take me to him."

"You got balls, cop." He sighed. "All right. Follow me."

Eric glanced at the locked door. "He's not in that one?"

"No." Kazi chuckled. "We're all safer with *that* door locked."

Eric hurried after Kazi, catching up with him at the door a few down from the one with the music. No music came from inside. Kazi typed in the code, the lock switched from red to green, and he shoved open the door. Eric entered a brightly lit room with a glass isolation chamber inside.

Zaine lay on a bed on top of the sheets, staring at the glass ceiling.

Relief washed over Eric. He hadn't realized how much he'd needed to see him, to know he was all right after the hell that had been the conservatory. Panic soon rushed in. The last time he'd seen Zaine, Eric had let Sebastien feed from him—would Zaine be pissed?

Kazi banged on the glass. "Hey, Z. You got a visitor."

Zaine turned his head. Shock blew his eyes wide. He blurred from the bed and pressed both hands to the glass, his face fraught. *"Eric?"* Did his voice quiver?

"Yeah, hey." Eric stopped at the glass and tried to smile.

Zaine's gaze roamed over him like it usually did, but it was different now, more intense, full of feeling and hurt and fear. Shame tried to overwhelm Eric.

"I'm okay," he said.

"How are you here?"

Eric thumbed over his shoulder toward Kazi. "They lied. They've been looking after me."

Zaine bared his fangs at Kazi. "You dickless bastard!" He slammed a fist against the glass.

At least Kazi winced, clearly feeling the words land hard. "Not my call." He backed off. "And just so you know, I was never here." He pointed at Zaine. "If you tell Mikalis about this, I'll set your bike on fire. Keep me out of it."

Kazi sauntered out, leaving Eric alone with Zaine on the other side of the glass.

Zaine's whole face betrayed a pain Eric knew well. He'd been lied to and it had cut him to the heart. Eric pressed a hand to the glass. Zaine mirrored it. "I'm sorry about what you saw. I was trying—"

"I'm so sorry," Zaine said. "I... was too fucking slow, too into stopping him. I should have gone to you—should have helped you first. I was out of it—"

"You have nothing to be sorry for."

Zaine pressed his forehead to the glass and closed his eyes. "I lost you."

Eric's heart flip-flopped behind his ribs. "Hey, I'm here now."

"I didn't think it could ever happen again... What I was feeling. I..." He opened his eyes. "I care about you. In ways I shouldn't—if you ask the Brotherhood. I know it's fast, and a lot, shit... I wouldn't blame you if you walked away, you should, but you have to know I care... I care like you're the one thing in this fucking world that makes sense. And I haven't felt like this since... forever. You should hate me, hate everything, especially the Brotherhood..." Zaine trailed off, swallowing hard.

"Those dickless assholes?" Eric shrugged. Nobody had ever said those things to Eric. He'd never had anyone tell him he was cared for, not like this. Nobody had looked at him like Zaine did now. As though he was *everything*. He smiled a bit shyly. "Who cares what they think?"

Zaine's face betrayed more pain. He pressed his hand to the other side of the glass over Eric's so they matched. "I'm not getting out of here this side of a decade."

"We'll see." Eric tapped in the code on the door lock and the glass door hissed open. He stepped inside. "I saw Kazi enter in the code."

Zaine laughed. "He let you see?"

"Maybe. Does it matter? You wanna get out of here?"

CHAPTER 24

aine

Eric was Zaine's long forgotten birthdays coming all at once. Not only was he alive, he waltzed in and unlocked the cell like all this was a dream and Zaine had summoned him from nothing.

He stood there all cocky, a bit pale and his voice wrecked, turning it gruff and low and delicious, and shit... Zaine couldn't hold back a second longer. He stepped close —moving too fast if Eric's widening eyes were any indication—and then he leaned in, stopping only to check Eric was okay with this. The hesitation almost killed him but he had to do this right. Eric had been through too much. Zaine almost didn't want to touch him, afraid he might break or poof away into a cloud of smoke, proving he wasn't here at all.

"If you're gonna kiss me, you'd better do it now—"

His lips met Eric's, warm and sweet, and the concrete box he'd packed his heart away in shattered open. Eric melted against him, fitting so perfectly in Zaine's arms that it was as if they'd been missing their other halves all along. The kiss was full of fireworks and feeling, and like all fireworks, over way too soon. Eric smiled. Zaine tasted that too. That perfect, slightly haunted smile. He tried to touch it with his thumb but Eric gave a soft, shy laugh, cinching Zaine's heart tighter.

Nobody would *ever* hurt Eric again. Zaine dropped his hand to gather up Eric's, which had found its way to his hip. "Any second now someone is going to look at those camera feeds, and you being here is definitely not allowed. Let's go." Zaine pulled him from the cell, Eric keyed in the code for the exterior door, and they were out, racing down the corridor.

"We can't go out the front," Zaine said, thoughts and heart racing. He'd soon be free with Eric. Eric was *alive*. Eric was here. He'd last seen Eric's body on a blood-soaked bed and now he was here, holding his hand, smiling at him. Zaine's heart was going to explode with feeling. "My bike... I know a way. Stick close to me. I've got this."

Eric tagged along behind, keeping pace as Zaine hurried down the corridors toward the old service stairwell. Nobody used it since they had the elevators but as soon as they dashed inside, the light came on, showing the way. Zaine didn't believe it was alarmed, but if it was, they'd know about it soon.

"Wait..." Eric puffed on the third-floor landing. "Just give me a second."

Zaine waited and tried not to stare, to drink the man in, to scrutinize his every inch, to make sure he wasn't in too much pain. He was weak from his ordeal but strong enough to come find him, to convince Kazi to let him in. That alone had to be some kind of miracle. Maybe Nyx had answered Zaine's prayers after all. How else was he alive and here? And he'd come for Zaine when he should have fled.

"You're staring." Eric smirked.

"I'm enjoying the moment. Just go with it."

A door slammed.

"Shit." Zaine grabbed his hand. "C'mon, we gotta run." He'd carry him if he had to, although Eric probably wouldn't agree.

They made it to the basement parking lot, the cars gleaming under harsh white lights. Zaine's bike glinted, waiting in her bay. "There she is. Get on." He snatched a set of keys from the nearby wall-safe, hurried to the bike, threw a leg over, and push-button-started the engine. Eric climbed on, knees hugging Zaine's thighs, and he grinned at the close contact. "Hold on." Eric's arms hooked around his waist and he pressed against Zaine's back. He could get used to this.

He roared the bike from the parking lot just as a pair of headlights flooded his rearview mirror. Shit, they'd been seen!

"I've got you. Just don't let go!" Zaine hunkered down, pulling Eric down with him, and the bike screamed out of the Atlas compound. The lights behind them soon vanished, too slow to keep up with the Ducati. But Zaine didn't slow. He raced away, faster, carving through the night.

Thank you, Nyx. I owe you one.

CHAPTER 25

ric

ZAINE CHECKED THE WINDOWS AGAIN, then the doors. "It's safe. Go wash up. I'll keep watch."

The motel was small and basic but functional. And clean. Eric showered, wishing he had a razor to shave with, and in front of the steamed-up bathroom mirror, he poked at the healing marks on his neck. The bandage had gotten wet, so he'd had to take it off. The bite was mostly bruises now, no open scabs.

"You okay in there?"

"Yeah." Eric stared at his reflection. What was he doing with Zaine? He cared for him, cared in ways that felt so right but couldn't be, could they? The Brotherhood, the nyktelios, vampires, gods. What was he supposed to do with all that?

"Eric?"

"Yeah?"

"If you don't open this door in five seconds, I'm coming in."

With a laugh, Eric opened the door and found Zaine with both arms braced against the doorframe, ready to break the door off its hinges. He smiled, but his icy blue eyes revealed all the hurt from thinking Eric dead and from before, when he'd lost another man he'd cared for.

"Are we safe here?" Eric asked.

"For now."

He leaned a shoulder against the doorframe. Zaine hadn't moved, was still braced against the frame, closely hemming Eric in, trapped there by the same indecision that played on his face. For someone so powerful, he had a vulnerable heart. Zaine looked at Eric, into him. Whatever was happening here between them, it felt right. Everything happening outside felt wrong. This, here, now, with Zaine, it was the first time Eric had felt at peace in weeks. Maybe since that night in his family's yard when his life had changed forever.

Zaine finally pushed off and backed away, then busied himself by dragging a chair to the window. He parted the drapes and peered outside. "Get some rest. I'll take first watch."

"You said we're safe."

"I said for now."

Eric had been resting for over a week. Resting was the last thing on his mind. The opposite, in fact. Their escape from the Brotherhood and the insane ride on the back of Zaine's bike had left him pumped. Despite all the madness, he hadn't felt this good in a long time. What he wanted was for Zaine to look at him with heat in his eyes like he had before. What he wanted was to push Zaine down on the bed and crawl on top of him until that damn fine man forgot all about the fear and lies and just *felt* Eric.

All those things Zaine had said about caring. He had to want it too. *Need* it.

Turning his head from the window, Zaine frowned. "You don't need to worry. I'm not going to hurt you."

It took a few seconds to realize he'd heard the spike in Eric's heartbeat. "I know. I was thinking about something else."

Zaine's eyes narrowed, then widened as he caught on. "That's..." He swallowed. "Not a good idea."

"Why?"

Zaine propped his head on his hand and peered out the window. "Because it doesn't end well."

That wasn't it at all. He was scared. Scared he'd hurt Eric again, but none of this had been his fault. And Eric was about to show him exactly that.

He crossed the floor and planted himself in Zaine's line of sight, blocking his view out the window. "I remember you making a promise back in that conservatory... Something about the two of us hooking up after we escaped?"

Zaine lifted his gaze, his eyes still full of apologies. "That was before you almost died."

Eric knelt, and just like that, Zaine's knees parted enough to let Eric lean closer if he wanted to. He definitely wanted to, but the destroyed expression on Zaine's face had him holding off. Maybe the others in the Brotherhood were as emotional as planks of wood, but Zaine wasn't. He felt everything, and he was hurting. Eric could take his mind off all that. Wanted to show him there was more to all this, more worth fighting for. There had to be, didn't there? Otherwise, why were they both here?

He slid a hand up Zaine's warm thigh, feeling firm muscle beneath the fabric of his pants. It always surprised Eric how hot Zaine was, literally.

Zaine caught his hand, trapping it against his leg. His face was serious. For a moment, Eric feared it would end there, but Zaine's internal wrangling must have ended because he raised Eric's hand to his mouth and settled a gentle kiss on his knuckles.

Shuffling closer, he slotted between Zaine's knees. So warm. What would it feel like to have all that strength splayed out under him? He didn't really do relationships—Sebastien had fucked him up enough that any relationship he'd tried to have hadn't stuck. His sexual experience boiled down to a few quick-and-dirty drunken fucks over the years, nothing like the promises in Zaine's eyes.

Zaine fluttered another soft kiss on Eric's knuckles, then his fingers, and as his tongue swept at a fingertip, Eric put his left hand to use by sweeping it up Zaine's thigh and angling for the scrunched fabric at his crotch, where the firm outline of his interested cock had begun to fill his pants.

Zaine leaned down, reaching out and slipping his hand to the nape of Eric's neck. He leaned in for the kiss, but Zaine frowned, stopping him. "If we do this," he said, "you have to lead. I can't..." Zaine wet his lips. "I need you to take control. I need to know you want this. That it's all you and not me driving it."

An exhilarated little flutter stole Eric's breath. "Exactly what I had in mind."

"I'm serious. Tell me what you want. I'll do *anything*." He breathed that last word over Eric's lips, and the thought alone almost had Eric groaning from raw desire. He'd wanted Zaine since he'd first seen him. But to have him like this, surrendering to him—the idea had Eric's heart pounding and his cock iron hard.

"You want me on my knees, I'm there." Zaine's fingers came around and skimmed Eric's cheek, brushing against bristle. "You mean everything to me. When I thought you were—"

As Eric pressed a finger to the vampire's lips, Zaine's eyes widened, and Eric swooped in, smothering whatever he was going to say beneath a savage kiss. When he pulled back, the vampire panted and his eyes shimmered, pupils full and dark. Eric lost himself in those wonderful eyes. "Just you and me and *this*." He palmed Zaine's cock through his pants. A growl bubbled through Zaine's clenched teeth and Eric's veins sizzled with want.

"Tell me where you want me."

"On the bed. Now."

Zaine jerked from the chair with Eric clutched against him, and he carried him to the bed in a blur of motion that left Eric's head spinning. Laughing, he shoved the vampire in the shoulder. Zaine flopped onto his back on the bed with Eric straddling his thighs. Yes, this was more like it. From Zaine's sideways smirk, he liked being under Eric too.

Eric braced an arm on either side of Zaine and lowered

himself to within kissing distance. “How many people get to see a Brotherhood vampire on his back?”

Zaine fought a laugh. “None who survive.”

“Hm,” Eric purred, then ignored Zaine’s attempt to take a kiss and skimmed his tongue down the man’s jaw to his neck. Zaine’s fingers scrunched into the back of Eric’s shirt, holding him down. Licking his neck, Eric tasted salt and sweetness and a uniquely Zaine spiciness. Zaine’s growl was all animal. He licked again and Zaine bucked under him.

“Sensitive?” Eric teased.

“Hm... very.”

Oh, that deep, devilish growl in Zaine’s voice. It resonated through Eric’s bones, made his body hum. Zaine’s hand unlocked its grip in Eric’s shirt and slid down his back, stopping to cup his ass and haul him down. Eric writhed against hard, hot muscles, and when he felt Zaine’s cock digging into the junction of his thigh and hip, Eric ground downward, seeking more heated friction. They both had too many layers on. Eric needed skin under his hands, between his teeth, needed to lick and twist and ride Zaine’s cock. He groaned his frustration at wanting all the things at once, making Zaine chuckle.

“Slow down, lover,” Zaine drawled. “I’m not going anywhere.”

CHAPTER 26

aine

Eric was setting Zaine ablaze. He wanted all of him everywhere, to feel and taste, wanted to see his face when he came, and Zaine planned on making him come hard, but it had to be his choice. Even now, with Eric's fingers fighting Zaine's shirt buttons, he wondered if he should stop this. Eric had been through so much. It had only been a week since he'd almost died. And before that, Sebastien's abuse, old and new, had to be raw in the man's mind. But he'd made it clear he wanted this, and Zaine, by Nyx, Zaine *ached* for this, for Eric to hold him, lick him, nibble with his blunt teeth on Zaine's neck like he had earlier, driving Zaine insane with need.

Eric made a frustrated growling sound—adorable coming from him—and then the buttons on Zaine's shirt flew apart and Eric's hot mouth sealed around Zaine's suddenly exposed nipple. "Gah…" Zaine bucked again, thrust a hand into Eric's hair, and lost himself to the feel of the man's warm, wet mouth teasing his skin.

This was too much.

He didn't deserve Eric.

Storm would have his balls for this.

And Zaine didn't give a shit.

Nothing short of the apocalypse could tear Zaine away now. Eric made quick work of Zaine's button and zipper and had his expert mouth around Zaine's cock in blinding speed, sucking him so deep Zaine lost the ability to form words and devolved into growls. So fierce, so precious, and a goddamned firework in bed too. Zaine was never letting him go.

Eric vanished suddenly, and Zaine whimpered at his loss—if anyone at the Brotherhood ever found out, he'd have to kill them. Eric, now without pants, threw off his T-shirt and wasted no time in climbing back onto the bed and taking Zaine's straining cock in his mouth.

Zaine had planned to tell him he was fucking gorgeous naked, but the second Eric's mouth sealed tight, all thoughts fluttered out of his head like a hoard of escaped butterflies. Zaine's fangs were out, and he hoped to Nyx that Eric wouldn't freak out because there wasn't a chance in hell of retracting them, not when his body was on fire with rabid need and desire and want for all things Eric. It was a damn good thing Eric was the one in control because if Zaine had had him under him, he'd struggle not to bite, and that had to be off the cards after seeing the mass of bruises painting Eric's neck.

Eric lifted off, rearing up on his knees. "Damn... wait... condom?"

With his cock throbbing between Eric's fingers, Zaine blinked, forgetting for a second how to think and what he meant. "Yeah— No, I mean... Only if you want to. Need to. Shit." He'd lost the ability to speak. "I'm immune to everything. And then there's the fact I haven't technically had sex in half a century, so..."

Eric laughed and then cut himself off. Zaine was serious. "Half a century?"

"I was locked up for most of it. I got creative with my hand." He wiggled his fingers.

Eric almost choked on a laugh. Half a century without sex? "I'd better make this good then, huh?"

"No pressure," Zaine purred. "Just go to town on me."

"Wait, you're immune to *everything*?"

"Nyktelios venom will turn me to dust. But anything else? I'm in the clear."

Eric's smirk turned wicked and his grip on Zaine's saliva-and-precum-slickened cock tightened. He took that wetness in his fingers, using it as lubricant, adjusted his position over Zaine, spread his ass, and lowered himself down. The exquisite tightness sealing around Zaine's cock stole a moan from somewhere inside his chest. Zaine gripped Eric's thighs as he seated himself hilt deep and then watched Eric's perfect body begin to rock. Eric's abs glistened wet, quivering as Zaine's cock skimmed that sensitive area inside his passage. His dick jutted, head slick with precum. "Let me touch you?"

"Yes." Eric rocked, riding hard. He squeezed his own nipple, mouth parted, and Zaine could feel himself beginning to flip over into either losing his load or his mind. He grasped Eric's cock and, with every one of his riding motions, Zaine worked him. Teeth bared, Eric watched Zaine's hand on his cock, and fuck if it didn't throb in his fist. The man liked it, liked what Zaine was, liked riding him, controlling him, and Zaine might be discovering a new appreciation of having Eric master him.

Eric's rhythm lost some of its smoothness and he garbled a sound that meant he was close to coming. Salivating, Zaine wished he could get his mouth around Eric's cock, but this was good enough—amazing even. Eric stopped rocking altogether and arched his back, surrendering his cock to Zaine's hand, then threw his head back. Come dashed Zaine's chest, warm on his skin, its scent sweet in the air.

Eric's eyes flashed and he rocked his hips again, taking Zaine deeper.

Zaine was already too high to come down, and instead of fighting to hold on, he let go. Pleasure numbed his thoughts and sizzled down his spine, and at the sight of Eric riding him, he spilled, unloading hard in ragged, savage waves, wringing him breathless until he was spent.

Eric fell forward and kissed him messily, artfully avoiding the fangs as Sebastien had probably taught him, then sucked on Zaine's lip and moaned into his mouth. Wrapping an arm around him, Zaine suddenly, desperately needed him skin to skin, heart to heart. He was pretty sure he loved this stubborn detective, but after four hundred years, if he'd learned anything, it was how to guard his heart. It didn't matter if Eric didn't care in the same way; Zaine was just grateful to have this moment with him. If it was all Eric ever wanted to give, then it was enough, but by Nyx he wished for more. So much more. If Eric would have him.

He wished for forever.

By the time Zaine emerged from the shower, Eric was dozing on the bed. Zaine crawled under the sheets next to him, tucked him close, and spooned him from behind as he listened to Eric's fierce warrior heart. There were other noises reverberating through the motel's flimsy walls: doors slamming, cars rumbling by, high heels clicking. But Eric's heart was the loudest of them all.

It was foolish in a hundred different ways.

This couldn't go anywhere. Eric had his life, his work, and Zaine was... not compatible with that. He would have to walk away, he knew it, which made this moment right here the most amazing of them all—out of his long lifetime, just this one little pocket with Eric tucked close, Zaine's warrior survivor. He'd probably laugh if he knew Zaine's thoughts. He'd throw Zaine that sly little smile, the one that said he was a lot cleverer than most people assumed.

The detective's heart rate quickened. Zaine didn't move, fearing he'd woken him and the moment would be stolen from him. Then Eric sighed, and his heart settled again. Zaine breathed him in. He knew the scent of his blood, but it was more than that now—Eric was inside of him. A part of him. The longer he lived, the more he believed people were all sums of their parts, and over the years, they collected new pieces, changing themselves in subtle ways. Making them better.

"I met Mikalis," Eric said, startling Zaine. The man's heart rate was so slow, he'd assumed he was still asleep. But a slow heart rate was good. It meant Eric was relaxed, content in Zaine's arms. He tried not to read too much into it.

"And you survived?" he asked.

"I don't wanna meet him in a dark alley."

"He can also be absolutely normal too, which is even more terrifying." Zaine propped his head on a hand and looped a stray curl of Eric's hair around his finger, delighting in its silky feel. Eric lay on his right side, exposing the bruises on the left side of his neck and trusting Zaine with his teeth only inches away. Maybe Eric wasn't aware of the significance, but Zaine was. Trust was everything, especially coming from Eric.

"What did Mikalis say?"

"To back off or suffer the consequences."

"And instead of listening to the three-thousand-year-old being, you ignored him and came looking for me?"

"He's *that* old?" Eric twisted and laid his head back on the pillow, looking up at Zaine. Hair mussed, his face all sleepy and sex-sated, he was more handsome than a thousand Greek statues, more alluring than the gods themselves.

"Nobody knows," Zaine said. "At least nobody who will tell me."

Eric gazed sleepy-eyed up at Zaine. "So how did you... I mean, how does it happen? You weren't born with fangs, I guess?"

Zaine smiled. "I was born the traditional way, in a tiny village in Norway under Danish rule. It doesn't exist anymore. It's a valley now, farmland."

"Danes? Like in Hamlet?"

"Around the same time. You a Shakespeare kinda person?"

"I was into a lot of things before... everything changed. I wanted to be a photographer. Had all the equipment, college lined up... Anyway, *that* didn't happen. Now I'm a cop. You know my story. Tell me about you."

Zaine watched his face fall and skimmed his fingers down Eric's cheek, revitalizing his smile. "It was a long time ago, but I was charged with protecting the village along with my *kærasti*. We were warriors."

"Kae-vas-ti? Did I say that right?"

"It means *loved one*. My lover... He was my everything." Zaine waved Eric's concerned expression away. "It was a long time ago. The memory is old."

Eric's smirk grew and Zaine knew what was coming. "Just say it..."

"You're a Viking?"

"No, but close. My ancestors were."

"Zaine's a Viking name?"

So curious, his Eric. He loved that about him. "My given name is Zophonias, which doesn't much roll off the tongue. So Zaine it is."

Eric bent an arm behind his head and studied Zaine, eyebrow raised. His gaze sizzled his skin. Zaine would never get enough of that appreciative look. "The blue eyes and blond hair make a lot more sense now. Although you don't sound like a Viking."

Zaine snorted. "Know many modern Vikings? If I talked in my native few-hundred-years-old accent, I wouldn't blend in, would I? As for my appearance, the blue eyes are a quirk of all nyktelios. Something to do with enhanced night vision, harnessing more light and reflecting it back. I don't know. Raiden is the science guy. You haven't met him yet. I'm just Search and Destroy."

"So what happened? How did you turn into *this*?" Eric arched an eyebrow and deliberately roamed his gaze over Zaine's chest.

"This fine example of Brotherhood prowess? My raiding party came across an abandoned village. Well, what we believed was abandoned. Unbeknown to my *kærasti* and me, three nyktelios had cleared it out and were sheltering in the buildings. We camped there and when dusk fell, they slaughtered everyone."

Eric's face fell again but not all the way. He kept some of the new light in his eyes. "But not you?"

"Not me."

"They left you behind as a witness. I know the feeling."

Zaine nodded. "They're like foxes in a henhouse, but these foxes left one chicken alive to play with. I don't remember much of it. Four hundred years is long enough to let go. But the nyk who turned me, he saw something in me. Wanted to fuck with me for longer than a few hours. For a while after the turning, there isn't much to remember." Zaine gestured at his head. "Conscious thought takes a back seat to survival. Storm found me a few years later, killed my sire, took me in."

"The big guy? Deep voice? Looks like Vin Diesel?"

"You met him too, huh? Yeah, to this day, I don't know

why Storm didn't kill me. He should have. But he said I told him something. I don't remember what. It must have been impressive for him not to dust me. Storm spent the next few years weaning me off the lust for hunt, teaching me another way—the Brotherhood way." Zaine winced. "It's an ongoing process."

"And here you are."

"Here I am. Still breaking the rules." It was worth it for this. For Eric.

"How does it work... the turning?" He'd asked it innocently. Fortunately, Zaine wasn't born yesterday.

He shook his head. "Don't think it."

"I'm not—"

"I see it in your eyes, Detective. You're thinking if you were more like me, like the rest, you could stop Sebastien, but the turning is a long, drawn-out process, fraught with risk, and even if it takes, you'd be a rabid nyktelios for years—assuming the Brotherhood didn't get to you first. It's not happening."

Eric's smile bloomed. He wasn't truly considering it, thankfully. "But I'd be immortal?" he asked.

"Not immortal, just real hard to kill. And *insane*. It's not worth the risk. *And* it's against the rules."

"*Now* he follows the rules," Eric teased and reached up to flick a lock of Zaine's hair back.

"In this, yeah." Zaine hooked a leg around Eric's thigh, pulling him even closer. His cock brushed Eric's leg, the contact reminding him how, not too long ago, Eric had ridden him hard and he'd loved every pounding inch of it. "Besides, I like you as you are."

"You *like* me?" Eric smirked.

Zaine growled, straddled both of Eric's legs, and sank lower down his fine body. "Nobody gets away with mocking me."

"No? What do you do to people who *mock* you?"

Zaine snorted. "I shouldn't tell you. You'll arrest me."

"Wait." Eric propped himself up on his elbows. "You don't actually murder people who tease you, right?"

"No." Zaine grinned, then flicked his tongue in the dip of Eric's navel. "Just frighten them." Diving lower, he found Eric's stiffening erection and encircled it with his fingers, blowing softly over his balls. Eric loosed a gurgling yelp and as his cock hardened, Zaine ran his tongue up its smooth length. "Some advice." He purred the words low in his throat. "Don't tease the vampire who has your cock between his fangs." And Zaine took him between his lips, keeping his gaze up, ensuring Eric was thoroughly on board with having a vampire deep throat him. Sebastien had probably done the same once, but Zaine planned to erase that bastard's touch from Eric's mind. He swept his tongue over Eric's slit. Thrusting his hands into Zaine's hair, Eric held him in place, driving him down.

Zaine's fangs ached to sink into flesh, but with him well-fed and rested, their ache only added to his pleasure in this moment, like his swollen and needy cock.

Eric let his head fall back. With every drag on his dick, his body trembled. His skin was flushed, sensitive. Zaine spread his hands over Eric's thighs, up to his waist, and everywhere he could reach, listening to his sawing breaths, feeling his hips twitch, needing to thrust. He loved this, loved hearing Eric's heart gallop, his body sing for Zaine. And when he came, Zaine swallowed him down, the ageless, primordial creature inside devouring all that Eric gave him.

As Eric hauled Zaine up for a kiss, he dropped his hand and stroked Zaine's dick, his eyes sleepy and face flushed.

All of this was too good. Zaine never wanted it to end, but like all good things, it inevitably would. And when the time came, he wasn't sure his heart would be able to take it.

CHAPTER 27

ric

He watched from the bed as Zaine threw on the replacement gun shoulder holsters over his shirt and fixed them into place. He'd retrieved the holsters from a rented safe deposit box on Canal Street, along with two guns and the cash they'd needed to pay for the motel. Eric had been too swept up in the thrill of the escape to question it then, but he wondered now why someone like Zaine needed a backup plan. "You have an emergency stash?"

"We all have them, should the Brotherhood be compromised." Zaine jerked the slide back on one of the two guns and checked the chamber, then the magazine, before loading it into place and slotting the gun home in its holster, the gestures so smooth they were clearly as familiar as breathing.

"Is that likely? The technology at Atlas looks impenetrable." He couldn't imagine anyone, government or otherwise, getting unauthorized access.

Zaine smiled at some past memory. "It's happened before."

"A nyk got inside?"

"In a manner of speaking." He threw on his jacket, hiding the guns, then glanced over his shoulder. "You should get dressed."

Something was wrong. Since dressing, Zaine's earlier softness had hardened into icy distance. "Yeah... sure." Zaine handed him his shirt. Their fingers skimmed, the touch fleeting. Eric looked up and caught his eye, but Zaine quickly locked down his expression.

"It wasn't a nyktelios," Zaine continued as Eric finished dressing. "A Brotherhood member went nyk and tried to burn it all down. There's a reason they take any lapse in control seriously. Hence, the tiny living quarters you found me in."

A Brotherhood member had turned on them from the inside? Eric buttoned up his shirt, silently turning over in his mind everything he'd learned. But his thoughts strayed back to how Zaine had so abruptly turned cold. Had Eric done something wrong? They'd been talking about the past, about Zaine's childhood and his *kærasti*, the lover he'd lost. Was that why he'd shut down? Eric didn't dare ask about what came *after*. There was only stopping Sebastien. But he'd secretly hoped maybe... they'd have an after. Back at Atlas, Zaine's words through the glass about caring, and last night when they'd lain together—he'd seemed all in until now.

He stood by the window checking his guns a second

time. When he looked over, he rubbed the back of his neck and averted his eyes again. "I have to contact the Brotherhood. Sebastien having access to those photos... He has someone on the inside. I didn't tell them before out of spite. Because I thought you were... gone. But Mikalis should know."

"So call him. Then we'll focus on tracking down Sebastien."

Zaine winced.

Eric wasn't a fool. He knew what this was. He was being shut out. He rose from the bed, adjusting his shirt cuffs. "That is what we're going to do, right?"

"He has my venom in him. He'll be holed up somewhere in a whole world of pain. There's only a few places he can go to heal where he won't be disturbed."

"Then I'm there. Let's do this."

"No." Zaine folded his arms.

"No?" Eric laughed. "What?"

"A nyk is at its most dangerous when it's dying. You've only seen the tame side of what we can do. If Sebastien sees you while in a ravenous state or has any idea you're close, he will rip you to shreds. I'm not letting that happen again."

Okay, he saw what this was. Zaine was the big bad vampire and Eric the damsel in distress, at least according to Zaine. But there was no way he was having his justice against Sebastien taken away. "I don't need you to protect me."

"Yeah, you do." Zaine's cheek twitched. "I'm not delivering you to him like a fucking Happy Meal."

Eric straightened and glared at the man he'd so thoroughly fucked not too long ago. Where was that caring side now? Where was Zaine's compassion? "This is my fight. Sebastien is my fight. I have to do this. I thought you understood—"

"Eric, you nearly died."

"And I'd do it again to see that bastard bleed."

"No, you won't. Damn it. You'll let me handle it." Zaine turned on his heel and flung open the door, striding outside.

What the fuck? Zaine couldn't do this. Eric rushed outside into the cool night air with the hum of nearby traffic and someone's TV too loud in one of the motel rooms. Throwing a leg over his bike, Zaine rocked it upright. He was leaving? "Hey—"

"Go back to your life," Zaine snarled.

"You're leaving me?"

"What does it look like?"

Eric's heart lurched, barely avoiding the hole threatening to swallow it. "You're just gonna fuck and run? You sonofabitch!"

Zaine winced but he couldn't even meet Eric's gaze. "It's not like that."

Eric grabbed the bike's bars, keeping Zaine from racing off and making damn sure he met Eric's glare. The ground felt as though it had tipped out from under him, and his place inside of everything was spiraling. He shouldn't have let Zaine get under his skin. He knew he didn't deserve good things; he never had. But he wanted Zaine to tell him to his face. "Then what is it like?"

Zaine's eyes lost every last ember of warmth, burning cold. "This couldn't last. You understand that, right? It was a blast. But our worlds don't ever cross. They can't, not without you getting hurt. It's how it has to be."

"Don't do this. I thought... I thought we had something." Jesus, he couldn't believe the vampire was making him say it, but it was the truth. He felt for Zaine in ways he hadn't felt for anyone before—honest and true things, not the twisted shit Sebastien had tried to make him believe was normal. Zaine was the best damn thing to happen to Eric in his whole life. And that was it? One night in a motel?

Zaine shook his head. "I'll stop Sebastien. You'll be safe. There's cash by the bed—"

"You bastard. You're leaving me cash after we fucked?" He flung his hands up and backed away from the bike. "Do you even hear yourself?"

Zaine grimaced and kicked the bike's stand up. "Don't look for me, and leave the Brotherhood well alone." He gunned the bike's engine, revving its cylinders and giving Eric no chance to reply, then pulled out of the parking lot and sped off without looking back.

Eric stood on the motel steps staring after him until the hum of traffic swallowed the sound of the bike's engine. He'd thought... What had he thought? That Zaine had wanted him in a way that meant something, not a fucking one-night stand. Jesus, he was an idiot. Why had he cared? Why had he gone looking for him, even broken him out of the Brotherhood's cells? Why had he bothered?

Because sometime in all of this, he'd damn well opened his heart, and Zaine had ripped it out.

Go back to his life? Just walk away, as though that were even possible?

"Sonofabitch!"

He dashed back inside their room and collected his jacket and the roll of hundred-dollar bills.

Walk away...

It was never gonna happen.

The Brotherhood could kiss his ass. Sebastien was his.

CHAPTER 28

ric

NATE GRINNED, set the take-out coffee down on Eric's desk, and propped his ass against the desk corner. "Good to have you back. You've had a rough few weeks, huh?"

"Something like that." Eric picked up the coffee and took a sip. Sweet and hot, exactly how he liked it. "Thanks, man. I needed that. So, bring me up to speed on what I've missed." It had been less than forty-eight hours since Zaine had walked away, vanishing from Eric's life as though turning into smoke, just a bad dream. He'd spent those days and nights digging up everything he could find on the Brotherhood, searching the internet for any bread-crumbs on the names Zaine had dropped despite Mikalis's warning not to. But information on them had been sparse. He'd needed more and ended up at the precinct searching police databases, digging up all the shit the Brotherhood kept hidden. Unexplained exsanguination deaths were a huge red flag, and all of the cases going back decades appeared to close within a week, wrapped up in neat little bows.

But now Nate had arrived with coffee, and Eric had to set aside the waking dream that had been the Brotherhood and Sebastien while Nate filled him in on the new cases. He'd had help from Bekkers, a kick-ass detective from the Fifth Precinct who Nate clearly had more than a general work interest in. For New York, it had been a quiet few weeks on the murder front.

They'd both reached the bottoms of their coffee cups by the time Nate had finished his briefing. "Hey." Eric set his cup down and leaned back in his chair. "What happened with the Capaldi case? Exsanguination?"

Nate shook his head. "Taken off my hands. Closed by the higher-ups. And the John Doe with the same wounds."

"Closed? Just like that?"

Nate shrugged. "Above our pay grades."

The Brotherhood had that kind of reach? Or Mikalis did. He could believe that scary piece of work had a leash on someone high up in the New York Police Department. "And... Vergil? Any sign of him? No body yet?"

"Nothing. Word on the street is he's been taken out like the rest of his crew, we just haven't found the remains yet. Got that to look forward to, I guess."

"Yeah."

"Won't be crying over that one, that's for sure."

The precinct had carried on in his absence like it always did, phones ringing, cases coming in and closing, the ebb and flow of New York and its people. There was a comfort in that, but Eric sat among it all now feeling like a rock in the stream, with all of it rushing around him. He'd seen things that defied nature, been a part of things that most of the world didn't believe in. And he was supposed to just *forget?*

"Hey, man, I'm glad you're okay," Nate said, catching Eric's melancholy. "Was worried there for a while."

He smiled at his partner and tilted his near-empty coffee cup as thanks. They hadn't known each other long, but Nate was a good guy. "Thanks for looking out for me. I appreciate it."

"Anytime. We're partners, right? You know you can come to me with anything."

"Yeah, man." Stacks of paperwork needed his attention and his email inbox showed two hundred emails. "I need to clear this shit."

"Sure. I have a few loose ends to tie up with Bekkers. I'll drop back in later, see if you're up for some fieldwork?"

"Yeah, do that." Eric sent a wave after Nate's disappearing figure and faced his computer screen. He searched the NYPD database for the Capaldi file and got hit with a fat RESTRICTED ACCESS warning. He needed the chief's login to go any further into the file, but the summary was available. *Closed.* The John Doe was linked to the Capaldi case, along with two others that were new cases. He couldn't get inside any of them, but he could plot the locations on a map of New York.

Capaldi and the related cases were linked to Sebastien. Eric's gut knew it, but finding the evidence to link the nyk with the victims was a whole lot harder than relying on a hunch.

He printed off the summary and knocked on the chief's door.

"Ah, Sharpe. Come in. How are you feeling? Sorry to hear about your loss."

He'd forgotten he was supposed to have had a bereavement in the family. "Thank you, yeah, it's been tough." Eric had always respected Chief Allen. He was Black, in his late forties, a stout figure of a man with a solid moral compass, and he was a stickler for doing things the "right way." He was a pillar the entire precinct leaned against and a huge part of why his precinct was one of the most successful. "May I?" Eric gestured at the chair by the desk and Allen dipped his chin. "I wanna run something by you. The Capaldi case? It was closed while I was away. Do you know anything about it?" Eric handed over the printout.

Allen scoured the sheet, taking it all in, then sniffed and leaned back in his creaking chair. "That's closed all right." He handed the sheet back. "Was there a specific something you wanted to know?"

"Well, yeah, like... How is it closed when there were no leads and no suspects a week ago?"

"Nate has briefed you?"

"Yes, and he doesn't know anything. Just that it was closed from the top."

Allen's silver-peppered eyebrows pinched into a frown. He beckoned for the file again, took it, and set it aside on a small stack of folders. "Leave it with me. I'll take a look."

"Yeah, okay." That was something, at least, but not enough. "I'd like access to the file."

"Do you have new evidence?"

"No. I just want to make sure my notes are complete."

Allen studied Eric. "I'll see what I can do."

His tone was a dismissal and Eric made for the door.

"Detective? Be careful, eh. Not much good ever came from kicking a hornet's nest." Allen held his gaze, conveying more with his stare than their entire conversation.

"Copy that, Chief."

Allen knew *something*, enough to warn Eric off. How far did the Brotherhood's reach go? Did the chief know there were creatures out there not entirely human? Or was this more about someone with political power pulling strings from above?

Eric was damn well going to find out.

HE SPENT the rest of the day stuck at his desk clearing emails, and for a few hours, he almost forgot how his life had recently flipped on its axis for a second time. Then his phone buzzed. The Brotherhood had left it inside his apartment along with his washed and fixed clothes—at least, he'd assumed it was them when he'd found it on returning home.

Unknown number: *Help me*

He stared at the screen. It wasn't Zaine. The Brotherhood had deleted Zaine's contact details from the phone, but Eric knew the number and this wasn't it.

Who is this? Eric sent back.

He waited, but no reply came through. After a few minutes of silence, he slipped the phone into his pocket and left his desk to grab a coffee from the pot in the precinct kitchen. Not the best of coffees, but it was wet and black and he needed the caffeine hit. His sleep schedule was screwed up from spending too long in the Brotherhood's basement. There hadn't been much time for sleep when he'd been on the run with Zaine either, between getting him off and having the vampire go down on him. Maybe it had been a dream? The more hours that passed, the more it felt as though none of it was real.

"Hey, man." Nate grabbed a cup and poured himself a coffee. "You all caught up with the files?"

"Huh? Sorry. Late night. Yeah. Almost."

Nate leaned back against the kitchen countertop, smiling ironically. "You gonna tell me about him?"

Eric's heart flopped over. "About who?"

"The guy you're seeing."

Jesus, he couldn't get anything by Nate. "I'm not." He laughed lightly.

"Okay, sure. Whatever you say. Those two coffee cups on your counter? Your weird hours? Secret text messages? You're not the only detective around here."

Eric sighed. If he didn't tell Nate something, the man would keep implying there was more going on. "Shit, I'm that obvious? I don't know—it's over anyway. If it was anything to begin with. It's complicated. And he's not around anymore." And he was going to stop there before his voice gave away too much. "It's all good."

Nate screwed up his face, not believing anything was "all good." "We should go out, you and me. Get wasted. Blow off steam."

"No offense—" Eric chuckled. "—but you're straight."

"Not a *date*. Can't you get wasted with your straight partner?"

"No." He laughed. "Yeah, I mean. Sure. You wanna get wasted, we can get wasted." He sure as shit needed the distraction. A night out might take his mind off *everything*. Like the fact Sebastien was still out there somewhere and Zaine was going it alone to try and stop him—after failing alone several times already. And if the Brotherhood found out, they'd lock Zaine up again. "When?" he asked, catching his free-falling thoughts.

"If nothing heavy comes in, tonight?"

"You wanna get wrecked on a school night?" He'd thought Nate too straitlaced and career focused to risk showing up at work hungover.

"Just say if you can't handle it, Sharpe." He smirked.

Eric laughed and showed him a tiny gap between his finger and thumb. "I'm about this far away from having a drinking problem, so yeah, I can handle it."

"Wow..." Nate grinned and was probably plotting Eric's downfall at the bottom of a bottle. "Hey, you got a visitor." He nodded toward Eric's desk, where a guy wearing a gray hooded top sat waiting. The hood was up, hiding his face. "You expecting someone?"

"Nothing on the schedule." He set his coffee down. "Put a pin in our date night. I'll be right back."

"Not a date," Nate called, laughing.

Eric circled around his desk. "Hi, do you need help?"

"D-Detective Sharpe?" A gruff, almost torn voice stuttered out from under the hood.

"Yeah." Eric sat at his desk, wishing he'd brought his coffee along. He tried to get a peek under the man's hood but saw only a pale chin. Then the man slowly lifted his head.

Silver eyes shone from under the hood and Eric's heart stuttered behind his ribs. Vergil Sonneman.

No, not possible.

Eric had shot him himself. Dead men did not come back, unless they were Sebastien. Unless they were... nyktelios.

Vergil's skin was so pale it almost glowed blue. His eyes fixed on Eric with laser intensity, the dark pupils shot, encased in silver.

"Easy." Eric lifted his hands. "Easy, Vergil."

"F-f-fuckin' cop." The words were mangled behind growls, but Eric heard their meaning.

He tried to recall what Zaine had said about newly turned nyks. Words like rabid and vicious stood out. Newly turned nyks were murder machines, that seemed to be the takeaway, and now one was sitting opposite Eric in a precinct full of cops.

"Vergil, listen to me." He kept his voice low. Nobody had noticed Vergil but they soon would if Eric didn't get him out of here. Fast. "I can help you—"

He slammed a hand onto Eric's desk, rattling the pens in their holder. *"F-fuckin' liar! Killed my crew."* He pointed a finger and twisted it in the air. *"Under. Cover. Cop."*

Nate started to head over, and that was the last thing Eric needed. One wrong move and Vergil would snap, tearing out the throat of whoever happened to be within reach. Nobody here knew the creature they had among them, and Eric had to keep it that way.

The phones continued to ring. Someone at the back of the bullpen laughed.

Nate's glare burned into Eric, and he shook his head, warning his partner off.

A growl bubbled out of Vergil—a sound no human should make. He snarled, pulling back his top lip. Two sharply curved teeth gleamed, and below those were a pair of incisors that were smaller but no less sharp. Teeth exactly like those had torn into Eric's neck, severing an artery. A flush of cold raced through Eric's veins, chasing the memory of how his body had turned to ice around him while he bled out on Sebastien's bed. "Vergil, come with me. Just you and me. Let's go somewhere to talk." He had to get him away from everyone. After that he'd figure out how to stop him or send him back to wherever he'd come from... From Sebastien?

Someone else laughed and Vergil's head snapped up, nostrils flaring. *"Cunt's... bleeding. Sweet... blood."*

"Hey, Vergil." Eric snapped his fingers and Vergil's glare locked back on him. "I'm the one you're here for. Did Sebastien send you?"

Vergil's face crumpled. *"Sebastien?"* He shrank inward, his shoulders folding, then thumped himself on the side of the head, once, twice, then again and again. *"Sebastiensebastiensebastien."*

Eric cracked open his desk drawer and discreetly withdrew his service Glock. There were no good outcomes for any confrontation with Vergil inside the precinct. He had to get him *outside*, away from people. "Hey, hey! Calm down."

Vergil stopped hitting himself but kept his head down and growled every breath.

"Okay, you and me, we're gonna take a walk."

Vergil didn't move, just stayed slumped in the chair and began to gently sway. His hood thankfully hid his face. Eric scooted around his desk and gripped Vergil's arm. "Easy," he said again when the man tensed. "Just you and me," he whispered against his ear. "You came here for me, remember. Sebastien said so, didn't he? Well, you got me, so let's go..." Vergil relented, rising out of the chair.

Nate's glare fixed on Eric but he gave a shake of his head and mouthed, *I've got this*. Hopefully, Nate would think Vergil was just a meth head who'd wandered in off the street.

Eric ushered Vergil out of the bullpen and into the stairwell as a couple of cops jogged up the steps toward him. There were still too many people around. He had to get Vergil *out* before whatever switch controlled him flipped in his head.

"*Killed my crew...*" Vergil growled.

"C'mon." Eric guided him down the stairs, all the way down to the underground parking lot, and shoved him through the swinging doors. Vergil stumbled ahead and whirled under a flickering overhead light. Growls bubbled out of him.

Eric checked the parking lot was empty and raised his gun. He couldn't kill him, not here and not with a gun. Zaine had made that clear. But he could hurt him and slow him down. "Where's your master? Where's Sebastien?"

Vergil swayed on his feet. *"Sent me."*

"Yeah, so where is he? Huh?"

Vergil snuffled. His lips parted, tongue tasting the air. *"You. Taste... sweet."*

"Uh-huh, here's what we're going to do. We're going to take my car and you're going to tell me where Sebastien is. Do you understand?"

A squad car crawled down the ramp into the parking lot. Eric holstered his gun and gathered Vergil to one side. He couldn't let him just walk out of there. Wherever Sebastien was, Zaine had said he'd be hurting. Maybe if Eric could get Vergil back to Sebastien, he could alert the Brotherhood to his location.

Vergil's grip shifted, twisting back on Eric's arm, and with a burst of strength, Vergil thrust forward, throwing Eric off his feet. His shoulder struck a nearby wall and he went for his gun as Vergil's teeth flashed, his jaws wide as he surged in for the kill. Eric couldn't get his gun up in time.

A gunshot boomed through the parking lot, and the side of Vergil's face blasted apart, raining blood and bone. His body jerked sideways as he stumbled into a parked squad car. Despite missing half his cheek and jaw, he whirled on the man who had shot him—Nate.

"Get down on the ground!" Nate yelled, gun cupped in his hands as he came closer.

Vergil loosed an inhuman roar and bolted toward him. Nate's gun boomed again, and Vergil's shoulders twisted but he kept on running. Another shot, and Vergil jerked. Another, and he stumbled and fell facedown a few strides from Nate, unmoving.

Nate blinked, frozen, and for a few seconds, only the

deafening gunshots rang in Eric's ears. Then came Nate's resounding, *"Fuck!"*

Eric reached for the car and tried to slow his breathing. Icy panic had wrapped around him, freezing him like a damn first-year cadet. Vergil's speed and strength had been too much for Eric.

If Nate hadn't shown up—

His partner moved in toward the body.

"Don't touch him," Eric wheezed, panic stealing his voice.

Nate crouched beside Vergil, checking for a pulse. "I need to call this in."

"No..." Eric croaked. "Get away." He stumbled toward the pair. Vergil was down, half his face gone. He'd be pissed but not dead. "Shit, Nate, get back!" Eric pulled his gun. Nate glanced behind him, and Vergil twitched into motion. His body bucked, muscles contorting.

"What the fu—"

Vergil grabbed for Nate, who reeled, knocked to his ass. Eric fired. And fired again. Vergil's body took the rounds like a damn punching bag but the impacts jerked him out of his frenzy to get to Nate. His growls rumbled, and then he took off loping away from Nate toward the exit.

"Oh no you don't..."

Eric bolted after him but Vergil's inhuman stride quickly outpaced his, and as he sprinted up the ramp, Eric knew he'd lose him. A horn honked, and by the time Eric reached the top of the ramp, there was no sign of Vergil, just the afternoon traffic and a few pedestrians giving him the side-eye. "Shit." Eric panted, holstering his gun again.

Nate jogged up alongside him. "How? How did he... How... I just... His face... "

"C'mon." Eric rubbed his eyes. "We need to get out of here."

"But we have to report it. They'd have heard the shots. I discharged my gun—"

"Can't report it. It'll just get shut down."

Nate paced, then planted his hands on his hips and glared. "That was Vergil Sonneman. What the hell is going on, Sharpe?"

There was no way around this, no lie that would explain how a man who had just had half his face blown away could get up and run off. He had to tell Nate everything. "Wanna get that drink?"

CHAPTER 29

aine

HE'D VISITED the three known addresses for Sebastien. All were fake, either staged or manned by a minimal housekeeping staff who claimed to rarely see Sebastien.

Despite the search yielding no results, one thing was certain: Sebastien's absence confirmed he was hurting. Every second, Zaine's venom crawled through his veins, trying to burn him up. It wouldn't kill him, only delivering venom to the jugular did that, but he'd be in agony, wishing Zaine's aim had hit its mark.

Sebastien was holed up somewhere—somewhere secure, somewhere dark, somewhere accessible so his feeders could replenish him.

Somewhere clever.

But short of riding around Midtown aimlessly, Zaine's resources were limited. His efforts alone had already proven to be lacking, and the Brotherhood might have discovered Sebastien's location by now.

He knew what he had to do.

Zaine's phone vibrated in his pocket. He pulled his bike to the side of the road, cut the engine, and glared at the name on the phone's screen. *Mikalis*. Like he'd known, somehow it would come to this.

Time to face the music.

Zaine breathed in, steeled himself, and answered the call. "Hey, listen, I'll come back in. I just need this to be over for Eric."

"Zaine—"

"I'm not off the rails, okay? I've never been more on them. This isn't Albuquerque all over again. It's about doing the right thing. Sometimes the Brotherhood lose sight of that—"

"Zaine, stop." Mikalis's voice could be soft and soothing or it could be glass, its edges sharp. Like it was now. "We have everything in hand. Step back."

That meant they'd found him. "Do you know where Sebastien is?"

"Come in."

"Is Eric safe?" Leaving him like he had... It had been a shitty thing to do but necessary. They had no future. None. The Brotherhood would see to that. The best outcome he could hope for was Eric moving on with his life. The *only* outcome.

"Zaine," Mikalis said again, "come in."

"I'm not coming in until I know Sebastien has been dusted. Do you have him? Have you gotten to him? Lock me up for a hundred years if you want, but I'm seeing this through. I don't trust you—"

A blast of oily black shadow riddled with sparks boiled in the air beside Zaine, and out stepped Mikalis wearing a midnight blue suit, his dark hair tied back in a ponytail loop.

"*Jesus!*" Zaine spluttered, almost dropping the phone.

"Not quite." The ages-old vampire smirked.

Zaine straightened, not buying Mikalis's smile. Snakes wore the same smile right before devouring their prey. He'd heard rumors Mikalis could *appear* but had never seen it. Until now.

He sighed through his nose, making an effort to relax even though his heart raced. Mikalis would hear its thumps as clear as Zaine could feel them behind his ribs. One of the first warnings Storm had given him, right after he'd been weaned off the chaos he'd spread as a nyks, was to treat Mikalis as though the master vampire could and would tear his throat out the second Zaine put a foot wrong. He might have shrugged it all off as bullshit if he hadn't witnessed it himself.

Mikalis would kill one of his own as readily as any nyks, should they betray him.

Circling around the front of Zaine's bike, Mikalis's dark-eyed gaze absorbed the sporadic street lighting and the passing trail of cars. At a glance, he was just a guy, but it didn't take long for that thin veneer to shift away, for Zaine's sight to see something beneath the man's skin. Some deeper, darker ancient part of him that had perhaps walked the earth longer than any other creature alive.

"Here's my problem," Mikalis began, casually tucking a

hand into his pants pocket. "The Brotherhood is and must forever be everything we stand for, everything we fight for. It is the reason we're here. Without it, we are no better than the creatures we hunt and kill. And how are we different from them?"

Zaine swallowed, accepting the dressing-down coming his way.

"We control that part of ourselves demanding chaos. That part Nyx herself seeded within us. You may think you are far removed from the divine, but her touch in you, albeit diluted by many generations, is just as strong as her touch is within me. Do not underestimate the power of chaos. We have rules for a reason, Zaine. They keep us safe, and we keep everyone else safe. The people who populate this world, we protect every single one as a whole."

He knew where this was going and shook his head. "I need to do this."

"Your *needs* are at best irrelevant, at worst bordering on selfish."

"It's not like that."

Mikalis sighed. "Love seeds chaos. You cannot have love and be among the Brotherhood. And if you're not part of the Brotherhood, you're against us."

"You really believe that?"

Mikalis held Zaine's gaze. He didn't blink, and those dark eyes carried a fine sliver of silvery light, like the pupils of cats' eyes narrowing to slits. "How many paths do you think I've crossed? How many loves have I let go? Trust me when I tell you it never ends well."

Zaine knew that. He'd said the same to Eric. But he

still wasn't sure he believed that to be the only way. Did Nyx truly wish this life on them?

"Go back to the compound. I have Sebastien in hand, you have my word. Eric will not be hurt. Everything else, including your escape from Atlas, we'll discuss in due course."

He couldn't argue with Mikalis, not without earning himself a few more decades in confinement. The vampire didn't argue; he overruled. And he clearly wasn't going to listen to anything Zaine said. He was older than the mountains, and just like a mountain, he was fucking immovable.

If being like Mikalis was what he had to look forward to, he didn't want it. He'd rather love for real, even if it was fleeting, than never love at all.

Zaine nodded. "All right."

Mikalis nodded too. "I'm not known for offering second chances. Don't disappoint me again, Zaine." The static-filled shadows boiled behind him, and without looking, he stepped backward and disappeared inside them, leaving Zaine alone on the sidewalk watching an unsuspecting world rush by.

CHAPTER 30

ric

ERIC HAD PICKED a bar farther from home than he'd usually venture to but within walking distance of his apartment, and there he'd told Nate everything. Half-truths wouldn't have cut it and he wasn't creative enough to think of a lie that would cover Vergil's breakdown and subsequent super strength and speed and the ability to walk off a few gunshot wounds to the face and chest.

Nate had begun skeptical, but as the drinks had flowed and Eric had talked, the more he had an answer for every one of Nate's questions, the more his partner came around to the idea of vampires in New York. "What did Sherlock say? When you eliminate the impossible, then whatever remains, however improbable, must be the truth."

"Yeah, except the truth *is* impossible. And he was probably high at the time." Nate threw back the dregs of his beer and waved the bartender over for another. "If I weren't drunk, I'd be hauling your ass in for a psych evaluation."

"Been there." Eric chinked his beer bottle with Nate's fresh one. "You'll have to shoot me to get me back."

Nate chuckled, took a swig of his beer, then picked at its label. "You've been dealing with this alone?"

"Pretty much, apart from Zaine..."

"Who brushed you off after getting laid. Asshole."

"Yeah." Couldn't think about Zaine, about where he might be. About Sebastien and Vergil and how he couldn't do a damn thing to help end it. Thinking on it made him feel helpless, and he'd vowed never to be helpless again.

"Hey, man, it's been... *interesting*." His partner half laughed. He'd probably wake up tomorrow and try and convince himself it wasn't as Eric had said. "But I guess I should call it a night. Get an Uber, head home."

"My place is closer. You're welcome to stay."

"You sure?"

"Yeah, honestly, after everything, I could do with the company."

"Dunno what kinda company I'll be, but sure. Thanks. I'll just..." He gestured at the back of the bar. "The restroom."

"Sure." After Nate left, Eric took his phone from his pocket and typed out a quick *Everything okay?* to Zaine's number. His finger hovered over send, then moved to delete.

Maybe Zaine *had* done him a favor by cutting him out. But he hadn't needed to be a dick about it. Or maybe he had, to make sure Eric didn't cling on—which he might have done. Zaine had been worth clinging on to. He laughed at himself and downed the beer. *Falling for the Viking vampire*, like his life was some kind of cheesy romance novel. Shit like that didn't happen in reality.

The earlier text *Help me* caught his eye among the messages. In a drunken fog, with the bar thumping and people laughing, the last few weeks didn't feel real and neither did all the crazy things he'd told Nate. If only he were insane, that would make things a whole lot easier. He stared at those two words: *Help me.*

Sebastien? he sent.

If it was the wrong number, then it wouldn't matter. Whoever got it would shrug it off. But what if Sebastien was holed up somewhere resting and he needed a feeder—a blood donor. If he was desperate enough, he might call Eric. And lead Eric right to him.

Nate was making his way back and no reply had come. Eric dropped the phone into his pocket and grabbed his coat. "Let's go."

They left the bar, stepping into the cold night air.

"Hey, thanks for this," Eric said. "I needed the downtime more than you know."

"Anytime, man. But tomorrow I'm hoping I wake up and it was all some twisted dream."

Eric snorted. "If only."

They stumbled back to Eric's apartment building, Nate chatting about Bekkers with way too much drunken enthusiasm. He'd regret confessing his feelings for her tomorrow. But until then, Eric let him talk about his crush and they both staggered up the stairs, trying to keep from waking his neighbors.

Nate fell against the wall beside Eric's apartment door and giggled. "Vampires in New York." He snickered.

"I thought you said you could handle your drink?" Eric fumbled his keys, unlocked the apartment door, and pushed inside, flicking on the lights as he entered the living area.

"Yeah, I may have embellished my abilities a bit."

The outside streetlight flooded light into the apartment through the open blinds, enough to see his way to the kitchen to grab a glass of water.

"You should hydrate," Eric said, filling a second glass. He turned and stared down the barrel of his partner's gun with Nate on the other end, suddenly clear-eyed and determined.

"Put the drinks down."

Eric lowered the glasses onto the countertop. "What—"

Nate narrowed his eyes. "Hand over your gun."

Eric's slow, alcohol-addled brain took a moment to process what was happening. "Nate, whatever this is, let's talk—"

"I've listened to you talk enough."

He sounded stone-cold sober while Eric's head swam, full of booze. He withdrew his Glock and set that down on the countertop. "What is this? You think I'm nuts, is that it?"

"Oh yeah, but not because of what you said." He jerked the gun. "Sit. Over there."

Eric maneuvered out from behind the counter and followed Nate's instructions to sit in the chair by the window. He kept his hands raised nonthreateningly while his thoughts whirred. Standing back, Nate kept his gaze trained down the barrel's sights. He'd either nursed one beer the whole night, or he could handle his drink better than Eric.

"Nate, c'mon..." This didn't make any sense. "What's going on? I told you the truth. I know it sounds crazy—"

"I believe you. Every word." He smiled his poster boy smile. "What I find impossible to accept is that you'd believe the Brotherhood over Sebastien."

Eric's gut plummeted through the floor. He swallowed, thoughts spiraling downward. *Oh no.* "You know Sebastien?"

Nate snorted and with his right hand, he pulled his left sleeve up, revealing bruises on his inner wrist. Eric had seen them on his partner before and thought nothing of them. Nate had explained it away once by saying he played tennis. "You know what that is? I know you do."

Nate knew Sebastien. He'd known everything, long before Eric had told him. "You're a feeder."

"Feeder?" Nate snorted. "I'm *chosen*."

Wincing, Eric lowered his hands and rubbed his face. "How long?"

"Long enough to know where my loyalties are. Unlike you. You walked away from him."

"You going to shoot me, Nate?" He wasn't a killer. Eric moved to stand but Nate's gun fired, splintering the chair's arm and peppering Eric with foam filling, shocking him back down. "Nate—what the fuck!"

"Do not move."

"What are you doing? Give me the gun. Whatever he told you is lies. You don't have to do this."

"Yes, he doessss..." A voice as rough as sandpaper hissed from the back of the apartment. The hunched figure emerged from the gloom. The body was bent and broken, shriveled and curled in like a spider carcass left in the sun. His fingers were crooked like twigs and hollow cheeks thinned his face.

Sebastien, but twisted and decayed.

Eric's throat dried. His heart pounded like a drum in his chest and head.

"The lifeblood flows strong inside you," Sebastien rasped.

Eric took his gaze from Sebastien, glancing at Nate just for a moment. The man's eyes had softened, his face flushed and jaw fallen slack. He wasn't alarmed at Sebastien's arrival, wasn't surprised. The spell Sebastien had him under went all the way down to the man's heart and mind. Sebastien had said he could ruin people, said he'd done worse, and here was Nate, Eric's friend, his partner—Sebastien's puppet.

It wasn't Nate's fault. He didn't know what he was doing, just that it felt good, felt right. He was the victim here. Eric knew that feeling well. He had to stop Nate from doing something he'd never forgive himself for.

Eric lunged for Nate. The gun boomed, and like a hook though his shoulder, he jerked back, almost whirling a complete three-sixty on his feet. Fire burned up his side. He let out a cry and fell back against the kitchen counter. Sebastien was on him suddenly, his heavy weight sprawled atop him, pinning him against the stool. He tore Eric's hand from the bullet wound and buried his mouth against the ruptured flesh. Sebastien's wet tongue probed, sweeping in, lapping.

Disgust and fear shivered through Eric. He bucked and tried to get a hand between him and Sebastien to pry him off, but even frail and desiccated, the vampire's strength was twice Eric's.

"It's you he needs—your blood," Nate was saying, his voice dull and hollow. "The rest of us weren't enough."

Us. How many feeders were there? Didn't matter. Eric had to get away.

His gun lay on the counter just out of reach. Nate still had his own gun raised. Eric would never make it out from under Sebastien and be able to grab his gun without Nate shooting him again.

The fire in his shoulder faded but the wound still throbbed, and the sickening sensation of Sebastien's tongue working in his flesh slithered through Eric's mind, trying to summon a scream.

He couldn't do this, couldn't be that boy. He couldn't damn well be the victim again and again. It had to end, here and now. He gathered the rage in his gut, the disgust twisting his heart, and levered Sebastien back. The vampire's fingers dug in, sharp nails sinking into the fabric of Eric's shirt and fixing to him like claws.

He couldn't be here under Sebastien again—he'd escaped him! He was more than a body to be drained. Pushing, muscles trembling with effort, Eric slowly, inch by inch, forced Sebastien back. For a moment it seemed as though he had him, then Sebastien jerked, readjusted his grip, and his teeth sank into Eric's shoulder. Venom pumped cool and slick, racing through his veins and desperate to reach his heart.

"Fuck you!" Eric seethed, still pushing, fighting with every breath, every beat of his heart like a hammer blow. The venom had him now, coiling around him. Maybe he was just losing his mind, but something inside him shifted, some part of him he hadn't known existed unfurled and raced to meet the cold trying to freeze him rigid. This new part of him burned fiercely. It felt like rage, like a lifetime of hating himself and what had been done to him—what *he* had done to others—boiling over, no longer contained.

Sebastien spluttered and blood dashed Eric's face.

Perhaps he was already mad because he was seeing impossible things, things like a man stepping from a veil of darkness and shadow, his eyes like pools of molten lava, his teeth twin scythes. The shadow man tore the gun from Nate's hand as though it was nothing more than a toy, caught Nate by the neck, and threw him across the room. The detective smacked against the wall and collapsed limp on the floor.

"No!" A surge of something poured into Eric's veins. He thrust both arms out and Sebastien flew back. In midair his form twisted, knotting and unknotting in a withered mass of flesh and blood and bone. It didn't make any sense.

And the shadow man, Eric knew him. He'd seen him before. Mikalis stood back, his blazing eyes narrowed on Eric.

"Kill Sebastien!" Eric yelled.

Mikalis leisurely turned his gaze from Eric toward Sebastien. He lunged, grabbed the writhing mass of vampire, and dragged him into an embrace. His fangs came down toward Sebastien's shifting neck—

Sebastien howled, the sound like nails on a chalkboard. He roared, whirling and twisting in Mikalis's grip and driving him backward into the wall and almost straight through it. Plaster and wood rained down, electric wires sparking.

Among the howls and vicious snarls, Eric grabbed his gun from the counter and aimed at the pair of wrestling creatures. Neither stayed still long enough for him to get a clean shot. Eric tried to get a fix on Sebastien's head—it wouldn't kill him, but it would slow him down long enough for Mikalis to finally get his teeth into him. A moment, a glimpse of Sebastien's twisted face, and Eric fired. The round tore through his jaw, splattering the back wall with blood, and Sebastien's scream wailed like a siren. There was a blast of the rotten fruit stench, and then two enormous leathery appendages sprang from Sebastien's back. He burst from Mikalis's grip and blasted straight through the apartment window, taking half the wall with him, and then was gone, vanished into the night.

Mikalis stared through the gaping hole in the wall and frowned. "Hm."

Hm? Fucking hm? Eric clutched his bleeding arm but kept the gun raised on Mikalis. Breathing hard, his body buzzed, ablaze but not with pain—with fire and strength and vengeance. His aim stayed true on Mikalis.

The vampire straightened, took a small black device from his pocket, and flicked a switch. The apartment lights died and the streetlight outside blinked out.

What... Eric slumped against the kitchen counter. "He's getting away."

"You—" Mikalis pointed at Eric. "—are coming with me." He slipped the device back into his pocket and sauntered toward the apartment door.

Eric swallowed. He dabbed at his shoulder, but where the bullet wound should have been, there was only a hole in his blood-soaked shirt. The wound... had healed?

"Detective." Mikalis said. "Don't make me ask again."

He had to go. Instinct told him Mikalis didn't ask anyone to ride along with him wherever they were going. "Yeah." He pushed off the counter and veered toward Nate's motionless body, fearing the worst.

"He's fine. Strong heartbeat." Mikalis opened the apartment door and strode out.

"Eric!" His neighbor Caroline stood outside her apartment door wrapped in a dressing gown and pink slippers. Her little dog saw Mikalis and scurried behind her legs.

"A gas explosion, ma'am," Mikalis said, tossing the words at her as he breezed by. "Nothing to be worried about. The authorities are on their way. Stay in your apartment."

"Eric?" Caroline blinked wide eyes.

"Yeah... It's all right. Do as he says." He followed Mikalis down the dark stairwell and out the building's front door, then hurried to keep up with his long stride. A black Jaguar waited ahead. Its alarm blipped, disarming, and Mikalis climbed in behind the wheel. Eric dashed to catch up and dropped into the passenger seat.

"Put your seat belt on." Mikalis roared the engine and

the car lurched away from the curb, rattling Eric in his seat like a pea in a can.

He fumbled with it, yanking on it several times before the mechanism finally let him pull the belt free and clip it across his chest. His shoulder drew his eye again. It still tingled. Blood stained his clothes, but any wound had vanished.

"You healed," Mikalis said, a statement, not a question. He leaned forward and peered at the dark sky, then shifted down a gear and sped up.

"Yeah..." Eric poked at the hole in his shirt.

"Interesting."

Interesting? Eric had just healed a bullet wound in minutes. That wasn't possible. Had Sebastien infected him with something? Shit, was he turning? "Am I—"

"No."

"Oh."

Mikalis glanced over. "But you are interesting."

"You said that." Eric's thoughts had begun to catch up with events. Sebastien had been waiting for him inside his apartment. Nate had known it, had lured him into letting his guard down. But he wasn't the only one using Eric. "You've been watching me."

"I have."

"You knew he'd show up. You used me as bait."

The vampire didn't bother to reply, just drove the Jaguar through the almost empty streets, breaking all the speed limits and running all the lights as though this was his own personal racetrack.

"What was the device you used to kill the lights?"

"EMP. Fries any camera footage, phones, makes it easier to work without human interference."

"You can't just... do what Sebastien did?" Eric wasn't even sure what he'd seen Sebastien do. It had looked like he'd turned into *something* with wings. "Fly after him?"

"I could but not with you. And you and I need to have a discussion."

"We do?"

"Yes." Mikalis smiled and ice returned to Eric's veins. "We definitely do."

Glancing at the sky, Eric searched for the silhouette of whatever creature Sebastien was now. He assumed Mikalis was looking at the sky every now and then for the same reason. "Where are we going?"

Mikalis suddenly slammed on the car's brakes and skidded to a halt outside a building Eric knew—Citegroup HQ, Capaldi's office building. He climbed from the car, prompting Eric to do the same, but the vampire didn't enter the building. Peering up at the glass frontage, he saw something so far up that Eric didn't have a chance in hell of seeing it. With a sigh, Mikalis climbed back inside the car and Eric followed. He glanced at Eric, his gaze less full of fire now, just a glacial iciness.

Eric swallowed again. He could smell the blood on himself and so could Mikalis. Was that about to be a problem? He'd miraculously fought off Sebastien, but he had no idea if he could do the same if this vampire attacked.

Mikalis stared some more. The silence stretched on.

Then the master vampire sighed again and pulled the car away from the curb. "Call Zaine. Tell him to meet us at Atlas."

Eric plucked the phone from his pocket and hesitated, wondering if he should reveal he knew Zaine's number from memory.

"There isn't much time," Mikalis said.

Eric dialed the number.

CHAPTER 31

aine

ERIC WAS on his way to Atlas. With Mikalis.

This was... bad.

He paced the dark foyer, striding through slices of moonlight streaking in through the glass doors.

Eric knew too much.

That was the only reason why Mikalis would be bringing him in that Zaine could think of. To make Eric disappear. Maybe even to have Zaine end him—as punishment.

Eric had called sounding fine, though a bit drained, but that was to be expected when trapped in a car with Mikalis. Zaine had wanted to ask if Mikalis had hurt him, but he'd known the master vampire would be listening in, and he couldn't do a damn thing to stop him.

He'd never win in a straight fight with Mikalis, but he could damn well try.

Kazi sauntered into the foyer and leaned against the reception desk. He folded his arms and arched an eyebrow.

Zaine stopped pacing. "Why are you here?"

"Boss's orders."

"Yeah, but why?"

He shrugged. "In case your man gets frisky?"

"In case I do, you mean," Zaine growled.

"Relax. If Mikalis wanted Eric dead, he would be already."

True enough. But that didn't stop Zaine's heart from trying to pound its way between his ribs. He stared through the doors out into the forecourt watching for the sweep of headlights that would signal their arrival. He'd attack Mikalis first, go straight for the vein. Surprise was his best weapon.

"Where's Storm?" Zaine asked.

"In the Ops Room."

"Why?"

Kazi rolled his eyes. "Breathe, Zaine. It's all good."

No, it wasn't all good. Something was up, something bad. "When has Mikalis *ever* brought a feeder back to Atlas?"

"Maybe he wants a snack?"

Zaine's fangs throbbed. His lip twitched, a snarl trying to rumble through.

Kazi's dark eyes lit up with the promise of violence. "Maybe I do."

"Touch Eric and I'll unload a clip in all that pretty—" He gestured at Kazi's face.

Kazi's smile faded. "Asshole."

"Dick."

"At least I keep mine in my pants."

"You're so old, you don't even know what yours is for."

Kazi huffed a half laugh, half growl.

Headlights blinked outside and Mikalis's sleek black Jaguar cruised to a halt in front of the doors. He climbed out, and then the passenger door opened and Eric emerged.

Blood.

So much blood on Eric's arm.

Zaine's mind snapped. He was through the door and rushing Mikalis before his thoughts had a chance to catch up with his reaction. The other vampire's steel-like fingers locked around Zaine's throat and in a blink, his back slammed into the side of the car, Mikalis pinning him down.

Without even baring his teeth, Mikalis said, "Rein it in, Zaine."

He couldn't. Someone had hurt Eric. His Eric. He was bleeding, in pain. Had Mikalis done this?

"Zaine?" Eric appeared in the corner of Zaine's eye, hip cocked, hair a mess, and a half smile on his lips. "Hey." He ran a hand through that mass of ruffled locks, sweeping it back from his eyes. "I'm fine."

Mikalis glared through his lashes. "I'm going to let you up. If you so much as raise your voice, you're going in confinement to cool off. Do you understand?"

He nodded, afraid his voice would come out as a growl. He only barely managed to tuck his fangs away—the damn things had a mind of their own when his blood was up. Mikalis stepped back and Zaine stood straight on his feet. He turned his attention to Eric again, wanting to rush to him and gather him in his arms, carry him off, and lock him in a room where he could take care of him. Nobody else would touch him. Eric was Zaine's, now and forever.

"Zaine," Mikalis said in warning, probably hearing Zaine's heart pound.

"I'm fine," he grouched.

Mikalis's heavy gaze burned.

"I said I'm fine. Back the fuck off."

Eric took the initiative and closed the distance to Zaine. "Hey..." He lifted a hand and his warm touch settled on Zaine's cheek.

He almost moaned from the relief of it. He'd hated leaving him, hated the things he'd had to say, and then seeing him with Mikalis... He opened his mouth to say he was sorry but caught Eric's expression going from soft admiration to cool indifference.

How could he make all that shit he'd said go away? How could he make this right?

Eric's smirk was sharp. He arched an eyebrow and landed a solid punch to Zaine's gut. Air whooshed from his lungs and his fangs dropped, his body arming for a fight.

"I think you know what that's for," Eric said sharply.

Kazi's barked laugh rang across the Atlas grounds, Zaine spluttered and coughed in disbelief more than pain, and Eric humphed, his face regretful and disappointed. "All right." The detective turned to Mikalis. "Take me in."

As Zaine propped himself against the car, he watched Eric fearlessly stroll into the Atlas building flanked by two of the world's most efficient and lethal predators.

If he hadn't been sure before, he was now. He loved that man.

CHAPTER 32

ric

ERIC HAD ONLY SEEN a small fraction of Atlas when he'd fled with Zaine. Mikalis led the way, passing polished steel doors and toughened glass walls. He wasn't entirely sure why he was here, just that Mikalis didn't seem interested in killing him and might even be open to the idea of sharing information regarding Sebastien. In fact, he seemed almost *too* interested in Eric. He'd seen Eric somehow overpower Sebastien, and then there was the healed shoulder. Maybe Mikalis would have an explanation because Eric sure didn't.

Kazi veered off into a room ahead, and then the big guy, Storm, arrived, his mean face blank as though they'd never met. Eric rode the elevator down with the pair. They weren't like Sebastien. They radiated danger but not in a way that wormed under Eric's skin, more an instinctual sense to back away slowly.

They entered a room full of medical equipment similar to the room he'd previously stayed in.

"We're here because...?" Eric asked, silently wishing he hadn't punched Zaine so that he could be here beside him now. He didn't think Storm and Mikalis wanted to hurt him, but there wouldn't be much he could do about it if they did.

Zaine had had the punch coming, though. He should never have treated Eric like something he could scrape off his shoe and be done with.

Storm positioned himself by the bank of machines. Mikalis leaned against the back wall, casually murderous. "Run his blood," Mikalis said. "I witnessed this man defend himself against a ravenous nyktelios *and* heal a bullet wound in less than five minutes."

"Shit," Storm said, drawing the word out. He glowered at Eric as though he'd like to stuff him under a microscope and pick him apart. Then the big man busied himself gathering a tray of medical equipment, including a large needle.

Eric rolled up his sleeve, anticipating what was to come. "I don't know what you're going to find that you haven't already."

"Have you—" Storm cleared his throat. "—been intimate with Zaine in any way?"

Eric laughed. "What does that have to do with anything?"

"A great deal," the man grumbled. "Did you exchange blood during those encounters?"

"What the fuck? No."

The vampire in question chose that moment to breeze into the room. Storm tensed. Mikalis didn't react at all.

"You don't have to tell them anything," Zaine said. "You don't even have to be here if you don't want to be. You're free to go. I'll make sure of it."

"Incorrect," Mikalis said. "At least until we get to the bottom of Eric's newfound abilities."

"His what?"

Eric showed Zaine his bloodied shoulder. "Bullet wound."

"You were shot?" Zaine started for Mikalis. "You said he wouldn't get hurt!"

"In my long and varied existence, a feeder hasn't once fought off a ravenous nyktelios. Neither has one healed substantial tissue damage within minutes. So Mr. Sharpe does in fact have to be here so that Storm can run some tests. Sharpe cannot be released into the general population until we have ascertained what's going on in his blood work. The only danger he's in, Zaine, is from you."

Zaine froze. Everyone in the room waited for him to make his next move—for his sake, Eric hoped it wasn't to swing at Mikalis—then he grabbed a chair, spun it around, and sat on it reversed with his arms resting over its back, broadcasting how he wasn't going anywhere anytime soon. "You okay with this?" he asked Eric.

"Sure. It's nothing they haven't already done."

Storm frowned at Zaine. "Are you going to cause problems?"

"No. I'm just sitting in. But if you hurt him in any way, I'll rip your damn arms off."

Eric's stubborn alley cat.

Storm rolled his eyes. "All right then." He picked up a needle and syringe and took a sample of Eric's blood, then slotted it into a machine.

"Tell me once you have the results." Mikalis left the room, taking a layer of suffocating tension with him.

"Eric, please remove your shirt," Storm said, a little softer. "Let's take a look at that shoulder. Make sure it's clean. Preternatural healing comes with its own pitfalls if foreign bodies aren't removed."

Eric obeyed, curiously content in Storm's large capable hands. The vampire poked and prodded him, cleaning the area as he worked. Zaine glared during the entire examination. Eric wasn't even sure he'd blinked. His gaze skipped from Eric's naked chest to his face, and when Zaine's gaze caught Eric's, Eric spared a small smile. He could give him that, even if he was pissed at him. Zaine's face lit up at the sight of it. He was a difficult man to stay mad at.

"What happened?" Zaine asked. "How'd you get shot?"

"Sebastien was waiting at my apartment. So was Mikalis."

"That sonofabitch," Zaine growled. "He vowed to keep you safe."

"They fought. So there's that. But Sebastien got away."

Zaine's eyebrows lifted. Storm stilled too. "He got away from Mikalis?" Zaine asked.

"Yeah, grew wings, if you can believe it, and took off out the window. Literally."

Storm glanced at Zaine.

"Shit." Zaine exhaled. "Sebastien is *ancient*."

"Your intel is full of holes," Storm told Zaine.

"Yeah... A lot of things are full of holes."

"It seems likely Sebastien *does* know Mikalis," Storm said, his deep voice rumbling. His big fingers massaged Eric's shoulder under Zaine's unblinking glare. "Well, you're healed all right. I can't explain it, but we'll see what the blood tests reveal. You're free to roam for now. Zaine, find Eric some clean clothes. Make him comfortable."

Zaine stood, his face troubled. "I'll take you on the tour now we're not on the run."

Eric hopped off the examination table. "Sure."

"Don't go too far," Storm warned. "Mikalis will want you present for the results."

Zaine relaxed the moment he led Eric from the room, and now they were alone, Eric found it easier to breathe. Storm was no less intimidating than Mikalis, just for different reasons. "The compound is impressive. The Brotherhood run an actual business here? That must take some impressive logistical sleight of hand."

Zaine smirked. "Atlas Technologies. It functions as a legitimate company on the surface. Employs a few hundred staff."

"Who happen to have a secret society of vampires working out of their building's basement."

"They have no idea who or what we are." Zaine's smile softened. "Atlas, the brain behind the Brotherhood, is Mikalis's baby. The operating system is so intelligent its practically sentient."

"Mikalis slides right under the radar, doesn't he?" Eric said, thinking of how all this happened on the outskirts of NYC and nobody had noticed.

"He's been hiding in plain sight a very long time."

Zaine stopped outside a door, thumped the keypad, and stepped into a room functioning as a bedroom. A few pictures were taped to the wall—views of green rolling hills and dramatic coastlines. A spare shoulder holster had been slung over a nearby chair, obviously Zaine's. The room was compact but comfy and kind of had that Zaine, leather, and soap smell.

"Your place?"

"Sometimes. I have an apartment in the city to keep up appearances." He opened the closet and gestured for Eric to take a look. "Most of it should fit you. We're not far off the same size."

Eric examined the contents of the closet and then casually admired Zaine's athletic build. He had broader shoulders, more muscle. Eric knew exactly how those muscles felt trembling under his own hands, so there was no mistaking them. He cleared his throat and pushed those thoughts aside. "Thanks but these will hang off me."

"You can walk around shirtless if you prefer, but shit's gonna be weird enough without you arriving bare-chested in the Ops Room." Zaine grabbed a pale blue shirt and held it up to Eric. "C'mon, turn around."

With a laugh, he did. His back sizzled from Zaine's closeness, his skin suddenly alive and extra sensitive to the vampire's touch. Just a brush here and there, but as Eric slotted his arms into the sleeves, his blood raced. Zaine's exhale near his ear shivered through him. He couldn't deny he wanted Zaine, but the last time they'd screwed around, Zaine had dropped him like a rock right after. He couldn't stand that again.

Zaine stepped around to face him and began to button the shirt. His knuckles skimmed Eric's chin, probably deliberately. Eric held his blue-eyed gaze and Zaine's smile grew. "I'm sorry for everything I said outside that motel. The truth is I care about you—a great deal. A lot more than I should."

Eric placed his hands over Zaine's as he was doing up the buttons, pausing him. "Don't ever pull that shit with me again."

He swallowed. "It was wrong. I wasn't... I didn't use you. I meant everything, before I left. I want you, Eric, in all ways." His voice softened to a whisper. "But I can't have you, and it's killing me."

It was crazy that in all this insanity, all this turmoil, Eric should find someone who made the world make sense, made his heart beat for different reasons, made him want to live. Okay, so that someone happened to be a four-hundred-year-old nonhuman, but Eric's connection with Zaine was unlike anything he'd experienced before. It went deeper than a passing attraction, as though some part of Zaine was stitched into his bones.

An array of emotions passed over Zaine's troubled face, and Eric knew none of the Brotherhood ever saw Zaine like this. They didn't know the real Zaine because the real man didn't have a place among them. The Brotherhood didn't care. If they cared, that made them vulnerable. Were they all so emotionally restrained?

Eric ran his fingertips over Zaine's nervous smile.

"Careful." Zaine's lips twitched. "I bite."

"You know, it's not a deal breaker."

Zaine chuckled. His hand came up to cup Eric's jaw. "We can't do this."

"We could." Eric leaned into his touch. As Eric saw it, life was fragile. He'd known it since he'd stood in his family's yard and watched his whole world turn to ash. Tomorrow he might die. Hell, he might die tonight. Maybe he and Zaine didn't have a future, but they definitely wouldn't have one if they didn't even try. He threaded the fingers of his free hand with Zaine's. "You've lived for so long, you've forgotten what it means to live in the moment."

Zaine's hand on Eric's chin skimmed around the back of his neck, the touch like a match to a fuse, setting his veins ablaze. His heat enveloped Eric's body, raising the fine hairs on his arms. "You're amazing. I've wanted to tell you since we met." Zaine drew him close, their lips brushing, breaths shared.

Nothing felt as right as this, as him.

Two knocks rapped on the door. "Hey, Z?" Kazi called from outside.

Zaine growled and Eric almost kissed the sound from his lips, but if he did that, he'd have to shove the vampire up against the wall and devour him whole, and they had company.

"Results are in. Mikalis wants you both in the Ops Room... Zaine?"

"Yeah. We'll be right down."

Eric wasn't getting a kiss then. That was probably just as well—

Zaine hauled him off his feet and into a furious, passionate kiss, the kind that set his soul on fire. He burned up right there, thrusting his tongue in, battling with Zaine's, narrowly avoiding his sharp fangs. His back hit the wall, and then Zaine got both hands under his ass, propping him up. Eric locked his legs around Zaine's waist, planning to never let him go.

The kiss broke apart and Eric chuckled, his gaze lost in Zaine's. The vampire grinned, close to laughing. "You ever been fucked off your feet, Detective?"

Eric snorted a laugh. He had definitely not been fucked off his feet, but Zaine had the strength to do it. "Is that a promise?"

"Oh yeah."

"So romantic."

"I'll buy you a thousand roses." He nudged Eric's mouth, teasing an almost-kiss. "Make love to you in a bed of them." Warm lips tickled Eric's mouth. "Worship every inch of you."

The sincere look on his face said he meant it too. "You're crazy," Eric said, laughing.

"Undoubtably."

Eric's heart ached the moment he caught the intensity in Zaine's eyes. He meant every word, and he was afraid too. A different fear to Eric's. He knew how this story ended. Eric died, tonight, tomorrow, next year, fifty years from now. Whenever it happened, it *had* to happen. "Hey... Maybe we can change our ending?"

Zaine's lashes fluttered closed and his barriers came down. "I'd better put you down before Mikalis appears in here." He carefully lowered Eric to his feet and backed off. He kept his smirk, though. Eric loved that smirk.

Brushing down his borrowed shirt, he fixed the last few

buttons, leaving it untucked. Zaine's soft smile would carry him through whatever happened next.

"You ready to meet the rest of the Blackrose Brotherhood assholes?" Zaine asked, hand on the doorknob.

"Let's do it."

CHAPTER 33

aine

ERIC'S STEPS slowed the second he entered the Ops Rom behind Zaine. It was a lot to take in—Atlas holoscreens and the smart table with its circle of leather chairs and the black rose motif at its center were like something out of a sci-fi thriller movie. The finances behind the Brotherhood operation had to be enormous.

"Eric," Mikalis said in greeting as he stood at the head of the table, face stoic and unreadable. Standing next to him, Storm loomed, his expression just as impossible to decipher.

Octavius was there sitting on the opposite side of the table wearing all white, which matched his mop of white hair. Kazi was sprawled in a chair at the other end of the table leaning on an elbow. Raiden wasn't there and neither was Thebeus. They were probably out on a job. Aiko sat cross-legged on the table next to Kazi. He saluted Zaine by tapping two fingers to his forehead and dropping his chin.

"Hey, Aiko, how were our European counterparts?" Zaine asked. It had been six months since he'd last seen Aiko as he'd gotten on a private plane bound for Europe.

"Busy. Nyk numbers are growing and it's not obvious why."

"Aiko will return to Prague at the end of the month," Mikalis explained, then gestured for Zaine and Eric to take a seat. "Storm, present your findings for the others."

Storm flicked his wrist and Eric's blood work results appeared in the form of graphs on the screens projected from the middle of the table.

"Eric Sharpe is an unremarkable human being," Storm said. "No offense."

Was it too soon to flip a desk? Zaine simmered in his seat. Eric didn't appear to react at all, just quietly observed the results.

"His red blood cell count is low, but that's to be expected from the trauma of the past few weeks. However, there are trace elements of nyktelios venom secreted during feeding to subdue their victims." Storm tapped the holo display and the screen zoomed in on an array of listed elements. Zaine checked them off inside his mind, his concern growing with every listed item. The silence in the room said the others had seen the significance of the list too.

"What is it?" Eric asked. "What are you all seeing?"

Storm folded his wide arms and asked Eric, "You're sure you didn't share blood during intercourse?"

"Fuck," Zaine snarled. "You really just asked that? What the hell is wrong with you?"

"It's a reasonable question," Mikalis said. "Considering the results."

After every damn thing, they still thought he was capable of turning Eric. "Your confidence in me is *inspiring*," he hissed. "Despite what you think, I do have some self-control. And no, we have not shared blood while we've fucked."

Eric's hand settled on Zaine's thigh under the table out of sight of the others. "Why is that important?" he asked, much calmer than Zaine.

"Reasonable question, my ass," Zaine muttered.

"That ass getting some action, Z?" Kazi drawled.

"Kazimir," Mikalis snapped. "Bait Zaine into reacting again and you'll be the one behind glass. Understand?"

Kazi swallowed and shrank back in his chair. "Got it."

Zaine showed him his middle finger.

Mikalis's heavy sigh said a lot more than words could. "All right, I can see my time is limited before someone here says or does something that will test my patience, and as we have a rogue nyktelios to catch, I'm not in the mood for drama. Zaine, you're not the first of the Brotherhood to have sex with a feeder, but Eric is the first to experience biological changes due to the act."

"Wait... What?" Eric leaned forward.

"Huh?" Zaine frowned. "Wait a second. You don't know he's changing because of... us." This was absurd. But also, someone in the Brotherhood had had sex with a feeder in the past? Not important, perhaps, but Zaine had damn well known they weren't all perfect.

"The facts are this: Eric has a measure of nyktelios abilities but without the need for fresh oxygenated blood to sustain those abilities. His blood work contains elements of our DNA but remains human. It's as though he's undergone a small change similar to that of the turning but nothing near those catastrophic physical alterations."

"That's impossible," Aiko said.

"I saw him repel an ancient nyktelios and heal a gunshot wound. Which brings us to the nyktelios, Sebastien. I have to ask you, Eric. Did Sebastien attempt to turn you?"

"By turning you mean sharing blood, right?" Eric asked to clarify.

"That's a part of the process, yes."

"No. Never."

"But you have a *close* relationship with Sebastien?"

"I... It's complicated."

Zaine pinched the bridge of his nose. Eric was faring better under questioning than he was.

"Why is there a nyktelios feeder in our Ops Room?" Octavius asked, his lofty tone high and mighty.

"Because Eric Sharpe has always been able to resist Sebastien, isn't that right? You did, in fact, almost kill him once?" Mikalis suggested.

"Yeah..."

Zaine laid his hand over Eric's.

"I did. I mean, I thought I'd killed him years ago, but I didn't have all the facts, so I couldn't know stabbing him in the heart wouldn't work."

"You've always been able to resist nyktelios venom, and

I want to know why that is. Storm will run more tests, Eric, which requires you to stay with us a while. Are you open to that?"

"Are we all pretending I have a choice?" he asked, eyeing the others, who stayed quiet. "Okay then. It's a good thing I want the answers as much as you do. But I also want Sebastien ended, and I'm not going to be shoved aside. So where is he and let's get it done. That is what you're all specialized to do, right? Kill nyktelios. So can we get on with that?"

Octavius stiffened. "Zaine, how much did you tell the feeder?"

"The *feeder* has a fucking name."

"Quiet!" Mikalis swiped Storm's documents off the screen and brought up Sebastien's file. "Sebien is not what or who he appears to be. He has clearly eluded the Brotherhood for some time. Zaine's preliminary intel barely scraped the surface. Sebien—Sebastien—is at least a thousand years old. The only way he has been able to slip by me for so long is with internal knowledge of our methods. He either had access to someone in the Brotherhood or still does. And that someone has aided his survival until now."

Eric's hand tightened on Zaine's leg. Sebastien's informer was unlikely to be anyone around this table. Mikalis's Brotherhood was tight. But Sebastien definitely had someone looking out for him.

"Nobody here need worry," Mikalis said. "I have absolute faith in you all. I'll make some enquires with other Brotherhood cells—"

"Can I ask *you* something?" Eric said, his cool gaze fixed on Mikalis.

"Go ahead."

"You mention Sebastien isn't who he appears to be. He said almost those exact words about you. Do you know him personally? Because all of this is personal to Sebastien, from kidnapping and torturing Zaine to his being here in New York. It's all for you. I was just a happy bonus. He wants you to notice him, Mikalis. Why is that?"

All eyes turned to Mikalis. "I don't know."

"What do you think he meant when he said that about you?"

"I genuinely do not know." Mikalis held Eric's gaze and Zaine felt his heart begin to flutter as the two of them locked horns. Eric was a damn good detective. He knew when something felt off, and Mikalis, right then, was definitely off. Zaine saw it too. The stillness in him, the way his expression rested in neutral. He was doing a damn good impression of someone who had nothing to hide—while hiding a lot.

"Moving on," Mikalis said. "Sebastien has been running his operation from the Citegroup building in Midtown. And that's where he's fled."

"Citegroup?" Eric leaned forward. "I picked up a case there. Body left in Times Square drained of blood. So that murder was Sebastien, right?"

"Yeah." Zaine could answer that one. "Capaldi was a feeder. He had some kind of altercation with Sebastien. Sebastien killed him and left him for the cops to find. Sloppy. I figured I'd rattle Sebastien's cage by turning up the heat on him. If he thought he was being fucked with, he'd focus on me, make mistakes. I hadn't planned on you getting involved."

"Wait, *you* left the body on the bench?" Eric frowned.

"Yeah. I didn't kill him, though. Just *moved* him."

Eric's frown cut deeper. "Did you have my case closed?"

"I did that," Mikalis said, and again Eric and Mikalis locked glares.

"You can do that? Just click your fingers and close a homicide case?"

"I can do a whole lot more, Detective. Now, if it's all right with you, I'd like to explain how we're going to bring down your tormentor. May I continue?"

"You think you're above the law?"

Mikalis pressed both hands to the table and leaned in. "Detective Sharpe, I was protecting humanity before modern civilization built the laws you sometimes have trouble upholding. Your laws are of no consequence to me."

"Yeah, I'm getting that."

Holy shit, Eric was either fearless or insanely stupid, staring down Mikalis like that. He probably wasn't aware of how he was tugging on a tiger's tail, but watching him make Mikalis squirm was hot. The faces of the others here confirmed it. Storm frowned, unhappy his bromantic partner was being put on the spot. Octavius looked as though he might burst a blood vessel in the next five seconds. Kazi glowered, and Aiko had his head tilted, fiercely studying Eric just out of his sight line.

"We'll find Sebastien inside this building," Mikalis continued, pointing out the 3D image of the Citegroup building. "There's construction work on floors one hundred twelve through fourteen. He'll be holed up there where he won't be disturbed. Thanks to Eric, he's weakened, and thanks to Zaine, he's envenomed. There will be no better time to finish him."

"He has multiple feeders," Eric said. "There may be victims in there."

"Unfortunate but not a concern."

"They're my concern," Eric said. "You've got all this equipment. And y'all can do five times what a human can do—"

"Fifteen times," Kazi said.

"I'd say more like twenty," Aiko added.

"Yeah, but his benchmark is Zaine, so..."

"Right," Aiko drawled. The pair grinned at Zaine.

"You see what I have to deal with?" Zaine told Eric with a smile. "Assholes. All of them."

Mikalis swiped the hovering images away. "If we wait any longer, the nyktelios will replenish himself. We go in tonight. And we go in hard. Octavius, I want you leading the op from nearby. Knock out the power when we arrive at the Citegroup building."

"Consider it done."

"Aiko and Kazi, you're with me. Storm, you're with Zaine."

"And Eric?" Zaine asked.

The room fell silent.

"He's with you," Mikalis finally said. "His life will be in your hands."

"My life is in my own hands," Eric said, "but thanks for the concern."

Mikalis glowered, then surprised everyone by cracking a smile. "Let's go."

Zaine hung back with Eric while the others filed from the room. “We should join them,” Zaine said, getting to his feet.

Eric nodded but didn’t rise. “If we discover people in there with Sebastien, I’m not leaving them.”

“I know what you’re trying to do, but those people... They won’t be like you. You heard what Storm said. You’ve always had a resistance to Sebastien. Others don’t. At best, they’ll be obstacles. At worst, they’ll try and kill you.”

Eric looked up and that fierceness Zaine so admired burned hotter than ever in his gaze. “He doesn’t get to destroy more lives.”

“All right. I’m with you. We’ll try and get them out. That’s the best I can promise.”

Satisfied, Eric stood, hesitating only when Zaine pinned him with his stare. “What?”

“You ever worn a double shoulder holster?”

CHAPTER 34

ric

THE MEETING HAD GONE AS WELL as expected. The Brotherhood were intimidating for a lot of reasons. Their technology gave them the ability to move through New York like ghosts. But when it came to the Brotherhood's individual operatives, each one was lethal. Eric didn't need to be a detective to see that. They'd had centuries to hone their skills and they'd come from very different worlds than Eric's. They'd adapted, but they were the same inside too. Vicious, deadly, cold. They didn't give a shit about the innocent people caught in the war.

Sebastien had said the same. Even Zaine had explained how they weren't the good guys. But they could be. With their skills, their expertise, they *could* save people. Someone just had to make them see how to change their ways, use their powers for good.

They returned to Zaine's room, where he handed over the shoulder holster and helped adjust it to Eric's body. "Wait here, I'll be right back." He left, and Eric drifted about the small quarters. Zaine lived sparsely. No family photos, just the scenery shots from his homeland. The Brotherhood life was a long, lonely one. Eric almost pitied them.

The door opened again and a blur of all white slammed into Eric, pinning him to the wall. Fingers closed around his neck, choking him. Blue eyes, snow-white hair.

"Watch your back, *feeder*," Octavius sneered, baring his fangs. "Accidents happen on ops. Feeders die. We wouldn't want you to be a victim."

Eric wheezed, fighting to fill his lungs, his chest jerking. His heart and head pounded as darkness rushed in, and then Octavius vanished, dropping Eric to his knees. He gasped for air, grabbed the nearby bed, and hauled himself onto its edge. *Breathe, just breathe*. He rubbed at his neck, his heart slowing and breaths settling.

Jesus... He hadn't even seen Octavius attack. He'd appeared and vanished again in seconds.

If he'd thought the members of the Brotherhood were in any way friendly, he'd just had that thought shattered.

He couldn't tell Zaine.

Zaine would lose his shit. He'd lash out at Octavius and get himself locked away when they needed him to bring down Sebastien. *Eric* needed him.

Octavius's threat was just posturing—just a warning. He could have snapped Eric's neck like a twig if he'd wanted to.

They didn't want a feeder among them. His point had been made.

Eric swallowed and sighed. "Stay away from Octavius."

THEY DROVE through Midtown in a conspicuous line of blacked-out vans. Their approach was obvious, but this was New York. Short of a bomb being detonated, nobody paid too much attention unless it impacted their daily commute.

It was late, or early—Eric wasn't sure which. He should have been tired, but his veins buzzed and his heart pumped. Finally they were closing in on Sebastien, and whatever went down, by dawn it would be over. Mikalis and the Brotherhood would make sure of that.

What came after that was something Eric hadn't yet figured out. Would the Brotherhood drop him like Zaine had? Just walk away? *Kill the nyk, move on*. That was their routine. But how was Eric supposed to go back to his life knowing everything he did? And what of the weird cocktail of changes happening in his blood?

He didn't think Mikalis would allow him to walk away, not anymore. Too much had changed.

"You okay?" Zaine asked. He drove, while Storm was in the back tapping away on his phone and putting his earpiece in.

"Yeah."

"He'll be ashes and gone soon."

"Yeah," Eric repeated.

Zaine's glance caught Storm in the rearview mirror. Eric didn't see what the big guy's reflection had to say.

"It's a lot... The Brotherhood, Mikalis, *this*," Zaine continued. "When we're done with Sebastien, you and me? We'll talk. About everything."

"Sure."

The Citegroup building shimmered ahead, a monolith of glass and steel stretching into the ink-dark sky, its top floor crowned by blinking lights.

The streetlights ahead plunged into darkness. Octavius's voice filtered through the earpieces they all wore. "Cameras are down. You have fourteen minutes to execute."

Zaine pulled their van to a halt outside the building. The Brotherhood teams spilled out as Eric climbed from the van. Nobody said a word. Mikalis's team vanished the second their feet hit the sidewalk, moving too fast for Eric to track, as though they were all ghosts disappearing in the shadows.

Storm and Zaine flanked Eric at the foot of the steps to the building's front entrance. Eric checked the pair of Glocks Zaine had loaned him. He had tried to offer Desert Eagles, and Eric had laughed. He wanted accuracy, not hand cannons. Of course, Zaine had taken the Eagles and looked scorching hot wearing them.

Storm gave the entrance door a robust shove, popping it open, and strode inside the foyer, which was lit only by emergency exit lights.

"Going up," Storm said, forcing open the elevator doors and entering the waiting car.

Eric entered, followed by Zaine. "It's working?"

Zaine tapped his earpiece. "Octavius, east elevator."

A moment later, the elevator lights flickered on, the car's doors closed, and the elevator jolted into motion.

"Bats would be so much quicker," Eric said, tapping his fingers against his thigh while watching the numbers count up.

"Bats?" Storm asked.

"I told Eric I turned into a bat to escape his apartment." Zaine smirked.

Storm waited a beat and said, "You *can't* turn into a bat?"

"No. What? Wait..." Zaine snorted. "You're fucking with me."

Storm shrugged a massive shoulder.

Zaine chuckled. "You can't turn into a bat, and even if you could, they'd be big-ass muscular bats too buff to fly, so don't even go there."

Storm's laugh was a deep rumble of thunder. Eric found himself warming to the big vampire. Storm slid his gaze sideways to Eric, sensing his attention. "Look out for yourself, all right? We didn't bring you here to babysit you."

"I get it."

He seemed to want to say more but swallowed whatever it was and glanced at Zaine, still chuckling to himself and watching the numbers climb. Something in the big vampire's gaze hinted at emotion. Storm was concerned, not so much for Eric but for Zaine. Interesting for a creature who wasn't supposed to *care*. He was worried about Zaine, about what would happen to him if Sebastien got to Eric. Eric was worried about that too.

Zaine had been locked up before when he'd lost

someone he loved, had almost turned back into the monster they hunted. The Brotherhood were bad, and Zaine bitched about them, but he was proud to be among them—even Eric could see that much. Storm had saved Zaine and the big vampire still watched over him.

The members of the Brotherhood weren't so complicated. And despite their own rules, they did care. It was just that none of them wanted to admit it.

The elevator numbers slowed. Zaine removed his guns, fingers resting on the barrels a twitch away from the triggers. Eric removed his own gun, happier with wielding just the one.

Zaine caught Eric's glance and grinned. "All right, let's get this bloodsucker."

The elevator doors opened.

CHAPTER 35

aine

ERIC WAS MORE than capable of saving his own ass, but that wasn't going to stop Zaine from keeping a close eye on him. Eric could heal, even had enough strength to fight off a dying Sebastien, but he could also die, and there was no way in hell Zaine was watching that happen a second time. Not on Zaine's watch.

The floor they'd exited the elevator on had been stripped, leaving bare plasterboard, metal trusses, and trailing wires not yet hooked up to the main electrical system. Dim emergency lighting cast a green hue down empty corridors, but multiple shadows crowded every corner. Shadows Eric wouldn't be able to see through.

Instinct urged Zaine to shove Eric back in that elevator car and get him as far away as possible. The detective would hate him for it, but he'd be alive.

A glance behind him revealed the man following close and Storm behind him, instinctively watching Eric's back.

They crept deeper into the mazelike layout. A breeze drifted between the flimsy walls, carrying the rich, coppery scent of old blood. Zaine's fangs ached and his venom glands behind the roof of his mouth felt heavy, ready to end Sebastien forever.

A body lay up ahead, sprawled in a doorway. Zaine didn't need to examine the woman to know she'd been drained and discarded. The gaping wound in her neck and lack of spilled blood made the cause of death very clear. Sebastien had been here.

Eric went down on his knee and checked her pulse. He couldn't know her heart had long ago ceased to beat. Zaine steeled his own heart and tried not to link Eric's fragile existence with that of the dead woman's. Sebastien didn't want Eric dead but he likely hadn't wanted that feeder dead ether. Killing a feeder was unproductive—it was also a sign of a nyktelios losing his shit. Sebastien was more dangerous now than he'd ever been. Like Zaine in the conservatory, if Sebastien got his hands on Eric while ravenous, he'd kill him.

The second body, a young man no older than nineteen, lay dead against a wall, propped there like a doll. Zaine recognized him as one of the boys from the club. Eric didn't bother to check him. There was no surviving the savage mess where his neck used to be.

Sebastien had torn through his nest of feeders. He might even have slaughtered them all. If he had, he could almost be back to full strength.

"Ten minutes," Octavius said though the earpiece.

Zaine stepped over another body and counted five more up ahead. Gritting his teeth, he glanced behind him and saw determination in Eric's eyes. With every new body they came across, Eric's sense of justice would boil ever hotter. The detective was lethal with a gun, generally calm, and definitely strong, but this was personal. Runaway emotions would get him killed.

A phone rang.

"Shit." Eric fumbled in his pocket, casting Zaine a sheepish expression for not having turned it off. He plucked the phone free. His brow pinched, and he raised it to his ear. "Yeah?" His eyes flicked to Zaine. "Yes, Sebastien. I hear you."

Zaine glanced at Storm. The big guy nodded and veered off down another corridor, searching the rest of the floor for Sebastien.

"I understand," Eric said into the phone. "All right." He lowered the phone. "He says if I go to him alone, he'll let you all live."

Zaine snorted. "Right. Nobody is falling for that shit." Except maybe Eric, who already looked defeated. "You know he's lying. He'll take you and go to ground. He'll make you disappear. That's not happening." He closed the distance between them and held out his hand for the phone. Eric sighed, handing it over. "Hey, Sebastien, remember me? That agony currently eating you up from the inside out, that's my venom—"

"Brotherhood puppet," Sebastien growled.

"Listen. Eric isn't yours. He made that clear years ago when he stabbed you in the heart. We're not handing him over. And you're not getting out of this building in anything other than a paper bag. The Brotherhood are here. And we're coming for you."

"Mikalis" he hissed, sounding as unhinged as any blood-starved nyktelios.

"You'd better believe it."

"Hm," the ancient vampire crooned, voice suddenly clear. "Good." The line went dead.

Zaine handed the phone back and saw Eric's worried gaze had fallen to a body they'd passed. "Hey... These people were already dead the second he bit them. He's just dragged it out for months, years maybe. There's nothing you or I could have done."

"Yeah."

Zaine was done with the *yeahs*. Eric was badass, brave, and strong, but he was also clinging to the threads holding him together.

Zaine holstered his guns, scooped Eric close, and breathed him in. The rigid tension melted from Eric's body, molding perfectly to Zaine's. "We've got this," Zaine whispered against his cheek. "Forget the others, forget the past. There's just you and me. We can do this." A whole lot of emotional pain crossed Eric's face, including guilt. "Together."

"I could have killed them," Eric whispered. "I did... before."

Zaine was going to kill that bloodsucking piece of shit, and he was damn well going to make sure Sebastien knew Eric had survived him. He sank a hand into Eric's hair and pulled the man closer still, cradling him. Eric buried his face against Zaine's neck. "After this, I'm taking you away...

A tropical island, I don't know. Nordic fucking cruise. Whatever. But there will be an after, all right?"

"A bed of roses?" Eric smiled, leaning back. Some of his bright spark returned to his eyes.

"Yes, definitely that."

A clang rang out somewhere on the floor and Eric eased from Zaine's arms. He nodded, his no-bullshit detective persona slipping back into place. Zaine nodded back and turned in the direction of the noise. Where the hell had Storm gotten to? He tapped his earpiece. "Storm? Check in."

Silence.

"Storm?"

Nothing.

"Octavius, locate Storm." Silence.

"Shit," Zaine hissed through his teeth. "Octavius, respond?"

Either the comms had glitched or Octavius had been compromised. Until comms returned, they were now all isolated. "All right." Zaine freed his guns again. "Let's do this the old-fashioned way. Search and destroy. Eric, you've got my back."

"Always."

Zaine threw his man a smile that meant more than he could know, and when Eric's tentative smile came back, his heart raced faster. He'd meant every word about taking him away somewhere. Zaine had chosen his path. If it came down to the Brotherhood or Eric, the answer was easy. It would always be Eric, Mikalis's consequences be damned.

CHAPTER 36

ric

He knew on the outside he appeared to have himself under control. He'd perfected that act years ago. Inside, however, fear and self-loathing had his heart tripping over itself and his thoughts spilling like sand through his efforts to try and stay calm. He'd thought he could do this, but the bodies... the feeders... They'd been nothing more than batteries to Sebastien, consumed and tossed away. Human beings with lives and families, loved ones. Just like Eric had once had. Just like the victims Sebastien had brought to Eric during those years he'd tried to forget. How Sebastien had delighted in making Eric watch as Sebastien had fed from them and fucked them, how they'd spent their last breaths begging for more and how Eric had wanted to watch, to be there, to know he was the special one—the one Sebastien always came back to.

He'd buried it all so deeply it could never hurt him again. But not deep enough.

If the Brotherhood learned what he'd done—how he'd killed and liked it—they'd probably kill him. Octavius would make good on his threat. Zaine would do something heroic and stupid to protect Eric, but Eric didn't deserve his love.

Was Eric any better than Sebastien?

He'd been poisoned—brainwashed, seduced, and manipulated—or so he'd thought. But Mikalis was right. Eric had some resistance to Sebastien, so maybe he'd had a choice in some of it all along.

He followed Zaine down the corridor through sheets of plastic hanging from doorways and along the trail of blood leading them like an arrow toward Sebastien.

Voices filtered through the air. Zaine glanced behind him and nodded at Eric, asking if he was all right. Eric nodded back, ignoring the internal whispers telling him to hold the Glock to his head and end it now, before the inevitable happened and Sebastien got his claws into Eric all over again. Insane thoughts. Wrong thoughts. But he couldn't chase them out of his head. Was he losing his mind?

The voices outside his head grew louder. One was definitely Mikalis, his accent distinct and smooth. The other was Sebastien's throaty animal-like growl.

"Hey," Zaine whispered. His hand settled warmly on Eric's shoulder. "You all right?"

"Yeah, I... just..."

Zaine drew Eric to one side behind a freshly painted

plasterboard wall and knelt with him, then peered into his eyes. "*Are* you all right?"

"I'm good." Eric brushed Zaine's hand off. "I just... Let's get this done, okay?"

"Listen, Sebastien is old. He can get inside your head, literally. Are you thinking clearly? Can you hear him? Hear voices?"

Eric puffed out and dropped his head back. "Yeah."

Zaine frowned. "That's what I thought... Whatever you're thinking, whatever he's telling you, it's not you."

Eric almost laughed. The voices telling him to kill himself sure sounded like his own thoughts.

Zaine hesitated then added, "I can hear Mikalis up ahead. Stay here. I'll be right back."

Alone, Eric sighed, frowned at the gun in his hand, and holstered it just in case. He shouldn't be here. He was a liability. He should remove the gun, flick off the safety, and when Zaine came back, put a bullet in his—

Eric clutched his head. *"Fuck!" You sonofabitch, get out of my head!*

Sebastien's deep, rolling laughter spilled through Eric's mind, sucking out his will. Despair rolled over him. The only solution was Sebastien—he had to get to him, to finish him, and the torment would stop.

A feverish hand smothered Eric's mouth, jerking his head back. He snapped his eyes open and stared straight at Vergil's face. The dead man grinned and peeled his lips back over two pairs of fangs. "Shhh." Vergil chuckled. "You're his now."

CHAPTER 37

aine

FROM HIS HUNCHED position in the shadows behind two large barrels of paint, Zaine watched Mikalis casually chat with the gargoyle-like creature Sebastien had become. He had tucked his brown leathery wings against his hunched back, and his face was a contorted echo of something human but full of teeth and blazing eyes. Black claws tipped long, gnarled fingers. Weak and broken, he'd shrugged off his human camouflage.

Mikalis stood several feet back, arms crossed, face mildly disapproving. "You disappoint me, Sebien."

Sebastien growled, flicking sharp fingers, and began to prowl around Mikalis. "You are unrecognizable. Where is the creature she made, where is the fire, where is the chaos?"

Mikalis tilted his head but let Sebastien circle him.

"Times change, as you well know. It's over. Surrender with honor or die in shame."

Sebastien's laugh rustled like paper. "*Memento mori*, Mikalis. Your day in the sun must be soon, no?"

"All this for what? To speak with me? So speak."

"If you do not know, then everything is as it should be," Sebastien said, gloating. His hideous form convulsed around deep laughter. "I know, Mikalis... I know the secrets you keep. Do *they* know?" Sebastien had circled all the way around and came to a halt standing in front of Mikalis. They were matched in height, although the nyktelios appeared much larger in his original form with his wings arching high. "Your precious Brotherhood. Do they know they march to the tune of your lies?"

Mikalis didn't answer, didn't move, didn't even breathe. He stood with his back to Zaine, so there was no way to read his face, but Zaine sensed his rage like an electric charge in the air.

"No?" Sebastien snickered. "What will happen when they discover you are not Nyx's precious messenger? When they discover you're not like them at all?" Sebastien leaned closer. So did Zaine. "When they learn... you're not nyktelios."

Mikalis's hand lashed out like the crack of a whip. He caught Sebastien by the neck. His wings snapping open, he punched Mikalis in the chest with the force of a wrecking ball, blasting him backward through three layers of plasterboard wall. Dust filled the air, rolling like smoke. And then Mikalis, lying on his side, peered through the haze, his gaze finding and fixing on Zaine. Mikalis's nod was almost imperceptible. *Almost.*

Zaine fired both guns in quick staccato bursts, emptying the clips into Sebastien and driving the vampire back with every round that pierced his chest. He fired until the triggers clicked empty. Sebastien bared his fangs and hissed, then thrust his wings downward and blasted through the ceiling to the floor above. Zaine bolted after him, leaping into the hole in the ceiling and climbing through, but the settling dust and darkness obscured Sebastien's escape. He would he here. Somewhere.

Zaine sniffed the air. Blood.

Safety signs declared No Entry. Barriers blocked routes into rooms where the windows had been boarded up. The wind howled through gaps in the construction, washing away Sebastien's scent.

Mikalis blurred into solid form beside Zaine. "He's surprisingly strong."

Zaine almost rolled his eyes. "You think?"

Mikalis gestured toward the junction coming up ahead. "You take the east side."

"Do you have comms contact with the others?"

"No, but—" He tapped his forehead. "Storm is a floor below dealing with a nest of zealous feeders. Octavius is offline. I've sent Aiko to him."

Unsurprisingly, Mikalis had almost everything under control. "The power will reboot in a few minutes," Zaine said.

"Then it's time we ended this. Go."

Zaine veered right. Out of ammo, he was at a disadvantage, but Sebastien had a few more holes in his chest to heal. A sign ahead warned of an exposed drop. A strong breeze flowed from that direction—likely an unfinished window. Sebastien might take to the air again but not without Eric. A twinge of guilt had Zaine's steps faltering. Eric should be here, right behind him, but if Sebastien was in his head, that made him too unpredictable. Zaine would circle back to him soon. He wouldn't sideline him for long. He needed him close for the final blow.

Almost as though his thoughts had dreamed him up, Eric's scent flowed over Zaine, carried on the wind. His heart spiked. He dashed past the warning sign into a room where a window gaped, unboarded and open to the elements. In front of the yawning hole, a near-rabid nyk had Eric clutched to his chest, fangs close to his throat, a hand over his mouth, and his other arm around Eric's waist.

"Whoa." Zaine raised his hands, showing the nyk they were empty. "Hey, easy there."

Eric's eyes fixed on Zaine, but not in fear. In rage.

The detective dropped his hand to cover the nyk's grip on his waist. Whether it was the rage that gave Eric strength or whatever changes were happening inside of him, he somehow jerked the nyk's arm back at an impossible angle to the brittle sound of bones snapping. The nyk howled and his fangs flashed, about to come down on the detective's neck.

Eric twisted and shoved.

The nyk teetered, his arms spread and hands grasping for anything to stop his free fall backward. Eric wasn't done. He backed up and kicked out, striking the nyk in the chest. The nyk reeled, his legs hitting the low windowsill, and he toppled backward, falling through the window.

Eric braced against the window frame as Zaine grasped the opposite side and peered down the outside of the high-rise. Wind swirled. The nyk plummeted as he clawed at the air, shrinking by the second.

His body struck the sidewalk with a satisfyingly dull thud.

"Is he coming back from that?" Eric asked.

"I doubt it, but we'll have Octavius check as soon as he's back online."

Eric's lips twitched into a half smile. "Good." The wind teased his hair and a touch of color flushed his cheeks. "That's for Grahams, you son of a bitch."

A dart of heated lust and pride and all the electric sensations Eric sparked alive in Zaine flashed through him. "Murder looks good on you."

"That's the second time I've killed him. It had better stick." He smirked. That smirk was Zaine's weakness. He could lose himself in admiring it. Admiring *Eric*.

His soft laugh ratcheted Zaine's need up another notch.

"You gotta stop looking at me like that," Eric said, laughing.

"Oh yeah? Says who?"

"We're in the—"

If Eric finished the sentence, Zaine didn't hear it through his sudden shift in weight and the brutal jerk on his arm. He felt himself fall, saw the long drop down the side of the building yawn wide in front of him again, only this time he was the one falling through it—

An abrupt snap pulled him to a halt midair. Claws dug into his shoulders, holding him aloft.

Fuck.

He didn't have wings.

Fuck!

He dangled.

Sebastien's laugh echoed above him and his claws dug deeper into Zaine's shoulders.

From the window several yards away, Eric had his Glock aimed at Sebastien. "Don't!"

"Shoot and your Brotherhood lover dies," Sebastien said in warning.

Don't look down, don't look down.

Zaine saw the agony of loss in Eric's eyes. He wouldn't survive the grief again.

Eric pointed the gun at his own head. "You want me, Sebastien?"

Sebastien's claws dug in even more. "You will not do it."

"No?" the detective sneered. "You really did a number on me. Fucked me up for years. I never recovered, not really. Never will, probably. I don't want to live with you in my head—"

"Don't, Sweet One... You must not," Sebastien whined.

Eric flexed his finger on the trigger, too damn close. "Set Zaine down somewhere safe."

The beat of Sebastien's wings blasted Zaine as he dangled, feet in the air. He couldn't reach up to grab Sebastien. Couldn't do a damn thing to stop this. His life, for what it was worth, lay in Eric's hands. "Eric, don't—"

Sebastien let go.

CHAPTER 38

ric

"No!"

Time slowed. Eric's heart jolted behind his ribs. He watched Zaine's face pale in horrible slow motion, watched him fall. Icy, vicious fury boiled through his veins. He swung the gun from his head, aimed between the eyes of Sebastien's monstrous form, and fired. The round punched though his skull, jerking his head back. His wings stopped beating, and the vampire fell too.

Now both were gone.

Eric blinked at the space where Zaine had been moments before.

He couldn't think it, couldn't look...

He grasped the windowsill and peered down. Sebastien corkscrewed in the air, limp wings causing him to spiral.

He couldn't see Zaine.

Where was he? Had he already... hit the ground?

"No." Eric backed away from the edge. He heard screams, maybe his own. He pressed the gun muzzle to his head, the hot metal hurting where it dug in. *No, no, no...* He couldn't do this anymore, couldn't be a part of this life. Zaine was the only damn thing that made any sense. He couldn't do this without him. Didn't want to live alone. His heart gaped, trying to swallow him. If he could tear it out, he would.

Why?

Why did everyone he love have to die?

The lights suddenly buzzed back on, flooding Eric in cool white light. On his knees, he blinked into the brightness, his body and mind numb. His skin prickled as if it was lined with razors. Everything hurt—his heart, his body, his soul. He blinked through blurred vision and saw a figure approach, like a ghost... or a dream.

Zaine was in front of him suddenly, kneeling, holding his face. "Eric? Eric—Hey!"

He wasn't here. He was dead.

Eric had just seen him fall.

Zaine threw his arms around him and pulled him close. He felt real and solid and smelled like Zaine, warm and spicy, like cinnamon and the home Eric hadn't known he'd been missing. He clutched at Zaine, firm and real. Here. Slowly, carefully, the pieces of his broken heart slotted back together. He pushed Zaine back, stared at his face, touched his worried smile.

"I'm okay." Zaine smiled. "I'm here..."

Mikalis approached with the limp and hideous form of Sebastien draped in his arms. The back of Sebastien's skull gaped open, exposing brain matter. But he wasn't dead. Weak, near death, but not there yet.

The vampire that had haunted Eric's dreams for over half his life bled from his ears and eyes, nose and mouth. His body was broken, but his chest still rose and fell. He still lived, still breathed.

Eric shoved at Zaine, pushing him off, and scrambled to his feet. "Kill him," he told Mikalis. "Kill him now."

"Of course." He knelt and laid Sebastien on the floor. Mikalis's sharp, curved fangs glistened. He leaned over Sebastien—

"Wait..." Eric swallowed hard. "Can you bring him around? Make him see us? Make him... hurt?"

"Eric..." Zaine, still on his knees, reached for him.

Eric raised a hand, warding him off. "No, don't stop this. Mikalis? Can you do that?"

"No."

"He has to know. He has to suffer. He can't die in his fucking sleep! You understand, don't you? I know you do. He has to see me!"

"I can't bring him around," Mikalis said again. "But you can."

"How? Tell me how."

"No." Zaine got to his feet. "No, this is fucked up. Eric, just let Mikalis end it. Have it over with."

Eric looked at Zaine, a man he'd thought dead, was unconvinced wasn't dead. Maybe this was what true madness felt like and none of this was real? But would it all hurt so much if it was a dream?

"What do I have to do?" he asked Mikalis.

The vampire stepped over Sebastien's body, took Eric's

hand in his warm fingers, and raised Eric's wrist to his lips. Mikalis's silver eyes fixed on him, waiting for permission. Eric nodded, and the master vampire struck, sinking his teeth deep. Lightning stabbed at Eric's heart—it wasn't like when Zaine did this, wasn't like that at all. Fire boiled through his chest and into his lungs. He choked on a scream—and then Mikalis withdrew, pulled Eric down to his knees, and held his bleeding wrist over Sebastien's lips.

Blood readily pulsed from the bite wound and ran between the injured vampire's lips.

Nothing happened.

For too long... nothing changed.

Then Sebastien's closed eyes twitched.

It was enough. A sign. He was waking up.

Mikalis drew Eric's wrist back to his mouth and swept his tongue over the free-flowing wounds, his eyes locking on Eric's again. The electric snap of power stole a single heartbeat from Eric's chest, and then Mikalis rocked back, dropping Eric's wrist. He didn't miss how Mikalis's eyes shone, how he swept his tongue across his lips, sweeping up every last drop of Eric's blood, or how he appeared to smile just for a glimmer of a second.

Sebastien's eyes opened.

Mikalis's hand slammed down, pinning Sebastien's broken body to the floor, and Eric cupped his old master's face in a gentle hand. He leaned over Sebastien, peering into his eyes as he'd done as a kid. The ghosts of their past lay between them, that of a boy begging a monster to love him. That boy was grown now, and he begged no more.

"For all the lives you stole, for the years you took from me, for my family, my little sister—know I never loved you. I killed you then, and you'll die now for good. You will never hurt another innocent soul."

Sebastien's arm shot up. His fingers clutched at Eric's arm. "Be careful... who you... trust."

Eric tore the vampire's wretched grip free and nodded to Mikalis. He struck again, but this time his bite sank into Sebastien's neck. Eric watched, breathing hard and fast as the venom slid in, watched as moment by moment Sebastien's skin tightened around his bones, watched it crack and split and gradually turn to sand, then dust.

When it was over, he met Mikalis's hard stare.

It *was* over. Sebastien was finally gone and never coming back. But there was a warning in Mikalis's gaze too, as though something else, something fundamental, had begun.

CHAPTER 39

aine

ERIC SHOOK off Zaine's efforts to help him to his feet, and then again in the elevator he didn't respond when Zaine asked if he was all right. Of course, he *wasn't* all right. Zaine had known that the moment Mikalis had carried him with his wings back to the top floor and he'd found Eric on his knees in pieces.

There had been no time to tell Eric how Mikalis had caught Zaine, rescued him really. Because he would have ended the same way as the earlier nyktelios if Mikalis hadn't stepped in—or flown in, as it happened.

They bundled back into the vans and sped away from the Citegroup building with everyone accounted for. The equipment had glitched, but Octavius had been watching them from a distance, and he'd dealt with the nyktelios

Eric had shoved from the window, delivering the killing bite.

A blast thundered suddenly, setting the night sky ablaze. Eric twisted in his seat and stared in the rearview mirror at the rising fireball. "What happened?"

Storm, from behind the wheel, said, "Cleanup."

"There were people in there... Feeders, but people."

"People die," Storm said.

Eric winced. The tension between them grew heavier with every breath. Zaine couldn't shake the feeling he'd done something wrong, something terrible.

"Let me out," Eric said several blocks later.

"I can't do that," Storm grumbled.

"Let me out, Storm."

"Mikalis wants everyone back at Atlas to debrief—"

"Let. Me. Out."

Zaine sighed. "Let him go. Mikalis can take it up with me."

Storm's gaze flicked to Zaine in the mirror. He pulled over and Eric hopped out, slamming the door behind him.

He watched his man walk down the sidewalk. The sun rose in the distance, bleeding the streets red and casting Eric's long shadow behind him. Zaine's heart ached as though that might be the last time he saw Eric Sharpe.

"Somehow, I fucked it up." It was all of it. Everything. The Brotherhood, Zaine, Eric's past, and how those things were tied up in knots. It was too much for Eric, too much for any man, but Eric had seen the ugly side of the Brotherhood, and he was clearly done with it. And done with Zaine.

Storm peeled off into the early morning traffic. "It's for the best."

Zaine slumped back in the seat. "Because every story ends the same, right."

THE BROTHERHOOD WENT ON, as inevitable as dawn and dusk, and a week after Sebastien's nest had been exposed and the vampire finally dusted, Zaine skimmed potential new nyktelios targets to track, gather intel on, and ultimately destroy. He used to love these beginning stages, finding possible nyks and going out into the world to observe them, gathering evidence for what would be their downfall.

But as the images flickered across Atlas's holoscreens, none of it got a rise out of him. With a few flicks of his fingers, he discarded the potential targets and brought up Atlas's observations of another target—Detective Eric Sharpe. Pictures of Eric fanned above the table: Eric waiting in line to grab coffee, sunglasses on, scanning the crowd. Eric entering his building. Eric checking his phone outside his precinct. Eric with another man, likely a possible new partner. Zaine scrolled through them all, catching Eric's smirk in one. He zoomed in and enlarged the picture. That damn smirk.

Eric was going to be okay.

He was a survivor.

He'd already picked himself up, dusted himself off, gone back to work, and was carrying on.

Without Zaine.

Which was, absolutely, for the best. What had Zaine been hoping for? A happy ever after? No Brotherhood member had ever had one, so why should he be any different?

"He's all right."

Zaine tensed at the sound of Mikalis's voice and considered swiping the files from sight, but Mikalis had already seen them.

The master vampire approached the table and studied the mosaic of images. "He went back to work the next day."

Mikalis was having Eric monitored using Atlas's vast access to camera networks but was probably using one of the Brotherhood on the ground too. Zaine would have been more surprised if Mikalis *hadn't* been tailing him. Eric knew *a lot.* He could be problematic for the Brotherhood. But he was smart. He wouldn't cause trouble.

What was there to say? Nothing. What was done was done, and Zaine knew in the end Mikalis had been right. The Brotherhood's world had to remain unseen, detached from humanity, protecting it but never a part of it.

"Do you see now why we cannot care?" Mikalis asked softly. He turned his gaze to Zaine, but instead of its usual cool clarity, there was some warmth in Mikalis's face. Some hint of pity maybe. Or regret?

"He's a good man," Zaine said a bit gruffly.

"Good men are often the first to fall." Mikalis spoke as though he'd said those words more than a few times over the decades. As though he had perhaps fallen into the same trap as Zaine more than once. He'd cared, and he'd been burned. "Sharpe will be monitored until we can ascertain whether he's a threat. If he exhibits any further unusual biological characteristics, we may have to bring him in."

Understandable. Zaine swiped the images away and closed Atlas's research program down. The lights dimmed, making the room feel smaller. "And what do I get? A few years in a glass box? For what it's worth, I didn't lose control. This really wasn't Albuquerque again. My only crime was to care, and that's over, so... Lock me up if you want, but I'd be more useful out there curbing rising nyktelios numbers."

"You disobeyed my orders. Orders that must be followed for our own good. You failed in your task to secure and extract the nyktelios—regardless of his age. You willfully broke out of containment, showing complete disregard for the Brotherhood way. If we all acted the way you did, there would be no Brotherhood."

Zaine swallowed and sighed through his nose. Leaning back in the chair, he lifted his gaze. "Yeah, you're right. But here's the thing... Sebastien had a few things to say before you killed him. Things about you and your secrets. It gets damn lonely in containment. I might let slip some of those things I heard... to Storm."

Mikalis stilled, for a few seconds not so much as breathing. Then, with a quick smile, he relaxed into motion again and leaned against the edge of the table. "Perhaps containment is unnecessary in this instance, as you clearly did not lose control."

Bingo. Zaine mirrored his smile and got to his feet. "We're on the same page." He headed for the door.

"Zaine?"

He turned and regarded their ageless and ancient master and how his piercing glare burned through Zaine. There was a threat there all right.

"The Brotherhood must always come first."

Zaine nodded. "*Memento mori.*" He left Mikalis in the Ops Room, grabbed his bike keys, threw on a jacket, and rode the elevator down to the parking garage to collect his bike. The Brotherhood were everything. They were his life, but he wasn't ready to let go of half his soul, not yet. There was one last thing he needed to do before that happened.

One last attempt to save his heart.

CHAPTER 40

ric

"CLOSE THE DOOR," Chief Allen said.

Eric closed the door, shutting out the precinct's background noise of ringing phones and chattering voices, and stood in front of the chief's desk, hands clasped behind his back.

Allen regarded Eric coolly, but his hardness soon thawed. He sighed and leaned back in his chair. "How are you, Sharpe?"

"Fine, Chief. Getting back into the flow of things."

"I heard from Nate's doctors today. He's recovering well. There was some significant damage, unfortunately, and he seems to be struggling with the treatment. It'll be a few months before he'll be returning to work. At the earliest."

Nate hadn't fared too well, and it had nothing to do

with the head injury he'd sustained during the "gas explosion" at Eric's apartment. He'd been hooked on Sebastien, probably for years. He might never recover.

"I'm going to assign you a new partner," Allen said after a moment of heavy silence. "How did you get on with Carmichael?"

He'd worked with Carmichael on a domestic homicide during the past few days. The man was solid. He'd probably be fine if Eric could muster enough energy to care. The only problem was that Eric had sleepwalked through the week, going through the motions and doing everything expected of him but feeling nothing. This world had lost interest for him now he knew another one existed.

He told the chief what he wanted to hear and wondered how long he'd be able to hold down his career. Six months, maybe. Tops.

Allen dismissed him, then called him back. "Sharpe?"

"Yes, Chief?"

Allen interlocked his fingers on the desktop and pressed his lips together. "Some crimes the law can't touch," he began. "Some wrongs can't be made right. At times, all we can do is try. And occasionally, if we're lucky, that's enough."

"Chief?"

Allen rubbed at his face and sighed again. "You remember I told you not to kick the hornet's nest?"

"Yeah..."

"Well, I don't know what nest you kicked and I don't want to know, but it'd be a damn shame if those hornets got the better of you. You know what I'm saying?"

He knew about the Brotherhood all right. Knew a lot more than Eric had realized.

"You're a good cop, Sharpe," Allen went on. "Maybe those hornets need a kick now and then. You hear me?"

"I hear you." Eric let the chief see his smile, and maybe something like his old zeal quickened his heart again.

"Now get back out there and do some good."

THE RESTAURANT he'd visited with Zaine gleamed with sparkling lights and bubbled with laughter, just like it had that night. Eric savored a few drinks at the bar, soaking up the atmosphere. He wasn't even sure why he'd come back. Maybe to capture the ghost of something he'd almost had but let slip through his fingers.

Zaine wasn't the Brotherhood. He was damn good at pretending to be like them, but the vampire hunter had a heart. Eric had seen it in his laugh, felt it in his soft, reverent touches. Four hundred years of pretending to be something because he had no choice. Normally, most people just had to do that for one lifetime.

Eric tipped his drink to Zaine, wherever he was, and hoped he never lost that heart. The Brotherhood needed it.

"Have you seen a guy around here? Tall, kinda lean, like he should survive on more than coffee and a righteous sense of justice?"

Eric smiled into his drink. He almost didn't want to turn his head, didn't want to see him, because he'd be that same stunning feast for the eyes that Eric hadn't been able to resist, and he'd have to resist him. "Now that I think of it, I have seen that guy."

Zaine slipped onto the neighboring stool and flicked a hand at the bartender for a drink. Eric had been right. He wore a casual, loose-fitting shirt and black pants, too casual for the office but too formal for the gym. The jacket hid his double holster, but it'd be there, tucked snugly against his sides.

"He said," Eric continued, "should some smart-ass Viking come asking after him, to tell him he was never here."

"That right?"

The bartender delivered Zaine's beer. He wrapped his fingers around it but didn't drink. He faced Eric and leaned an arm on the bar, unashamedly raking his gaze over him.

"You got a message for him?" Eric asked.

"Yeah." Zaine's smile faltered. "Tell him I'm sorry. Tell him I never meant to hurt him. Tell him... he was the best thing to happen to me in four long centuries. Tell him there's a Nordic cruise with his name on it. Has he ever seen the northern lights?"

Eric couldn't help but smile, even as it hurt. "No. I haven't." He met Zaine's soft gaze and as his smile slowly faded, Eric's heart felt heavier. What was Zaine doing here? What did he hope for?

"You wanna get out of here?" Zaine asked, wicked delight playing in his icy blue eyes.

"Why?"

Zaine blinked. "I, er... I was thinking you could take a ride with me?"

He wanted to. He wanted it so badly he almost said yes just for the hell of it, but tomorrow morning his heart would break all over again. Zaine would never leave the Brotherhood, and the Brotherhood would never allow it.

Zaine straightened and turned toward the bar as he picked at his beer label. "Would you tell him, even if it ends here, I'll love him... always."

The word hit him like a punch to the gut. "That's not fair."

"It's the truth."

"What do you want from me?" The words sounded a lot harsher than he'd planned, but they came from a place of feeling. A place so damaged, Eric couldn't afford another crack to the foundations.

Zaine set his drink down and glared back. "I want you."

"What about the Brotherhood? Huh? What about tomorrow when you walk away again?"

"I don't have the answers," Zaine said too loudly. "I wish I did." A few nearby diners glanced over. "Just... ride with me, *please*."

He hadn't known Zaine could look so pained. His face had fallen as though his heart had been crushed in his chest.

"You want me to get down on my knees and beg? I will." Zaine started to climb off the stool.

Eric hopped off his own stool, grabbed Zaine's hand, and hauled him upright before he could make a fool of himself. "Stop—"

Zaine plastered himself close and smirked. "Ride with me."

"Zaine—"

"Please..." His knuckles skimmed Eric's face, sending ripples through him. "I have a surprise for you."

"You don't take no for an answer, do you?" Eric said, his resistance falling away.

"Because, *kærasti*, you haven't actually said no."

"*Kærasti?*" Eric echoed, fighting his own smile as he tried not to mangle the strange accent.

"Darling."

Eric sighed. What a fool he'd been, thinking he could resist this man. "All right." Zaine overpaid for the drinks, leaving cash on the bar, and ushered Eric out the door. It would have been a lie to deny that his heart raced whenever Zaine reached for him, when their fingers brushed, or when Zaine kicked his bike upright and Eric climbed on, folding his arms around the vampire's waist.

Maybe this wasn't going to last, maybe it would break his heart tomorrow, but he'd told Zaine to live in the moment, and as Zaine sped his bike through the dazzling New York streets, Eric planned to do exactly that. And make the moment last forever.

CHAPTER 41

aine

He hadn't actually planned on the bike ride. The idea had come to him as soon as he'd seen Eric at the bar—exactly where he'd hoped he'd be. And now he wished the ride would never end. With Eric pressed close, his heart racing, his body a siren song to Zaine's withered soul, there was nowhere else in the world or in time he'd rather be.

But there was somewhere he *had* planned to be.

He pulled the bike up outside his apartment building—a converted boathouse in the redeveloped Hudson Yards area. It was modest in comparison to the neighboring multimillion-dollar high-rises, but he preferred it that way. Eric climbed off the bike and looked quizzically at the stairs going up the quirky timber-and-steel building. He didn't say a word as he climbed them after Zaine, only smiled when he entered the top-floor apartment after him.

The Hudson sparkled outside the windows and Zaine couldn't have imagined it better. But now that he had Eric here, nerves fluttered low in his belly. He didn't *get* nervous.

"Nice place." Eric sauntered toward the large picture window. "This is what money and time gets you, huh?"

"Something like that." Zaine watched him standing there silhouetted by New York, the epitome of bravery. The survivor. He couldn't wait any longer, and closing the distance, he slipped his arms around Eric's waist and drew the man back against his chest, relishing how he leaned into him, yielding without resistance.

"I have a plan," Zaine said, breathing in the smell of Eric's aftershave and the man himself, breathing him down into the depths of his memory where he could keep him, even if he walked away tomorrow. "I need you, Eric. And the Brotherhood need you, although they'll never admit it. You're right. We could help people. And I think you're the man to show them—us—how."

"Me? Why would they even listen?"

"We'll make them listen."

"I don't know—"

Eric turned in his arms and he pressed a finger to the man's lips, making his eyes widen.

"Before we talk about that... Come with me." He dropped a hand, took Eric's in his, and drew him toward the closed bedroom door. Eric was already frowning. Zaine knew what he was thinking but he hoped what lay behind the door would at least convince him Zaine was serious about all of this, about him. The closer he got to the door, the more his heart pounded and the more he feared he was about to expose his heart, only to have it crushed if Eric said no.

Stepping aside, he gestured for Eric to open the door. His heart had forced its way up his throat and he wasn't even sure he could speak. He hadn't expected this to mean so much. "Go ahead."

Eric's frown turned curious, lifted by a suspicious smile. He opened the door.

CHAPTER 42

aine

A BLANKET of roses and petals covered the vast king-sized bed. It was, in fact, a bed of roses. Eric drifted closer. He wasn't saying anything. Why wasn't he saying anything?

"This..." he croaked. "You did this..."

Zaine swooped in and wrapped strong arms around Eric's waist. He purred a rumbling sound and growled in Eric's ear, "For you."

He was almost too afraid to look at Eric's face, to see his thoughts there. He'd faced a thousand-year-old nyktelios without fear, but right then, handing Eric his heart, he was terrified. He let go, strode to the bed, and turned, making himself meet Eric's gaze. His expression wasn't too bad. Confused, maybe, but his smirk was twitching. Eric swallowed, shifted on his feet, opened his mouth, then closed it again. "I, er... Damn, I just..." He dragged a hand down his chin and bowed his head.

Zaine's heart shriveled behind his ribs. All right, it was all right... Eric didn't want this. Zaine would take it like a man. Later, he'd beat the shit out of a nyktelios, but right now he'd swallow it. Because he loved and respected Eric, his space, and whatever he needed. Even if that wasn't Zaine.

"Fuck." Eric sighed. "I'm..." He lifted his head. Unshed tears made his eyes shine.

Zaine moved too fast, startling a gasp from Eric's sweet lips. Lips he brushed with his own. "I don't know what to do," Zaine said, "but I know I want us. I'll fight for us. For you. If the Brotherhood refuse to accept this—accept us —" He twined his fingers with Eric's, feeling his tremble. "—that's their choice. I'll walk away from them, never from you. Never from you again." Zaine pressed Eric's hand to his chest over his heart. "This is yours. If you'll have it. Have me?"

Eric's glistening eyes lifted. His mouth twisted, his expression fraught with some unknown pain. Then, whatever battle raged inside him, he won. His mouth crashed into Zaine's. He flung his arms over the vampire's shoulders and pulled him down into a devastating kiss. All Zaine's fears vanished, gone in the flash burn of heat Eric's kiss scorched through his soul. He scooped Eric into his arms, lifted him off his feet, and lost himself to the feel of the man he loved, loving him in return. It had to be love, didn't it—nothing else had set Zaine's heart alight like this.

Eric gasped free, kissed down Zaine's jaw, then nipped at his neck, spilling sharp needles of pleasure down his back. He groaned, maybe growled, then dug his fingers into Eric's ass, grinding him against Zaine's aching cock. Propped in Zaine's arms, Eric leaned back. His warm hands cupped Zaine's face and he peered into his eyes. "If we're doing this, I need to know, Zaine. I need you to give me your word."

"Anything, *kærasti*."

"You're a part of my world and I'm a part of yours. It has to be this way. We can make it work. Don't shut me out."

Zaine believed that. Together, they would make it work. "Side by side."

Eric frowned, suddenly so serious, then his mouth ravaged Zaine's. "Now fuck me off my feet, vampire," he mumbled into the kiss.

"Hm. Gladly."

CHAPTER 43

ric

EVERYTHING HE'D BEEN afraid of, all the emptiness he'd carried with him since Sebastien's demise—it vanished the moment Zaine's hot mouth skimmed his neck. He knew what it cost Zaine to kiss him there, could feel the tension strumming through the vampire's body. Zaine lit Eric up in all ways. He'd never get enough of the passionate, deadly, stronghearted man.

Zaine carried him to the bed and set him down among the sweet-smelling roses with a startling gentleness. His blue eyes blazed silver at their edges. He prowled down Eric's body—his gaze never leaving Eric's as his fingers worked to undo the shirt buttons. It seemed impossible that Eric should be worthy of his love, but it was there in his eyes, in the way his mouth gently skimmed Eric's, and how his hands, capable of devastating strength, gathered

Eric's shirt to the sides and exposed his middle, where Zaine's tongue swept next.

He might burn up then, combust from lust. Was that even a thing?

Zaine chuckled. Eric grabbed his face, hauled him higher, and thrust his tongue between his lips, needing to taste all of him. Zaine's possessive growls rumbled through him. "You're mine, Eric Sharpe."

"Hm," Eric purred, nudging noses. "Show me."

Zaine worked furiously at Eric's fly and yanked off his pants, then went down on him in one swoop, leaving no time for Eric to catch his breath. He groaned through his teeth, grasped Zaine's already messy hair, and thrust deep between his lips, driving into the sweet, tight warmth. Zaine's tongue swirled, tasting and teasing, and he looked up, blue eyes like sparkling gems. They were beautiful really, the Brotherhood. Each and every one of them was fierce and painfully cold but immortal, righteous—living fragments of a different world. They didn't see themselves as beautiful, but Zaine was. At least to Eric.

Zaine lifted off his cock and prowled up his chest. "You're looking at me as though having deep and meaningful thoughts while I have your cock between my fangs."

"Sorry?"

"No, I love it. Eye-fuck me some more, Detective."

"Then go down on me again, Viking."

"As you wish."

He did, and Eric threw his head back, surrendering to the ripples of pleasure and giving his body and mind to Zaine. When Zaine's finger explored his hole, he moaned something about wanting more, and Zaine gave him that too. Until there was nothing but rising waves of ecstasy about to break over him. He clutched Zaine's face, met his gaze, and silently demanded *more*.

Shifting onto his knees, Zaine opened his fly and freed his hard cock. From the bedside table, he grabbed a bottle of oil, and in the next moment, with their gazes locked and Eric's legs spread, Zaine's heated length pushed against his hole, widening and opening him. The vampire shuddered, exhaled, and groaned against Eric's neck. "You're the reason I'm alive." He kissed him, mouth savagely owning Eric in a way that made his back arch and his body demand all Zaine could give.

As soon as Zaine encircled Eric's cock, he knew he wouldn't last. And with a few powerful strokes from Zaine, the cresting wave he'd been chasing broke and he spilled. Zaine's thrusting quickened, his eyes fierce and teeth low and exposed inside his mouth. The vampire came with a ferocious growl and shuddered into him, then slumped over, still holding his weight up but smothering Eric in warmth.

Zaine lifted his head and smiled down at him. His fingers stroked Eric's face, their softness a treat. "I am not worthy."

"Funny, I was thinking the same."

Zaine bowed his head and pressed his forehead to Eric's so that all Eric could see were those dazzling eyes and the man's achingly handsome face. "I love you, you know," Eric said. "It's real. I feel it. It feels like freedom."

Zaine breathed in and exhaled hard, then rolling onto his side, he tucked Eric close. "When I'm with you, it feels as though we could conquer the world."

"Maybe we can?" Eric's heart warmed, the moment so perfect it made all the heartache and horror worth it.

"Oh? You have a plan?"

"I think I do."

WITH ZAINE beside him and his NYPD badge at his hip, Eric walked into Atlas. Kazi was waiting inside. He pushed off the back wall, his disapproving gaze already fixed on Zaine. "This is a bad idea, Z."

"Your opinion is noted, but we've got this."

Kazi stepped aside without slowing their pace and said, "I'll come see you in confinement."

Zaine flashed Eric a smile as they entered the elevator. "He won't put me in confinement." His confidence almost had Eric believing it. But he also knew Mikalis lived by his firm rules, and he and Zaine were about to upset all that. It was for the best. Mikalis had to see that.

The Brotherhood had the potential to really do some good. If Mikalis allowed it.

Zaine stepped into the Ops room with Eric right behind him.

Storm and Mikalis abruptly ended their conversation as Octavius quickly swept the contents of the Atlas screens away. "Zaine, what is *he* doing here?" Octavius snarled. Ice touched Eric's spine, even from across the room.

Mikalis shot Octavius a silencing glance. "Leave us."

"No, it's fine," Zaine said. "Aiko can stay too."

Jesus, Eric hadn't even *seen* Aiko lurking at the back of

the room. He came into sight now, shorter in height than the others but no less threatening.

"Here's how it's going to be." Zaine parked his ass against the edge of the table. "Eventually, we all know you'd have hauled Eric in. For all your talk of observation, having him roam free would never sit well with you." Mikalis's eyes narrowed, but Zaine plowed on. "You'd have found some excuse, some reason to squirrel him away. One, I'm not letting that happen, and two, neither is Eric. So here's the deal." Zaine turned his gaze to Eric.

All the Brotherhood glared at him now, the weight of their judgmental stares like a ten-ton weight. "I'll work with you as an NYPD detective. Alert you to any new suspicious nyktelios activity—"

"We have Atlas for that," Octavius said. "We don't need a feeder giving us orders."

"You're a piece of work, huh," Eric said. "Do I threaten you? Is that it? Is there something about this"—Eric gestured at himself, then Zaine—"that offends you?"

"I don't listen to feeders." He stood and looked to Mikalis for backup, but he was too engrossed in studying Eric.

"He's not a feeder," Mikalis finally said. "But he is something." He folded his arms and dipped his chin. "Go on."

Eric wasn't sure if he should thank Mikalis. He hadn't forgotten the vampire's teeth sliding into his wrist, or how Mikalis's eyes had darkened with desire during those personal few seconds between them. But he didn't want to linger on it either. So much of this he was still trying to navigate, and he needed the Brotherhood on his side to do that. "As I was saying—"

Octavius blurred from his position at the table and vanished, moving too fast for Eric to track.

"He'll get over it." Zaine encouraged Eric with a nod. "Go on."

Eric cleared his throat. "I'll give you information you can't find on computers, word on the street, a line of communication in the NYPD, postmortem reports, and you get access to whatever is going on inside me. In return, the Brotherhood will reconsider its rule regarding helping people."

"Helping people doesn't solve the nyktelios problem," Storm said, entering the conversation.

"A problem you've been trying to solve for several millennia. Maybe it's time you tried another way?"

Aiko approached the table, entering Eric's field of vision. He preferred the vampire where he could see him. "Helping people gets messy."

"With your unlimited resources and centuries of experience, you can't handle some mess?"

The room fell silent except for the hum of the air conditioning. Everyone watched Mikalis for his response.

"Nyktelios numbers are rising," he said. "The Brotherhood remain strong, but it's not enough. We need more if we're going to end this war."

Eric swallowed and said, "Sebastien told me something was coming *for you*, Mikalis. He was proud of that fact. Atlas can't track everything, and the Brotherhood numbers *aren't* increasing. You need to start thinking outside your three-thousand-year-old box. The nyktelios aren't going away. They're getting stronger. Are you?"

Mikalis's left eyebrow lifted.

"Just because you've done something the same way forever doesn't make it right," Zaine said, as though he'd said the same before.

"You make a compelling argument but I have my concerns regarding your relationship with Zaine and how it clouds both your judgments."

"I love him," Eric said. "And that should be no concern of yours."

Aiko spluttered something in Japanese that was probably a curse word and Storm's glower turned thunderous.

"He's right," Zaine said. "You think caring makes us weak, but you've got it all wrong. Eric and I are stronger together. You've forgotten that, Mikalis. Or maybe you don't want to remember? Whatever the reason, I've never wanted to fight more than I do now, knowing I have something—*someone*—to fight for."

"All right, thank you, Zaine," Mikalis said. "And Eric. I think you've made your point. I'll consider this. However, understand that should the nyktelios realize Eric is working with us, he'll become a target, putting him in danger."

"Let them come," Eric said.

Mikalis held his gaze. "I genuinely can't decide if you're brave or foolish."

"Both. I think." His heart pounded in a good way. This felt like something, like progress, as though he'd finally broken through the wall that had been holding him back since Sebastien's abuse. He wanted to make a difference, wanted to make sure the nyktelios didn't get their claws into more people, and if they did, Eric was going to make damn sure the Brotherhood tried to save those people, even if it was like pushing water uphill. But it would be a start. He'd be doing some good. And he wouldn't be alone.

EPILOGUE

Mikalis

ATLAS DISPLAYED a mosaic of multicolored graphs that were showing a steady uptick as they unpicked the genetic makeup of Eric Sharpe's blood work. The more the graphic twitched and grew, the more concerned Mikalis became.

"You ever seen anything like that?" Storm asked. The stalwart Brotherhood member stood beside Mikalis, arms crossed, stance immovable.

"No."

Detective Eric Sharpe was not a feeder, he wasn't riddled with nyk venom, wasn't intoxicated by a desire he couldn't control, and according to both the detective and Zaine, Zaine hadn't tried to transition him to nyktelios. They weren't lying. Mikalis knew liars. But Sharpe's blood *was* undergoing preternatural changes at the molecular level, changes only the goddess herself could perform.

"Tainted sample?" Storm suggested.

"I took this sample myself."

Storm's face turned troubled. "It explains how he's able to heal and his growing strength."

"But little else."

Storm sighed. "You know what this suggests?" Mikalis had an idea but he let Storm continue. "He won't age, not physically."

Mikalis had come to the same conclusion. Eric Sharpe was going to be with them for a very long time. At least he'd surrendered himself voluntarily. Zaine had been right—Mikalis could not have allowed him to walk free.

"Leave this with me. And Storm, don't tell the others. Not yet."

Storm nodded and left the Ops room. Finally alone, Mikalis again regarded the data and dancing graphics. Eric Sharpe defied everything they knew about the nyktelios, about themselves. Sharpe's existence was a problem. And Mikalis disliked problems.

Swiping the screen, he summoned the system commands, selected everything in Eric Sharpe's file, and hesitated, his finger hovering over Delete. If the others discovered what Eric was, the Brotherhood would fall. And the Brotherhood were everything. The Brotherhood must continue, irrespective of any cost.

Mikalis hit Delete.

~

The Blackrose Brotherhood series continues in Violent Mistake.

When ex-investigate journalist Felix Qiaud, gets a little too close to the Brotherhood, Mikalis issues Kazi with the kill-order. It's nothing Kazi hasn't done before, but at the crucial moment, Kazi and Quaid are kidnapped by a Nyx-worshipping cult. Now the pair must work together to escape the cult and avoid Mikalis's wrath.
Enemies become lovers in the next steamy Blackrose Brotherhood book.

Buy or borrow it now from Amazon.

ALSO BY ARIANA NASH

Sign up to Ariana's newsletter so you don't miss all the news.

www.ariananashbooks.com

***

Shadows of London

(Five book urban fantasy series)

A sexy assassin, a billionaire boss with secrets, and magic bubbling up through the streets of London. All in a days work for artifact agent, John "Dom" Domenici.

Start the Shadows of London series with Twisted Pretty Things

***

Silk & Steel Series

(Complete four book dark fantasy series)

Elf assassin Eroan, falls for the dragon prince Lysander, in this heart-shattering star-crossed lovers tale.

"(Silk & Steel) will appeal to fans of CS Pacat's Captive Prince and Jex Lane's Beautiful Monsters." *R. A. Steffan, author of The Last Vampire.*

"A few pages in and I'm already hooked." - *Jex Lane, author of Beautiful Monsters.*

"The characters yank, twist, and shatter your heartstrings." - *Goodreads review*

Start the adventure with Silk & Steel, Silk & Steel #1

Primal Sin

(Complete trilogy)

Angels and demons fight for love over London's battle-scarred streets.

Start the sinfully dark journey today, with **Primal Sin #1**

ABOUT THE AUTHOR

Born to wolves, Rainbow Award winner Ariana Nash only ventures from the Cornish moors when the moon is fat and the night alive with myths and legends. She captures those myths in glass jars and returning home, weaves them into stories filled with forbidden desires, fantasy realms, and wicked delights.

Sign up to her newsletter and get a free ebook here: https://www.subscribepage.com/silk-steel

Printed in Great Britain
by Amazon